FLINT
and
MIRROR

FLINT
and
MIRROR

JOHN CROWLEY

TOR

A TOM DOHERTY ASSOCIATES BOOK
NEW YORK

This is a work of fiction. All of the characters, organizations, and events portrayed in this novel are either products of the author's imagination or are used fictitiously.

FLINT AND MIRROR

A Tor Book
Published by Tom Doherty Associates
120 Broadway
New York, NY 10271

www.tor-forge.com

Tor® is a registered trademark of Macmillan Publishing Group, LLC.

Library of Congress Cataloging-in-Publication Data

Names: Crowley, John, 1942– author.
Title: Flint and mirror / John Crowley.
Description: First Edition. | New York : Tor, 2022. |
"A Tom Doherty Associates Book."
Identifiers: LCCN 2021062782 (print) | LCCN 2021062783 (ebook) |
ISBN 9781250817525 (hardcover) | ISBN 9781250817532 (ebook)
Classification: LCC PS3553.R597 F55 2022 (print) |
LCC PS3553.R597 (ebook) | DDC 813/.54—dc23
LC record available at https://lccn.loc.gov/2021062782
LC ebook record available at https://lccn.loc.gov/2021062783

Our books may be purchased in bulk for promotional,
educational, or business use. Please contact your local bookseller
or the Macmillan Corporate and Premium Sales Department
at 1-800-221-7945, extension 5442, or by email at
MacmillanSpecialMarkets@macmillan.com.

First Edition: 2022

Printed in the United States of America

0 9 8 7 6 5 4 3 2 1

But I know that all things that happen are not due to chance and happenstance alone but are brought about by intelligences who have constraints—but who have wills as well.

CONFITEOR

everyone agreed: it had grown colder in Rome in these latter days.

The damp chill of winter lasted longer, the great stone houses and palaces of the noble *rioni* remained cold when spring came. The churches were colder still. The warm blue Italian skies of former times blazed as ever in innumerable paintings, but were less true now. In truth the whole world had grown colder, from China to Brazil, but Hugh O'Neill, Earl of Tyrone, didn't know that; his own land—which he had not seen in a decade—was still green, still warm, in his mind. England, yes, had been cold: when as a boy he had dwelt there, he had gone with his fosterers the Sidneys and walked out on the frozen Thames river, hard as granite, where buildings and arcades of ice had been put up, lit at night by candles and cressets that seemed to shiver in the cold; sleighs flitted past as on a broad highway, drawn by horses with studded shoes, casting off a glitter of ice with every step.

How long ago that was.

The apartments in the Palazzo Salviati that the Pope had provided to the Earl were furnished with charcoal braziers, but the tall windows weren't glazed, and the Earl refused to batten the shutters at nightfall. He slept through the night wrapped in the rugs of his couch, sitting up, his head propped on pillows like a sick man. A naked sword within hand's reach. He thought that on any night he might be murdered by agents of one or another of the powers he had striven with, or betrayed, or failed. The King of Spain's son. The English Crown. His own clan and liegemen. Sanctissimus himself, or his cardinals for the matter of that: they might soon tire of the Earl's endless pleas for money and arms whereby he might return to Ireland, of his plotting when *in vino plenus* with his fellow exiles—this one brooding on vengeance, that one mad for justice—who might themselves hate him secretly. A pillow over his face as he slept. But the great and beautiful ones, the legions of earth and air, whom most of all he had failed and who had failed him in turn—they could not reach him here to punish or to harm: could no more leave that island than he could return to it.

But it was summer now, a blessing; on waking he felt it, this long day breaking, somehow suddenly. His bedchamber door was rapped on lightly and opened; his attendants brought a basin of water for him to wash in, white towels for his hands and face. He rose, pushing aside the bedclothes and standing up with an old man's groan, naked. Would his lordship break his fast, he was asked, or attend Mass first? The Earl looked down on himself, the red curls of his breast gone gray, the scars and welts where no hair grew. The land that was himself, in all its history. Was he well or ill? He could not say. He would hear Mass, he said. He was helped into the long wadded coat that the Romans wear at morning, *vestaglia, robe de chambre,* and took the hands of the men on either side of him while he put his feet, twisted and knuckly and seeming not his own, into velvet slippers. He drank the posset given him. He thought of turning back to bed. He belted the robe, thanked his attendants, who stepped away backward from him bowing and out the door, a thing which always charmed him. With a great yawn, a gulp of morning, he awoke entirely at last.

The Salviati palace contained a small chapel where each morning the Archbishop said Mass, as he was required by canon law to do, and wished to do. His daily congregation was small: the palace's serving nuns, a superannuated monsignor, the Archbishop's secretary. And the Earl of Tyrone, taking a gilded chair at a *prie-dieu* between the two rows of benches. When the Archbishop entered, followed by his server, he touched O'Neill on his shoulder as he passed, smiling, looking toward the Mass vessels and the Gospel open on the altar.

Peter Lombard, Archbishop of Armagh in Ulster, had never entered his See. He had been a bright Munster boy, sent off to Oxford and then the Continent to study; earned a doctorate at the Catholic college of Louvain in Belgium. When he came to Rome he so impressed Pope Clement VII that he ascended quickly through several appointments and soon was made Archbishop. He was the obvious choice for Armagh, but though he was anointed and given the ring and crozier he could never reach his seat in Ulster; couldn't be shepherd to his flock, couldn't marry or bury, couldn't say a High Mass for them on holy-days. Catholic clergy in Ireland were being imprisoned, exiled, hanged, and butchered. He would have gone to Ireland anyway but the Holy Father forbade it, and instead made Peter his Domestic Prelate, with a good income attached. The Irish exiles in Rome were made his concern. Like his friend Hugh O'Neill, he would never leave Rome, nor ever stand again on Irish soil.

I will go unto the altar of God, he said, hands lifted to the standing crucifix on the altar. And in the soft Latin of the Italian church the server answered: *To God who gave joy to my youth.* The Earl whispered in concert with the priest, he in Irish, the priest in Latin: *Why do you turn me away, why am I made to go on in sorrow, while my enemy afflicts me?* How many times in how many ages had that question been asked, the Earl wondered, and how often gone unanswered. He felt his tears arise, as they did often now, at small things, at nothing.

Midway in the Mass the Archbishop raised the circle of bread that had become transformed, bread into body; then wine into blood. The nuns rose and in a line, gray ghosts, approached the rail to partake. *Panis angelicus.* On this day the Earl would not. He could not; he had not confessed, had not done his penance, his sins had not been forgiven.

⁓

Hugh O'Neill attended divine service most mornings; in the evenings, if he did not engage in visionary plots and plans with other old Irishmen like himself, he sat with the Archbishop in his chambers, for the Archbishop, author of the huge *De regno Hiberniæ sanctorum insula commentarius,* his account of the saints and defenders of the Irish realm, wished to compile the intimate knowledge that Hugh O'Neill had of the events of the last Irish defense against the heretic. He was the Earl's historian; he put questions and wrote down what Hugh answered, when he could answer: the names and clans of old companions, the course of battles lost or won, the years and months and days of them; the letters of supplication or refusal, the oaths sworn and broken. The voice of the old Queen: Hugh would not tell the Archbishop how it was that he had come to hear that voice, and spoke instead of a sort of sense he had had, or a sensitivity to the procession of events: that he could know them at a distance, or in a time yet to come.

On Fridays he was a penitent: the Archbishop was his confessor, sat alone knee to knee with the Earl, his face turned away and his hand at times hiding his eyes, listening without speaking, unless what he heard needed explication or inquiry. In their tall cages the Archbishop's turtle-doves moaned, flitting pointlessly, gifts of the new Pope, Paul V. Here too Hugh was allowed a chair, was not made to lower himself to his knees, from which posture (he had said to the Archbishop) he might never rise again. And with head lowered, he confessed. *Bless me, Father, for I have sinned, in thought, word, and deed.*

A week's sins could be told in the tenth part of an hour; the old Earl had few of what the priest called Occasions of Sin now. Hugh O'Neill's confessions were not of present *peccata* but of the sins of his whole lived life, not so different from the history the Archbishop was writing, except that in the written history the crimes that the Earl acknowledged were excluded, whereas in confession they were probed and totted up with care. The nightly history-telling began at the beginning of Hugh's coming of age and went toward the end, to these rooms in Rome; the Friday confessions, however, had started at the end—the end of all the wars and all the battles in the wars and the things done in the battles and after them—and went backward, toward the beginning. Each week the Earl and his confessor turned back a little further, seeking what must be honestly spoken of now, all that he should have done and did not do, what he did and should not have done. Hugh O'Neill had never been an observant son of the Church; when it was advantageous he would enter a church, or kneel with his captains before a hunted priest in the wilderness for a blessing, but what things he had done as a warrior, as a leader, as the O'Neill and the champion of Ireland's and his own clan's rights and freedoms—those he would not have called sins; and even now in the face of the Archbishop's gentle questioning he sometimes resisted. When he could say no more, baffled by himself, and they had reached a place to stop, they arose together and exchanged a kiss of peace.

In the course of the years of exile, the Earl's and the Archbishop's, these two histories of Hugh O'Neill—of his acts and of his soul— reached the moment in his life where they crossed, like two riders each headed for the other's starting point: as one went toward the end, to matters hardest to speak of, so full of failures and defeats, the other reached the years of youth and childhood, when he went unschooled in grace and sin, and mostly learned to do things, to ride and run and throw the javelin, wrestle and brag, wake and sleep in the green world.

one

FLINT AND MIRROR

RATH

It was in the spring that his fosterers the O'Hagans brought Hugh O'Neill to the castle at Dungannon. It was a great progress in the boy Hugh's eyes, twenty or thirty horses jingling with brass trappings, carts bearing gifts for his O'Neill uncles at Dungannon, red cattle lowing in the van, gallowglass and archers and women in bright scarves, O'Hagans and McMahons and their dependents. And he knew that he, but ten years old, was the center of that progress, on a dappled pony, with a new mantle wrapped around his skinny body and a new ring on his finger.

He kept seeming to recognize the environs of the castle, and scanned the horizon for it, and questioned his cousin Phelim, who had come to fetch him to Dungannon, how far it was every hour until Phelim grew annoyed and told him to ask next when he saw it. When at last he did see it, a fugitive sun was just then looking out, and sunshine glanced off the wet, lime-washed walls of its palisades and made it seem bright and near and dim and far at once, heart-catching, for to Hugh the stone tower and its clay and thatch outbuildings were all the castles he had ever heard of in songs. He kicked his pony hard, and though Phelim and the laughing women called to him and reached out to keep him, he raced on, up the long muddy track that rose up to a knoll where now a knot of riders were gathering, their javelins high and slim and black against the sun: his uncles and cousins O'Neill, who when they saw the pony called and cheered him on.

Through the next weeks he was made much of, and it excited him; he ran everywhere, an undersized, red-headed imp, his stringy legs pink with cold and his high voice too loud. Everywhere the big hands of his uncles touched him and petted him, and they laughed at his extravagances and his stories, and when he killed a rabbit they praised him and held him aloft among them as though it had been twenty stags. At night he slept among them, rolled in among their great odorous shaggy shapes where they lay around the open turf fire that burned in the center of the hall. Sleepless and alert long into the night he watched the smoke ascend to the opening in the roof and listened to his uncles and cousins snoring and talking and breaking wind after their ale.

That there was a reason, perhaps not a good one and kept secret from him, why on this visit he should be put first ahead of older cousins, given first choice from the thick stews in which lumps of butter dissolved, and listened to when he spoke, Hugh felt but could not have said. Now and again he caught one or another of the men regarding him steadily, sadly, as though he were to be pitied; and again, a woman would sometimes, in the middle of some brag he was making, fold him in her arms and hug him hard. He was in a story whose plot he didn't know, and it made him the more restless and wild. Once when running into the hall he caught his uncle Turlough Luineach and a woman of his having an argument, he shouting at her to leave these matters to men; when she saw Hugh, the woman came to him, pulled his mantle around him and brushed leaves and burrs from it. "Will they have him dressed up in an English suit then for the rest of his life?" she said over her shoulder to Turlough Luineach, who was drinking angrily by the fire.

"His grandfather Conn had a suit of English clothes," Turlough said into his cup. "A fine suit of black velvet, I remember, with gold buttons and a black velvet hat. With a white plume in it!" he shouted, and Hugh couldn't tell if he was angry at the woman, or Hugh, or himself. The woman began crying; she drew her scarf over her face and left the hall. Turlough glanced once at Hugh, and spat into the fire.

Nights they sat in the light of the fire and the great reeking candle of reeds and butter, drinking Dungannon beer and Spanish wine and talking. Their talk was one subject only: the O'Neills. Whatever else came up in talk or song related to that long history, whether it was the strangeness—stupidity or guile, either could be argued—of the English colonials; or the raids and counter-raids of neighboring clans; or stories out of the far past. Hugh couldn't always tell, and perhaps his elders weren't always sure, what of the story had happened a thousand years ago and what of it was happening now. Heroes rose up and raided, slew their enemies, and carried off their cattle and their women; O'Neills were crowned *ard Rí*, High King, at Tara. There was mention of their ancestor Niall of the Nine

Hostages and of the high king Julius Caesar; of Brian Boru and Cuchulain, who lived long ago, and of the King of Spain's daughter, yet to come; of Shane O'Neill, now living, and his fierce Scots red-shanks. Hugh's grandfather Conn had been *an Ò Neill*, the O'Neill, head of his clan and its septs; but he had let the English dub him Earl of Tyrone. There had always been an O'Neill, invested at the crowning stone at Tullahogue to the sound of St. Patrick's bell; but Conn O'Neill, Earl of Tyrone, had knelt before King Harry over the sea, and had promised to plant corn, and learn English. And when he lay dying he said that a man was a fool to trust the English.

Within the tangled histories, each strand bright and clear and beaded with unforgotten incident but inextricably bound up with every other, Hugh could perceive his own story: how his grandfather had never settled the succession of his title of *an Ò Neill;* how Hugh's uncle Shane had risen up and slain his own half-brother Matthew, who was Conn's bastard son and Hugh's father, and now Shane called himself the O'Neill and claimed all Ulster for his own, and raided his cousins' lands whenever he chose with his six fierce sons; how he, Hugh, had true claim to what Shane had usurped. Sometimes all this was as clear to him as the branchings of a winter-naked tree against the sky; sometimes not. The English . . . there was the confusion. Like a cinder in his eye, they baffled his clear sight.

Turlough Luineach tells with relish: "Then comes up Sir Henry Sidney with all his power, and Shane? Can Shane stand against him? He cannot! It's as much as he can do to save his own skin. And that only by leaping into the Blackwater and swimming away. I'll drink the Lord Deputy's health for that, a good friend to Conn's true heir . . ."

Or, "What do they ask?" a *brehon*, a lawgiver, states. "You bend a knee to the Queen, and offer all your lands. She takes them and gives you the title Earl—and all your lands back again. *Surrender and regrant*," he said in English: "You are then as her *urragh*, but nothing has changed . . ."

"And they are sworn then to help you against your enemies," says Turlough.

"No," says another, "*you* against *theirs*, even if it be a man sworn to you or your own kinsman whom they've taken a hatred to. Conn was right: a man is a fool to trust them."

"Think of Earl Desmond, imprisoned now in London, who trusted them."

"Desmond is a thing of theirs. He is a Norman, he has their blood. Not the O'Neills."

"*Fubún*," says the blind poet O'Mahon in a quiet high voice that stills them all:

> Fubún *on the gray foreign gun,*
> Fubún *on the golden chain;*
> Fubún *on the court that talks English,*
> Fubún *on the denial of Mary's son.*

Hugh listens, turning from one speaker to the other, frightened by the poet's potent curse. He feels the attention of the O'Neills on him.

~~~

"In Ireland there are five kingdoms," O'Mahon the poet said. "One in each of the five directions. There was a time when each of the kingdoms had her king, and a court, and a castle-seat with lime-washed towers; battlements of spears, and armies young and laughing."

"There was a High King then too," said Hugh, seated at O'Mahon's feet in the grass, still green at Hallowtide. From the hill where they sat the Great Lake could just be seen, turning from silver to gold as the light went. The roving herds of cattle—Ulster's wealth—moved over the folded land. All this is O'Neill territory, and always forever has been.

"There was indeed once a High King," O'Mahon said.

"And will be again."

The wind stirred the poet's white hair. O'Mahon could not see Hugh, his cousin, but—he said—he could see the wind. "Now cousin," he said. "See how well the world is made. Each kingdom of Ireland has its own renown: Connaught in the west for learning and for magic, the writing of books and annals, and the dwelling-places of saints. In the north, Ulster"—he swept his hand over lands he couldn't see—"for courage, battles, and warriors. Leinster in the east for hospitality, for open doors and feasting, cauldrons never empty. Munster in the south for labor, for kerns and ploughmen, weaving and droving, birth and death."

Hugh, looking over the long view, the winding of the river where clouds were gathered now, asked: "Which is the greatest?"

"Which," O'Mahon said, pretending to ponder this. "Which do *you* think?"

"Ulster," said Hugh O'Neill of Ulster. "Because of the warriors. Cuchulain was of Ulster, who beat them all."

"Ah."

"Wisdom and magic are good," Hugh conceded. "Hosting is good. But warriors can beat them."

O'Mahon nodded to no one. "The greatest kingdom," he said, "is Munster."

Hugh said nothing to that. O'Mahon's hand sought for his shoulder and rested upon it, and Hugh knew he meant to explain. "In every kingdom," he said, "the North, the South, the East, and the West, there is also a north, a south, an east, a west. Isn't that so?"

"Yes," Hugh said. He could point to them: left, right, ahead, behind. Ulster is in the north, and yet in Ulster there is also a north, the north of the north: that's where his bad uncle Shane ruled. And so in that north, Shane's north, there must be again a north and a south, an east and a west. And then again . . .

"Listen," O'Mahon said. "Into each kingdom comes wisdom from the west, about what the world is and how it came to be. Courage from the north, to defend the world from what would swallow it up. Hospitality from the east to praise both learning and courage, and reward the kings who keep the world as it is. But before all these things, there is a world at all: a world to learn about, to defend, to praise, to keep. It is from Munster at first that the world comes to be."

"Oh," Hugh said, no wiser. "But you said that there were *five* kingdoms."

"So I did. And so it is said."

Connaught, Ulster, Leinster, Munster. "What is the fifth kingdom?"

"Well, cousin," O'Mahon said, "what is it then?"

"Meath," Hugh guessed. "Where Tara is, where the kings were crowned."

"That's fine country. Not north or south or east or west but in the middle."

He said no more about that, and Hugh felt sure that the answer might be otherwise. "Where else could it be?" he asked. O'Mahon only smiled. Hugh wondered if, blind as he was, he knew when he smiled and that others saw it. A kind of shudder fled along his spine, cold in the low sun. "But then," he said, "it might be far away."

"It might," O'Mahon said. "It might be far away, or it might be close." He chewed on nothing for a moment, and then he said: "Tell me this, cousin: Where is the center of the world?"

That was an old riddle; even boy Hugh knew the answer to it, his uncle Phelim's *brehon* had asked it of him. There are five directions to the world: four of them are north, south, east, and west, and where is the fifth? He knew how to name it, but just at that moment, sitting with bare legs crossed in the ferns in sight of the tower of Dungannon, he did not want to give it.

⌘

In Easter week there appeared out of a silvery morning mist from the southeast a slow procession of horses and men on foot. Even if Hugh watching from the tower had not seen the red and gold banner of the Lord Deputy of Ireland shaken out suddenly by the rainy breeze, he would have known that these were English and not Irish, for the men were a neat, dark cross moving together smartly: a van, the flag in the center where the Lord Deputy rode flanked by his *shot*, men with long guns over their shoulders; and a rear guard with a shambling ox-drawn cart.

He climbed down from the tower calling out the news, but the visitors had been seen already, and Phelim and the O'Hagan and Turlough were already mounting in the courtyard to ride and meet them. Hugh shouted at the horse-boys to bring his pony.

"You stay," Phelim said, pulling on his gloves of English leather.

"I won't," Hugh said, and pushed the horse-boy: "Go on!"

Phelim's horse began shaking his head and dancing away, and Phelim, pulling angrily at his bridle, commanded Hugh to obey; between the horse and Hugh disobeying him, he was getting red in the face, and Hugh was on the pony's back, laughing, before Phelim could take any action against him. Turlough had watched all this without speaking; now he raised a hand to silence Phelim and drew Hugh to his side.

"They might as well see him now as later," he said, and brushed back Hugh's hair with an oddly gentle gesture.

~⁓~

The two groups, English and Irish, stood for a time some distance apart with a marshy stream running between them, while heralds met formally in the middle and carried greetings back and forth. Then the Lord Deputy, in a gesture of condescension, rode forward with only his standard-bearer, splashing across the water and waving a gloved hand to Turlough; at that, Turlough rode down to meet him halfway, and leapt off his horse to take the Lord Deputy's bridle and shake his hand.

Watching these careful approaches Hugh began to feel less forward. He moved his pony back behind Phelim's snorting bay. Sir Henry Sidney was huge: his mouth full of white teeth opened in a black beard that reached up nearly to his eyes, which were small and also black; his great thighs, in hose and high boots, made the slim sword that hung from his baldric look as harmless as a toy. His broad chest was enclosed in a breastplate like a tun; Hugh didn't know its deep stomach was partly false, in the current fashion, but it looked big enough to hold him whole. Sir Henry raised an arm encased in a sleeve more dagged and gathered and complex than any garment Hugh had ever seen, and the squadron behind began to move up, and just then the Lord Deputy's bright eyes found Hugh.

In later years Hugh O'Neill would come to feel that there was within him a kind of treasure-chest or strong-box where certain moments in his life were kept, whole: some of them grand, some terrible, some oddly trivial, all perfect and complete with every sensation and feeling they had contained. Among the oldest which the box would hold was this one, when his uncle Turlough, leading the Deputy's horse, brought him to Hugh, and the Deputy reached down a massive hand and took Hugh's arm like a twig he might break, and spoke to him in English. All preserved: the huge laughing head, the jingle of the horses' trappings, and the sharp odor of their fresh droppings, even the soft glitter of condensing dewdrops on the silver surface of Sir Henry's armor. Dreaming or awake, in

London, in Rome, this moment would now and again be taken out and shown him, a green and silver opal, and make him wonder.

~~~~~

The negotiations leading to Sir Henry's taking Hugh O'Neill away with him to England as his ward went on for some days. The O'Neill's *brehon*, lawyer and lawgiver, translated Sir Henry's English for those who knew none; Sir Henry was patient and careful. Patient, while the Dungannon O'Neills rehearsed again the long story of their wrongs at Shane's hands. Careful not to commit himself to more than he directly promised: that he would be a good friend to the Baron Dungannon, as he called Hugh, while at the same time intimating that large honors could come of it, chiefly the earldom of Tyrone, which since Conn's death had remained in the Queen's gift, unbestowed.

He gave to Hugh a little sheath knife with a small emerald of peculiar hue set in the ivory hilt; he told Hugh that the gem was taken from a Spanish treasure-ship sailing from Peru on the other side of the world. Hugh, excluded from their negotiations, would sit with the women and turn the little knife in his hands, wondering what could be meant by the other side of the world. When it began to grow clear to him that he was meant to go to England with Sir Henry, he grew shy and silent, not daring even to ask what it would be like there. He tried to imagine England: he thought of a vast stone place, like the cathedral of Armagh multiplied over and over, where the sun did not shine.

At dinner Sir Henry saw him loitering at the door of the hall, peeking in. He raised his cup and called to him. "Come, my young lord," he said, and the Irish smiled and laughed at the compliment, though Hugh, whose English was slight, wasn't sure they weren't mocking him. Hands urged him forward, and rather than be pushed before Sir Henry, Hugh stood as tall as he could, his hand on the little knife at his belt, and walked up before the vast man.

"My lord, are you content to go to England with me?"

"I am, if my uncles send me."

"Well, so they do. You will see the Queen there." Hugh answered nothing to this, quite unable to picture the Queen. Sir Henry put a hand on Hugh's shoulder, where it lay like a stone weight. "I have a son near you in age. Well, something younger. His name is Philip."

"Phelim?"

"Philip. Philip is an English name. Come, shall we go tomorrow?" Sir Henry looked around, smiling at his hosts. Hugh was being teased: tomorrow was fixed.

"Tomorrow is too soon," Hugh said, attempting a big voice of Turlough's but feeling only sudden terror. Laughter around him made him snap his head around to see who mocked him. Shame overcame terror. "If it please your Lordship, we will go. Tomorrow. To England." They cheered at that, and Sir Henry's head bobbed slowly up and down like an ox's.

Hugh bowed and turned away, suppressing until he reached the door of the hall a desire to run. Once past the door, he fled: out of the castle, down the muddy lane between the outbuildings, past the lounging O'Hagans on watch, out into the gray night fields over which slow banks of mist lay undulating. Without stopping he ran along a beaten way up through the damp grass, out and up the long rise of earth that lay between Dungannon and the ancient mounds beyond. He kept on, to where a riven oak thrust up, had thrust up for as long as anyone knew, like a tensed black arm and gnarled hand.

Near the oak, almost hidden in the grass, were straight lines of worn mossy stones that marked where once a monastic house had stood; a hummocky sunken place had been its cellar. It was here that Hugh had killed, almost by accident, his first rabbit. He had not been thinking, that day, about hunting, but only sitting on a stone with his face tilted upward into the sun thinking of nothing, his javelin across his lap. When he opened his eyes, the sunlit ground was a coruscating darkness, except for the brown shape of the rabbit in the center of vision, near enough almost to touch. Since then he had felt the place was lucky for him, though he wouldn't have ventured there at night; now he found himself there, almost before he had decided on it, almost before the voices and faces in the hall had settled out of consciousness. He had nearly reached the oak when he saw that someone sat on the old stones.

"Who is it there?" said the man, without turning to look. "Is it Hugh O'Neill?"

"It is," said Hugh, wondering how blind O'Mahon nearly always knew who was approaching him. Nearby a man of the O'Hagans lay with his head pillowed on his arm, asleep; he'd have brought the poet here, tasked to protect him.

"Come here, then, Hugh." Still not turning to him—why should he? and yet it was unsettling—O'Mahon touched the stone seat beside him. "Sit. Do you have iron about you, cousin?"

"I have a knife."

"Take it off, will you? And put it a distance away."

He did as he was told, sticking the little knife in a spiky tree-stump some paces off; somehow the poet's gentle tone brooked neither resistance nor reply.

"Tomorrow," O'Mahon said when Hugh sat next to him again, "you go to England."

"Yes." Hugh felt ashamed to admit it here, even though it had been in no sense his choice; he didn't even like to hear the poet say the place's name.

"It's well you came here, then. For there are . . . personages who wish to say farewell to you. And give you a commandment. And a promise."

The poet wasn't smiling; his face was lean and composed behind a thin fair beard nearly transparent. His bald eyes, as though filled with milk and water, looked not so much blind as simply unused: a baby's eyes. "Behind you," he said, and Hugh looked quickly around, "in the old cellar there, lives one who will come forth in a moment, only you ought not to speak to him."

The cellar-place was obscure; any of its humps, which seemed to shift vaguely in the darkness, might have been someone.

"And beyond, from the rath"—O'Mahon pointed with certainty, though he didn't look, toward the broad ancient tumulus far off, riding blackly like a whale above the white shoals of mist—"now comes out a certain prince, and to him also you should not speak."

Hugh's heart had turned small and hard and beat painfully. He tried to say *Sidhe* but the word would not be said. He looked from the cellar to the rath to the cellar again—and there, a certain tussock darker than the rest grew arms and hands and began with slow patience to pull itself out of the earth. Then a sound as of a great stamping animal came from ahead of him, and, turning, he saw that out of the dark featureless mass of the rath something was proceeding toward him, something like a huge windblown cloak or a quickly oaring boat with a black luffing sail or a stampeding caparisoned horse. He felt a chill shiver up his back. At a sound behind him he turned again, to see a little thick black man, now fully out of the earth, glaring dourly at him (the glints of his eyes all that could be seen of his face) and staggering toward him under the weight of a black chest he carried in his stringy, rooty arms.

An owl hooted, quite near Hugh; he flung his head around and saw it, all white, gliding silently ahead of the Prince who came toward Hugh, of whom and whose steed Hugh could still make nothing but that they were vast, and were perhaps one being, except that now he perceived gray hands perhaps holding reins, and a circlet of gold where a brow might be. The white owl swept near Hugh's head, and with a silent wingbeat climbed to a perch in the riven oak.

There was a brief clap as of thunder behind him. The little black man had set down his chest. Now he glared up at the Prince before him and shook his head slowly, truculently; his huge black hat was like a tussock of grass, but there nodded in it, Hugh saw, a white feather delicate as snow. Beside Hugh, O'Mahon sat unchanged, his hands resting on his knees; but then he raised his head, for the Prince had drawn a sword.

It was as though an unseen hand manipulated a bright bar of moonlight; it had neither hilt nor point, but it was doubtless a sword. The Prince who bore it was furious, that was certain too: he thrust the sword imperiously toward the little man, who cried out with a shriek like gale-tormented branches rubbing, and stamped his feet; but, though resisting, his hands pulled open the lid of his chest. Hugh could see that there was nothing inside but limitless darkness. The little man thrust an arm deep inside and drew out something; then, approaching with deep reluctance only as near as he had to, he held it out to Hugh.

Hugh took it; it was deathly cold. There was the sound of a heavy cape snapped, and when Hugh turned to look, the Prince was already away down the dark air, gathering in his stormy hugeness as he went. The owl sailed after him. As it went away, a white feather fell, and floated zigzag down toward Hugh.

Behind Hugh, a dark hummock in the cellar-place had, for a moment, the glint of angry eyes, and then did not.

Ahead of him, across the fields, a brown mousing owl swept low over the silvery grass.

Hugh had in his hands a rudely carven flint, growing warm from his hand's heat, and a white owl's feather.

"The flint is the commandment," O'Mahon said, as if nothing extraordinary at all had happened, "and the feather is the promise."

"What does the commandment mean?"

"I don't know."

They sat a time in silence. The Moon, amber as old whiskey, appeared between the white-fringed hem of the clouds and the gray heads of the eastern hills. "Will I ever return?" Hugh asked, though he could almost not speak for the painful stone in his throat.

"Yes," O'Mahon said, and rose.

Hugh was shivering now. The O'Hagan kern awoke with a start, as from a dream, and sought for his charge, the poet; O'Mahon took Hugh's hand and with his staff going before him by a step, he went down the way toward the castle. If Sir Henry had known how late into the night Hugh had sat out of doors, he would have been alarmed; the night air, especially in Ireland, was well known to be pernicious.

"Goodbye then, cousin," Hugh said, at the castle gate.

"Goodbye, Hugh O'Neill." O'Mahon smiled. "If they give you a velvet hat to wear in England, your white feather will look fine in it."

Sir Henry Sidney, though he would not have said it to the Irish, was quite clear in his dispatches to the London council why he took up Hugh O'Neill. Not only was it policy for the English to support the weaker man in any quarrel between Irish dynasts, and thus prevent the growth of any over-mighty subject; it also seemed to Sir Henry that, like an eyas falcon, a young Irish lord if taken early enough might later come more willingly to the English wrist. Said otherwise: he was bringing Hugh to England as he might the cub of a beast to a bright and well-ordered menagerie, to tame him.

For that reason, and despite his wife's doubts, he set Hugh O'Neill companion to his own son Philip; and for the same reason he requested his son-in-law the Earl of Leicester to be Hugh's patron at court. "A boy poor in goods," he wrote Leicester, "and full feebly friended."

The Earl of Leicester, in conversation with the Queen, turned a nice simile, comparing his new Irish client to the grafted fruit-trees the Earl's gardeners made: by care and close binding, the hardy Irish apple might be given English roots, though born in Irish soil; and once having them, could not then be separated from them.

"Pray sir, then," the Queen said smiling, "his fruits be good."

"With good husbandry, Madame," Leicester said, "his fruits will be to your Majesty's taste." And he brought forward the boy, ten years old, his proud hair deep red, almost the color of the morocco-leather binding of a little prayer-book the Queen held in her left hand. His pale face and upturned nose were Irish; his eyes were emeralds. Two things the Queen loved were red hair and jewels; she put out her long ringed hand and brushed Hugh's hair.

"Our cousin of Ireland," she said.

He didn't dare raise his red-lashed eyes to her after he had made the courtesy that the Earl had carefully instructed him in; while they talked about him above his head in a courtly southern English he couldn't follow, he looked at the Queen's dress.

She seemed in fact to be wearing several. As though she were some fabulous many-walled fort, mined and breached, through the slashings and partings of her outer dress another could be seen, and where that was opened there was another, and lace beneath that. The outer wall was all jeweled, beaded with tiny seed-pearls as though with dew, worked and embroidered in many patterns of leaf, vine, flower. On her petticoat were pictured monsters of the sea, snorting sea-horses and leviathans with mouths like port-cullises. And on the outer garment's inner side, turned out to reveal them, were sewn a hundred disembodied eyes and ears. Hugh could believe that with those eyes and ears the Queen could see and hear, so that even as he looked at her clothing her clothing observed him. He raised his eyes to her white face framed in stiff lace, her hair dressed in pearls and silver.

Hugh saw then that the power of the Queen resided in her dress. She was bound up in it as magically as the children of Lir were bound up in the forms of swans. The willowy, long-legged courtiers, gartered and wearing slim English swords, moved as in a dance in circles and waves around her when she moved. When she left the chamber (she did not speak to Hugh again, but once her quick, bird eye lighted on him) she drew her ladies-in-waiting after her as though she caught up rustling fallen leaves in her train. The Earl later told Hugh that the Queen had a thousand such gowns and petticoats and farthingales, each more splendid than the last.

A screen elaborately carved—nymphs and satyrs, grape-clusters, incongruous armorial bearings picked out in gold leaf—had concealed from the chamber the Queen's chief counselor, Lord Burghley, and Dr. John Dee, her consulting physician and astrologer; but through the piercings of the screen they had seen and heard.

"That boy," Burghley said softly. "The red-headed one."

"Yes," said Dr. Dee. "The Irish boy."

"Sir Henry Sidney is his patron. He has been brought here to be schooled in English ways. There have been others. Her gracious Majesty believes she can win their hearts and their loyalty. They do learn manners and graces, but they return to their island, and their brutish natures well up again. There is no way to keep them bound to us in those fastnesses."

"I know not for certain," said Dr. Dee, combing his great beard with his fingers, "but it may be that there are ways."

"*Doctissime vir,*" said Burghley, "if there be ways, let us use them."

OBSIDIAN

a light snow lay on the roads and cottages when Hugh O'Neill and Philip Sidney, Sir Henry's son, went from Penshurst, the Sidney house in Kent, up to Mortlake to visit John Dee. There was a jouncing, canopied cart filled with rugs and cushions but the boys preferred to ride with the attendants, until the cold pinched them too deeply through the fine thin gloves and hose they wore. Hugh, careful now in matters of dress, would not have said that his English clothes were useless for keeping out cold compared to a shaggy Waterford mantle with a hood; but he seemed to be always cold and comfortless, somehow naked, in breeches and short cloaks.

Philip, rubbing his hands, his narrow blue-clad buttocks clenched, dismounted and threw his reins to the attendant. When Hugh had climbed in, they pulled shut the curtains and huddled together under the rugs, each laughing at the other's shivers. They talked of the Doctor, as they called Dee, with whom Philip was already studying Latin and Greek and mathematics—Hugh, though the older of the two, had had no lessons as yet, though they'd been promised him. They talked of what they would do when they were grown up and were knights, reweaving with themselves as the heroes the stories of Arthur and Guy of Warwick and the rest. When the two of them played at heroes on their ponies in the fields of Penshurst, Hugh could never bully Philip into taking the lesser part: *I will be a wandering knight, and you must be my esquire.* Philip Sidney knew the tales, and he knew (almost before he knew anything else of the world) that the son of an Irish chieftain could not have ascendancy even in play over the son of an English knight.

But whenever Philip had Hugh at stick-swordspoint in a combat, utterly defeated, Hugh would leap up and summon from the hills and forests a sudden host of helpers who slew Philip's merely mortal companions. Or he postulated a crow who was a great princess he had long ago aided, whose feet he could grasp and be carried to safety, or an oak tree that would open and hide him away.

It wasn't fair, Philip would cry, these sudden hosts that Hugh sang forth in harsh unmusical Irish. They didn't fit any rules, they had nothing to do with the triumph of good knights over evil ones, and why anyway did they only help Hugh?

"Because my family once did them a great service," Hugh said to Philip in the rocking wagon. The matter was never going to be resolved.

"Suppose my family had."

"Guy of Warwick hasn't any family."

"I say now that he does, and so he does."

"And there aren't . . . fairy-folk in England." That term carefully chosen.

"For sure there are."

"No there are not, and if there were how could you summon them? Do you think they understand English at all?"

"I will summon them in Latin. *Veni, venite, spiritus sylvani, dives fluminarum . . .*"

Hugh kicked at the covers and at Philip, laughing. Latin!

Once, they'd taken the issue to the wisest man they knew, excepting Doctor Dee himself, whom they didn't dare to ask: Buckle, the Penshurst gamekeeper.

"There was fairies here," he said to them. His enormous gnarled hands honed a long knife back and forth, back and forth on a whetstone. "But that was before King Harry's time, when I was a boy and said the Ave-Mary."

"See there!" said Philip.

"Gone," said Hugh.

"My grandam saw them," said Buckle. "Saw one sucking on the goat's pap like any kid, and so the goat were dry when she came to milk it. But not now in this new age." Back and forth went the blade, and Buckle tested it on the dark and ridgy pad of his thumb.

"Where did they go?" Philip asked.

"Away," Buckle said. "Gone away with the friars and the Mass and the Holy Blood of Hailes."

"But where?" Hugh said.

A smile altered all the deep crags and lines of Buckle's face. "Tell me," he said, "young master, where your lap goes when you stand up."

Doctor Dee's wife, Jane, gave the boys a posset of ale and hot milk to warm them, and when they had drunk it the Doctor offered them a choice: they might read in whatever books of his they liked, or work with his mathematical tools and study his maps, which he had unrolled on a long table, with compass and square laid on them. Philip chose a book, a rhymed romance that Doctor Dee chuckled at; the boy nested himself in cushions, opened his book, and was soon asleep *like a mouse in cotton-wool*, Jane Dee said. Hugh bent over the maps with the Doctor, whose round spectacles enlarged his eyes weirdly, his long beard nearly trailing across the sheets.

What Hugh had first to learn was that the maps showed the world not as a man walking in it sees it, but as a bird flying high over it. High, high: Doctor Dee showed him on a map of England the length of the journey from Penshurst to Mortlake, and it was no longer than the joint of his thumb. And then England and Ireland too grew small and insignificant when Doctor Dee unrolled a map of the whole wide world. Or half of it: the world, he told Hugh, is round as a ball, and this was a picture of but one half. A ball! Hung by God in the middle of the firmament, the great stars going around it in their spheres and the fixed stars in theirs. The world *did* have another side.

"This," the Doctor said, "is the Irish island, across St. George's Channel. Birds may fly across from there to here in the half-part of a day."

Hugh thought: the children of Lir.

"All these lands of Ireland, Wales, and Scotland"—his long finger showed them—"are the estate of the British Crown, of our Imperial Queen, whose sworn servant you are." He smiled warmly, looking down upon Hugh.

"So also am I," said Philip, who'd awakened and come behind them.

"And so you are." He turned again to his maps. "But look you. It is not only these Isles Britannicæ that belong to her. In right, these lands to the North, of the Danes and the Norwayans, they are hers too, by virtue of their old Kings her ancestors—though it were inadvisable to lay claim to them now. And farther too, beyond the ocean sea."

He began to tell them of lands far to the west, of Estotiland and Grœnland, of Atlantis. He talked of King Malgo and King Arthur, of Lord Madoc and Saint Brendan the Great; of Sebastian Caboto and John Caboto, who reached the shores of Atlantis almost before Columbus sailed. They, and others after, had set foot upon those lands and claimed them for kings from whom Elizabeth descended; and so they adhere to the British Crown. And to resume them under her rule the Queen need ask no leave of Spaniard or of Portingale.

"I will find new lands too, for the Queen," Philip said. "And you shall come too, to guide me. And Hugh shall be my esquire!"

Hugh O'Neill was silent, thinking: the kings of Ireland did not yield their lands to the English. The Irish lands were held by other kings, and other peoples altogether, from a time before time. And if a new true king could be crowned at Tara, that king would win those lands again.

~

It was time now for the boys to return to Kent. Outside, the serving-men could be heard mounting up, their spurs and trappings jingling.

"Now give my love and duty to your father," Doctor Dee said to Philip, "and take this gift from me, to guide you when you are grown, and set out upon those adventures you seek." He took from his table a small book, unbound and sewn with heavy thread. It was not printed but written in the Doctor's own fine hand, and the title said *General and Rare Memorials Pertayning to the Perfect Arte of Navigation.* Philip took it in his hands with a sort of baffled awe, aware of the honor, uncertain of the use; he sat and opened it.

"And for my new friend of Hibernia," he said. "Come with me." He took Hugh away to a corner of his astonishingly crowded room, pushed aside a glowing globe of pale brown crystal in a stand, lifted a dish of gems, and with an *Ah!* he picked up something that Hugh did not at first see.

"This," Doctor Dee said, "I will give you as my gift, in memorial of this day, if you will but promise me one thing. That you will keep it, always, on your person, and part with it never nor to no one." Hugh didn't know what to say to this, but the Doctor went on speaking as though Hugh had indeed promised. "This, young master, is a thing of which there is but one in the world. The uses of it will be borne in upon you when the need for them is great."

What he then put into Hugh's hand was an oval of black glass, glass more black than any he had ever seen, black too black to look right at, yet he could see that it reflected back to him his own face, as though he had come upon a stranger in the dark. It was bound in gold, and hung from a gold chain. On the back the surface of the gold was marked with a sign Hugh had never seen before: he touched the engraved lines with a finger.

"*Monas hieroglyphica*," said Doctor Dee. He lifted the little obsidian mirror from Hugh's hand by its brittle chain, hung it around the boy's neck. When Hugh again looked into the black sheen of it he saw neither himself nor any other thing; but his skin burned and his heart was hot. He looked to the Doctor, who only tucked the thing away within Hugh's doublet.

When he was at Penshurst again and alone—it was not an easy thing to be alone in the Sidney house, with the lords and ladies and officers of the Queen coming and going, and Philip's beautiful sister teasing, and the servants passing this way and that—Hugh opened his shirt and took in his fingers the thing the Doctor had given him. The privy (where he sat) was cold and dim. He touched the raised figure in the gold of the back, which looked a little like a crowned mannikin but likely was not, and turned it over. In the mirror was a face, but now not his own; for it wasn't like looking into a mirror at all, but like looking through a spy-hole into another place, a spy-hole through which someone in that place looked back at him. The person looking at him was the Queen of England.

On the Impregnation of Mirrors was not a book or a treatise or a Work; it wouldn't survive the wandering life that John Dee was to embark upon as the times and the heavens turned. It was just a few sheets, folded octavo and written in the Doctor's scribble hand, and no one not the Doctor would have been able to practice what it laid out, for certain necessary elements and motions went unwritten except in the Doctor's breast. Only one mirror of those that he had worked the art upon had succeeded entirely, only one had drawn the lines of time and space together so as to transmit the spirit of the owner to the eye of the possessor.

The making of it began with a paradox. If the impregnation of a mirror required that the one who first looked into it be its owner, then no other could ever have looked into it before, not he who silvered the glass, not she who polished the steel. How could the maker not be the owner? John Dee had seen the solution. There was one perfect mirror that needed no silvering, no polishing: it needed only to be discovered, detected, its smooth side inferred, then taken from the ground and secreted before even the finder's eye fell upon its face. He knew of many such fragments, taken from the lava fields of Greece or the Turkish lands, first found, as Pliny saith, by the traveller Obsius; his own he'd found on a lesser field, in Scotland. He remembered the cold hill, the fragments sharp as knives; his eyes kept steadily on the fast-flying clouds above while his fingers felt for the perfectest one, pocketing it unlooked-at.

He had placed it in the Queen's hand himself. Slipping it from where it hid in a purse of kidskin, feeling for its smoother side: which he held up to her face for a long moment, as long a moment as he dared, before giving it to her to examine. She seemed dazzled by it, amazed, though she had seen similar obsidian chips before. None like this one: Doctor Dee had bestirred its latent powers by prayer—and also by means that he had learned from helpers he would not name, not in the hearing of this Court.

And then forever there was the Queen's face within, and more than her face, her very self: her thought, her command, her power to entrance, how well the Doctor knew it. She had not asked to keep it—the one outcome he had feared. No, she had given it back to him with a gracious nod, and turned to other matters, for it was his. And now it was not his. Having taken its owner's face and nature, it could be handled, and the Doctor had milled it and framed it in gold and given it to the Irish boy to be sole the receiver of what the Queen, the sole giver, might give.

It may be there are ways.

Doctor Dee at month's end stood on a Welsh headland from where, on this clear day, the Irish coast could just be seen across St. George's Channel. The sun was setting behind the inland hills of the other island, making them seem large and near with the golden brightness. There where the sun set, Hugh O'Neill was one day to become a great chief; the Doctor's informants had let him know of it. In those years to come the little Irish chiefs and the old Irish lords would press Hugh to make a single kingdom out of the island that had never been one before, and to push out the English for good. But Hugh O'Neill—whether he ever came to know it or did not—was as though tethered by a long leash, the one end about his neck, the other held in the Queen's hand, though she too might never know of it; and the tug of it, of her thought and will and desire and need, would keep the man in check. She could turn to other matters, the greater world, more dangers.

And turn to Doctor Dee himself as well, his needs, his scope.

He turned from the sea. A single cloud like a great beast streaked with blood went away to the north with the wind, changing as it went.

A GRAY GOOSE

*t*he English did not like it at all that Shane O'Neill had given to himself the ancient title of *an Ò Neill*. This style fit nothing in the English system of knights, barons, lords, dukes, and marquises all arrayed in their ranks beneath their monarch. "The O'Neill" named nothing to them but a clan chieftain, a warlord, a despoiler. Shane O'Neill was a murderer: his father Bacach, whose name meant *cripple,* was the O'Neill before him, but Bacach quarreled with his son, and he ended dying in a dungeon of Shane's. The English didn't mind any of that, nor did it count for much with them that Shane had killed his brother Matthew, who claimed the title that Shane thought should be his. But thereupon Shane had gathered the clan at the rock of Tullahogue, where long ago O'Neill kings were crowned. There he took the white staff from the O'Hagans and declared himself the O'Neill, and his kerne and gallowglass made a great noise beating their swords upon their shields and screaming. And all the dead chiefs of the O'Neills could be heard murmuring their approval in the wind: so it was said.

That was what had roused the English: the massing of an Irish army, the claims of great power blessed by old gods and still-potent forebears.

The new Lord Deputy of Ireland, Sir Henry Sidney's successor, knew enough about the society wherein Shane and his rivals arose and their alliances were made. He ordered Shane to appear before him to account for his rebellious behavior, and acknowledge the Queen's authority over his lands and his person. To which Shane made no answer. Months of pursuit and encounter followed as English captains and English soldiery tried to bring Shane to heel, to teach him his duty and his manners. He fought them off time and again, and Hugh in Sir Henry Sidney's house heard of it at table and said little or nothing. When Shane at last capitulated, it was not from Sir Henry that Hugh heard the news, but from Philip: how Shane, weary, sick of living rough, had agreed to a *composition:* he would come in to Dublin, and thence to Windsor, there to "kneel before the Queen," Philip said grandly to Hugh, "and beg her pardon, and he will *kiss the hem of her garment*. And Hugh—you will be there to see it!"

~~~~~

Jewels in their ears, tiny jewels woven into the stiff fabrics of their coats, great jewels on their fingers and thumbs, jewels catching the jeweled light from high stained-glass windows: the Queen's courtiers stand on the steps below the throne and roundabout, in rough order of precedence or royal favor; knuckles on hips, gloved hands lying lightly on jeweled swords. In high seats are ambassadors from several lands, in finery of their own. Henry Sidney and his son Philip; Hugh O'Neill in black figured silk, white ruff at his neck, a white feather he'd placed in his velvet cap. The company stirs as though a wind passes through: doors are opened, trumpets and a herald with a scroll announce the arrival of a man the English don't know how to name. They will not call him "the O'Neill," no matter that he claims the honor, and he is not yet by the grace of God and the Queen's majesty Earl of Tyrone. A wit has decided he shall be "the *Great* O'Neill, cousin to Saint Patrick, friend to Queen Elizabeth, and foe to all the world beside." This piece of condescension has circulated, is being traded about even as the man appears (a murmur runs through those witnessing, though the Queen is as motionless as an idol). Swathed in a voluminous saffron tunic, boots to his thighs, taking great slow steps as though sleep-walking, his eyes are fixed on the Queen as on a goal. Behind him come two rows of henchmen, all in old-fashioned leaf mail from knee to neck and bearing each a three-foot battle-axe before him. All shaven and shorn but for the glib of hair falling over their eyes, all dressed in wolfskins.

So the story would be told ever after, a story that Hugh would hear from Englishmen who'd claim they witnessed it, who had stood there—they'd say—as the strange vision passed by. For sure it passed by Hugh O'Neill: Shane strode on without seeing him, wouldn't have known him anyway. But the wolfskins of the English story were mere shaggy enveloping Irish mantles, all different; the soldiers' woolen trews were bound in thongs of leather. Their chosen weapons were all different too, each his own. Three-foot-long battle-axes! Hugh would smile to be told that, and he'd nod, and let it be.

When Shane came near the throne he suddenly stopped still, let out a great yowl, and fell to his knees, then prostrate, forehead to the stones. He began loudly to beg the Queen's pardon, in English, and in Irish proclaim his innocence: innocence of the death of his father Conn Bacach, of the murder of his brother Matthew, he himself a plain gentleman wanting only peace and to do service for the Queen his liege. There was some tittering at this gibberish, which only Hugh of those watching could understand much of. Hugh wondered, seeing his uncle's length stretched before the carpeted steps that he himself had climbed, if now the Queen would project herself into Shane's soul as she had into his, Hugh's; and, if he was one day to be the O'Neill himself, would he too lie weeping before her, begging forgiveness? If he bore her with him always, how would he not?

Sir Henry didn't believe that Shane would abide by any commitment he made to the Queen and to the English powers in Ireland. Nor had he trusted any of the other Gael comers-in with their tears and avowals. What he did trust was that any one of them might at any time turn on another, as Shane had done, and relieve the English commanders of the work of suppression. By the time an English army took the field the warring Gaels could be expected to have done one another in, or the one to have harmed the other badly enough to make him no threat after.

As the Butlers in the south of the island had done to the Earl of Desmond. Sir Henry smiled to think of that, even as the Queen and her counselors prepared to depart the chamber, leaving Shane to the lawyers and the judges. The Great O'Neill! As, in after years, perhaps the boy Hugh might be—another thorn in the English side, unless he learned the lessons now put before him. Sir Henry laughed at the thought, his hands on the shoulders of his son and his ward, and the boys looked up to see what amused him.

Desmond!

"We shall go a-visiting this night, my lads," he said.

~⁓~

What had he done, the Earl of Desmond?

Hugh hadn't travelled to the south of Ireland, to Munster where the poet O'Mahon said the world began, and out of which came all the things that are: and Death one of the things. But he knew the stories of its great ones, the Geraldines, the Burkes, the Butlers, who had come to Ireland long ago with an English king. They'd driven out the old princes of that land, the Fomoire giants and the sons of Mil, or perhaps it was a different foe they met with there. They built castles such as they had had in England, four-square with a tower at each corner. They went into battle armored, rode armored horses, married Irish wives, and called themselves *earls:* of Desmond and Ormond, Kildare and Thomond and Clanricarde. In time they were English only in what they believed they remembered and the blood they boasted of; many spoke little English, and had secretaries to write and read documents, make cases in English courts. And when the new English came then to take land and enforce English laws, the earls opposed them.

That's what Hugh O'Neill knew.

When the Queen had withdrawn, Henry Sidney took his boys down to the Privy Stair and to the river, where watermen called for fares. The winter twilight had settled on the dark water; a scarf of cloud was drawn over the Moon. When he had summoned a boat Sir Henry put the boys aboard and got in himself, tipping the little craft with his bulk. *Southwark,* he told the waterman. *St. Leger House, his stair.*

"Where the Earl of Desmond is kept," said Philip in Hugh's ear. The waterman standing in the prow, his long oar seeming to search the black water, looked back at them, and with no reason to, shook his head and laughed.

At the water-stairs of Warham St. Leger's house, the boat put in with delicate exactness—the waterman winked at the boys as he took his coin from Sir Henry. Already servants with lamps were coming down from the house to bring them in.

Sir Henry and Sir Warham had much to talk of, concerns they shared as officers of the Crown who had governed Ireland under various titles in different years. Sir Henry drew his son to his side— there were good lessons he could learn in this house. When Sir Warham had taken Hugh's hand and questioned him briefly, Hugh was sent away with an armed serving-man of the house, summoned to take him through the gathering night. He would meet a great man, Sir Henry told him, and might talk with him in in his own tongue. "Remember me to his Grace," he said, with that wide wolfish smile, the smile that Hugh had first seen at the stream in Dungannon.

He was led out a different door from the one they'd gone in; he followed an *eight-foot-high iron-bound serving-man* bearing a lamp, his thick boots better than Hugh's fine slippers for the puddled way. Past the shuttered chandleries and a black chapel and into a street of taverns small and large, some no bigger than a little Irish bothy, some like good houses. The man stopped at a middling one, and after hanging his lamp on a peg by the door, he sat down heavily on a bench there, and adjusted his short sword and his cudgel.

"Go in, young maister," he said with a strange gentleness. "You'll know your man." He raised his eyes to the blank night sky. "And if it please 'ee, ask the landlord there to send out a minim of sherris sack, warmed with the poker for this cold night."

Hugh turned the ring on the door and pushed it open. There was a fire, and lamps lit, and voices, though few folk. Every one turned to see Hugh enter. One man, seated alone at a table, seemed to make a center in the room, as though alight while the others were dark. Yet he was gaunt, and weak-seeming, his hair thin and lank, his eyes hollow; a bottle before him. How it was that Hugh O'Neill could name the man, he didn't know; but he put off his hat and bowed, not deeply but respectfully, and he said—in English and then in Irish—*greetings, my lord of Desmond. How is it with your Lordship?* And the ill man regarded him and smiled, for he also knew to whom he spoke.

It was not well with his lordship.

On a May morning two years before, not far from a ford called Affane on the Blackwater River, Gerald Fitzgerald, the Earl of Desmond, and his neighbor Thomas Butler, the Earl of Ormond, with their allies and dependents, fought a battle: their feuding had lasted for generations, and this battle would be the last they would fight for sway and rule in Munster.

So said Earl Desmond to Hugh O'Neill in the Southwark inn: the last.

Butler and his O'Kennedys and Kilpatricks and Burkes had driven Desmond and his MacCarthys and O'Sullivans and McSheehys into the Blackwater River to be cut down in great numbers: Geraldines on the field that day were killed in the hundreds. As Desmond was rallying the last of his supporters—he told Hugh—a pistol was fired at him, striking him in the thigh, causing him to fall from his horse, to lie in the mud unable to rise, the thigh-bone broken. *I know the man who fired that shot,* he told Hugh, but it might as well have been that Desmond—who had long been ill and was never strong, a cripple who had needed help even to mount a horse—had simply been thrown, or lost his seat. In any case the Butlers lifted the helpless man to their shoulders like a slain stag, and mocked him, saying *Where now is the mighty Earl of Desmond?* And Gerald had answered—he told Hugh with a ghastly grin—*Where he belongs, on the necks of the Butlers!* As though he'd won, and not lost all.

"The worst of the crime," Desmond said to Hugh, "the very worst in the Queen's eyes, was that we and the Butlers flew our ancient flags as we went into battle. And how should we not? Yet the Queen believed and still believes that the land of Munster is England, and no man or army shall raise a standard there or contend with others for his ancient lands and rights. And she ordered the Butlers and we Fitzgeralds alike, to England, to stand before her, and beg her pardon."

The triumphant Butlers came in willingly enough: the Butler Earl of Ormond, "Black Tom," and his cohort, bringing Desmond Fitzgerald on a litter, laid helpless before the Queen. Sicker than he had been when he fell in the field Affane, his wound untended to, still in the filth of the garment he wore then. Able to speak only to assent, to beg for pardon, a whisper the Queen must lean forward from her chair to hear.

"She forgave Tom Butler," the Earl said now to Hugh. "For he was her playmate in girlhood, playmate and who knows what more, and she despised me always. *He* was forgiven and sent home. I was sent as a traitor to the Tower."

The innkeeper appeared at Desmond's side, took away the empty bottle, and placed another wrapped in straw before him, and solemnly drew the cork. Hugh put the request of Sir Warham's serving-man to him, and got a cold nod. Desmond lifted a finger, and the innkeeper placed a cup before Hugh; the Earl filled it full.

"More than any of that, though," he said, his voice grown dimmer. "Tom Butler is a Protestant, and a firm and strict one, strange as it might seem. I am of the old faith, the true faith, as you are, young Ulsterman."

It was so. All the North beyond the Pale of Dublin was of the true faith. Yet Hugh felt gather in the room an air of challenge and stress, drawn around him like an eeler's net, and thought he knew why: he touched his breast, the thick doublet that covered the Doctor's gift. "She has forgiven you now, my lord? So that you may live in Sir Warham's house?"

"If you can say *live*," the Earl of Desmond said. He drank again, poured wine again for both. "There is a tale told of my ancestor, who loved a woman of the other world. He did not know she was what she was, look you, but she seemed only a beautiful woman he encountered bathing. He stole her cloak from her, and without it she could not flee nor transform herself into another shape, and so he had her, and she told him that if he had not taken the cloak he never would have. And from that event she bore him a son. And she told him before she departed into her otherworld place in Knockainey Hill, that if he loved that son at all, he was *never to show surprise* at anything he did."

"Was it your father's father?" Hugh asked. He swallowed wine, feeling that strange entanglement around him withdraw, as though in avoidance.

"Oh, farther back than that, far farther," said the Earl. "But here is the thing of it. That son was a great leaper. At a feast he was challenged to show his skill. And from right where he stood, he leapt"—here the Earl swept his white hand into the air—"*right into a bottle* that was there on the board. Then he leapt out again."

Hugh laughed aloud, and the drinkers looked toward him, and away again.

"But you see," said Desmond, whose voice was growing thinner with every breath, "his father then said *he never thought the boy had any such power as that!* And with his marveling, he lost the son, just as the mother had foretold he would. For the son left the hall, and they at the feast followed and watched him go to the river-bank, and though he had seemed a man like any man, when his foot touched the water he became a gray goose and swam away, and never returned."

He lifted the bottle before him, and made to pour from it, but then put it down again. "I am not such a leaper," he said. "I can leap into a bottle, you see. But I can't leap out again."

Two figures that Hugh had before seen leaning together on a seat by the fire now stood as at a signal. They were so alike, swaddled in the same mantles, holding the same ragged staffs, that Hugh thought they must be twins, or one man multiplied. Without a word they came to stand at either side of the Earl, who lifted his hands for them to take. They brought him to his feet. From the chair he had occupied they took up a heavy cloak, and wrapped it around him with practiced skill. Then with one on either side of him he began to progress toward the door, his feet as though only pretending to take steps, like a puppet.

Hugh rose and stood aside, bowing low at his passing, but Desmond drew him to his side, and put his lips to Hugh's ear. *She sees me always*, he whispered. Then he was carried out, and borne down the slimy street, his helpers guiding him to his bed, or to another pot-house. St. Leger's serving-man rose from his bench, took up his lamp, burning low now, and walked before Hugh down the way he had come.

That night, in the bed in Sir Warham's house he shared with Philip, Hugh awoke seeing in the darkness the Queen's face, fading into glowing nothing. *She sees me always.* He lay unmoving, neither asleep nor awake, seeing the black surface of the river he had walked along. And a gray goose, moving strongly over the stirred water toward the far bank, which was not crowded with houses and wharves but stony and edged with reed-beds. As the bird came near to shore it lifted great pinions, and beat up out of the river into the dark air, shedding water as it rose.

TIR-OEN

It was seven years after he had come to England when Hugh O'Neill was returned to Ulster. The quiet boy had grown into a quiet young man, solid, careful. He had hardly spoken Irish or heard it spoken in all that time, except in memory. He was not yet the O'Neill, he was not Earl of Tyrone, but nor was he any other man. On the journey over the sea, Sir Henry Sidney—returning to Ireland to be Lord Deputy again, at the Queen's command—told Hugh that Hugh's half-brother Brian had been murdered, and it was certain that Brian's murderers had been sent by Shane. Hugh's distant uncle Turlough Luineach was now Shane's *tanist* or heir presumptive, and the English favored him—whatever that might mean for Turlough's benefit, to which the English would never commit in advance: perhaps an empty title—wealth and sway—or nothing at all. By the English designations, Hugh was himself only Baron Dungannon. All that he wanted for himself was to remain within the Queen's compass, which was at once large and close, generous and strait.

On Irish soil again, with English soldiers in his train and around his neck an English engine whose power he did not fully know. Clad as all rising young Englishmen were clad in that season of that year, he rode through Dublin and was not hailed or cheered. Who was on his side, who could he count on? There were the O'Hagans, who were loyal but poor, and the O'Donnells of Tyrconnell, sons of the fierce Scotswoman Ineen Duvh (the "Dark Girl"), who were as often O'Neill foes as friends. And Englishmen: Henry Sidney for certain, the Queen's men Burghley and Walsingham, who had taken his hand at his departure and smiled—surely they wished him well. They'd seen Shane O'Neill prostrate before the Queen, and some had known Shane's father, Conn O'Neill, and had remarked on the white feather Hugh wore always in his cap. At Court his patron the Earl of Leicester had whispered to him *And so the title for the earldom is undecided?* Hugh had learned more than courtly English from them, about their land and his own. Their eyes were colder than their hands.

The castle-tower of Dungannon still stood, but many of the old chiefs and their adherents who had feasted and quarreled there were scattered, fighting each other, or gone south to fight the incoming English settlers along with the heirs of Desmond. But at the news of the Baron Dungannon come home again they had begun returning, more every day. There were women still there in the castle, and from them he learned that his mother had died in a house of the O'Hagans.

"It is ill times," said blind O'Mahon, who had remained.

"It is."

O'Mahon lay on his couch, wrapped in a heavy mantle. "Well, you have grown, cousin. And in many ways too."

"I am the one I was," Hugh said.

"Tell me," O'Mahon said. "Once in a place nearby, up that mile to the crest of the hill, where a holy house once stood . . ."

"I remember," Hugh said.

"A thing was given you."

"Yes."

You may keep a thing about you, in one pocket or purse or another, and forget you have it; think to toss it away now and then and yet never do—not because it's of value but only because it's *yours*, a bit of yourself, and has long been. So the little carven flint had lain here and there throughout Hugh's growing up, getting lost and then turning up again. It didn't seem now to be what it had been: a thing of cold power, with a purpose of its own, too heavy for its size. It had become a small old stone, scratched with the figure of a man that a child might draw.

He felt here and there in his clothes and came upon it: felt it leap into his hand as soon as it could. He drew it out and for a foolish moment thought to display it to the blind man. "I have it still," he said.

"Will you go with me tomorrow, again up to that place?"

"If you like, cousin."

The next evening O'Mahon took O'Neill's arm, and together they went to the stables and chose horses for the journey. Hugh led O'Mahon to his old horse, who would be his eyes, as the journey was one the horse knew well enough. After an hour's ride they reached the place where the earth had opened on that night. They rode on past the riven oak, and there they left the horses. O'Mahon took Hugh's arm again; he knew well where he went but wanted help so as not to stumble on the way. "I have walked these paths since I was born," he said. "And before." They climbed the low hill that Hugh had known in childhood, when he had first come to this country with his O'Hagan fosterers; but then there had been tall trees, now cut, and beyond the trees the river, the fields of corn and pasture where cattle moved. Now fallow and bare.

"Day goes," the poet said, as though he saw it. Amid the low rolling of the hills there was the one hill taller and of a shape not made by wind and water, but by hands—it was easy to tell. Nearly six hundred rods around, but smaller somehow now than when he had seen it as a boy. "This hour is the border of day and night, as the river is the border of here and there. What cannot be known by day or night shows itself at twilight."

"You know these things, who can't see them?"

"My eyes are a border too, cousin. At which I forever stand."

They waited in silence there while the sky turned black above and to a pale, red-streaked green in the west. A mist gathered in the hollows. Hugh O'Neill would not later remember the moment, if there was a moment, when a host came forth, if it did, and stood there against the rath, hard to see but surely there in Hugh's sight. Growing in numbers as he watched, mounted and afoot.

"The foreign queen you love and serve," O'Mahon said. "She cares nothing for you but this: that you keep this Isle in subjection for her sake, until and when she can fill it with her hungry subjects and poor relations, to take from it what they will."

The ghost warriors were clearer now. Hugh could almost hear the rustle they made and the rattle of their arms. The Old Ones, the *Sidhe*.

"They command you to fight, Hugh O'Neill of the O'Neills. To lead. The O'Neill you will be, and what more you do not know. But you are not unfriended."

The warriors formed and reformed in the dark, their steeds turning in place, their lances like saplings in wind: as though impatient for him to cry out to them in supplication, or call them to his side.

The commandment, Hugh thought: the flint in his hand. But he could say nothing to them, not with his voice, not in his heart. Soon the border of night and day was closed, and he could see them no more. It was as though a great wind had snatched away his clothes, his velvets and silks, kidskin gloves, bonnet and ruff, and left him naked, a child again, not knowing where to turn.

⁓

There was a woman at that time living on the island of Achill off the coast of Donegal in the west of Ireland; her name was Gráinne O'Malley, and she was mistress over a force of sea-reivers that raided up and down the Isles, to Scotland and south as far as Brittany. She had built herself a castle on Achill and another on Clare Island and her long galleys went out from Clew Bay to raid, and she commanded them herself from the deck of the largest. When young she was "the crop-haired girl" who wore boy's clothes and made herself such a nuisance that her father took her aboard his vessels on his trading trips to Spain, and left his son at home. She could read and write, and knew pistols as well as the cutlass. It was said that she and her family were wreckers who built fires on headlands to bring ships to destruction, which her people then could profit from: any man who said that was her enemy, and would feel the sting of that enmity. She was encircled by enemies who were as often friends: the wild O'Flahertys who seemed to kill for pleasure, the McMahons of the interior, the Scots MacDonnells and their hosts of Scots redshanks, who had settled in the glen of Antrim and claimed it for their own. She was some thirty or forty years old and had become a force all through the Mayo coast when, on an early spring morning, a courier came to Dungannon and there asked to speak to Hugh O'Neill, now himself a man of twenty, his beard red and thick. He had a message, he said, for the *lord tanist*, from the lady Gráinne. He was brought into the kitchen, offered food and drink, but accepted only water. Word was sent to Hugh. It was a silent hour until he stood at the kitchen door.

"Why," said Hugh, "do you call me that? *Tanist*."

The courier rose from his seat and put his hands together behind his back. "Are you not, sir?"

"The heir of Shane O'Neill is an uncle of mine," Hugh said. "Turlough Luineach. Duly elected." The bland face of the courier did not alter. "Where is the message you have brought?"

"It is not written down. I have it in memory."

Hugh sat at the table. The women and the boys cooking and sweeping drew away. The courier took his seat again. "I have heard that your mistress is a learned woman," Hugh said. "Writes in English, and in Latin too."

"True," said the courier. "Yet now and then it seems to her good that no paper bear her thoughts, lest it fall into wrong hands."

Hugh studied the slim figure. "Has your horse been seen to?" he asked.

"I came on no horse. I run on my own legs."

"A long way, and in bad weather."

"There was much to see, much to pity also."

A silence came between them, like a third person at the table, who then departed. "Tell me what your lady wishes me to know," Hugh said.

"That *an Ò Neill*, Shane, your uncle, is now at war with the Scots MacDonnells in Antrim, allies of my lady. Shane has this summer gone to war against them that he might make Antrim a part of his own realm."

"Sorley Boye MacDonnell is their leader there," Hugh said. "A Scots chief."

"Shane has lately attacked Sorley Boye and taken him prisoner, and broken the power of the Scots. Sorley himself he keeps in a tower and will not feed him, and he is like to die of it. My lady Gráinne asks for your help against Shane, in aid of the Scots MacDonnells, her friends."

Hugh thought: What have I to do with MacDonnells? The face of the courier had not altered, and his white hands lay unmoving in his lap. Sir Henry Sidney had built a ring of little forts and breastworks along the border of the western lands that Shane claimed, lands that were in reality the lands of the Earl of Tyrone, who was not Shane, nor was it Hugh: for that title was in the granting of the Crown. Sidney would be very glad to hear of the end of Shane, in whatever manner that end might come.

"Tell your Lady Gráinne," he said with care, "that though she is a pirate and a reiver on the sea she may have her freedom and live long. Dublin and the English care nothing for that."

"No, they do not," said the courier.

"And if there be a way that she can find to reconcile Shane and the MacDonnells, and to settle the question of the glens of Antrim, that would be a fine thing."

The two young men—one at least was young, and the other young-seeming, or ageless, it could not be easily said what he might be in years—were silent awhile, till Hugh, restless in his seat, leaned forward to the other. "A reconciling. Let Shane release old Sorley Boye and the MacDonnells will rejoice. And Sir Henry in Dublin will forgive Shane his crimes, and take down those fortifications. The Scots settlements in Antrim will be undisturbed. Do you see?"

The courier didn't reply.

"I too will forgive him," Hugh said, his head suddenly hot with a power he hadn't known he would express. "I will. And as an offering of friendship I will give a quantity of gold to be divided among the MacDonnell chiefs, the *flatha*, at a meeting of all in the Ulster camp of the MacDonnells, which Gráinne O'Malley must call for. Do you understand? Open some barrels of *uisquebagh* and all will drink to the new peace, even Sorley Boye, when he has had meat."

The courier waited unmoving for more. Then he said: "This answer I should bring to my lady?"

"Yes."

The courier—it was not easy to detect, but Hugh could see it—was smiling faintly, as though pleased, or did he mock? He rose then from his seat, still smiling. With a slight tilt to his head—not a bow, not a nod—he stepped backward from Hugh's presence, then turned to leave the kitchen.

Hugh thought: He had not been fed, not given drink or any sustenance, which was wrong, though the man hadn't asked or demanded it, as was his right. He got up and went to the narrow window that looked to the west. He could just see the courier, going away, taking long easy strides up the hill into the growing dusk.

Conn Bacach O'Neill, the first of the O'Neills to be named Earl of Tyrone, had loved a woman named Alison, the daughter, or it may have been the wife, of a blacksmith called Kelly. Conn got Alison with child, and the child was named Matthew, and he was the father in turn of Hugh and his brother Brian. Shane, legitimate son of Conn, was set aside by his father in favor of Matthew—Conn must have loved Alison greatly, to take such a step—and it became the lifelong work of Shane, *Sean an Diomais,* Shane the Proud, to secure for himself the title of the O'Neill and his right to the earlship by the easiest way, which was the successive murders of Matthew and Matthew's sons. Before Shane could find the boy Hugh, he had been taken away to England by Sir Henry Sidney, who knew very well what titles he had claim to, if he could stay alive to keep them.

Now Hugh O'Neill waited.

It wasn't a month, it was not more than the nights between half-Moon and new Moon, when news came to him from Sir Henry in Dublin: a packet, with the seal of the Lord Deputy, handed to him by a red-coated English messenger on a morning he was out with his horses and his cousins. The packet, when undone of its ribbons, ordered Hugh O'Neill and a list of other names (many he knew, not all) to come to Dublin city at the command of the Queen, there to make a further confession of the wrongs they had done and the crimes they had committed against the Crown and the peace of the land. Sir Henry added a note in his own rapid hand, telling Hugh that the head of his uncle Shane, pickled in a pipkin, had been brought to Dublin, and at the Lord Deputy's order was now stuck up on a pike at the city gate. It was still there, a grinning death's-head that might be anyone's, when Hugh O'Neill and a body of his men came to Dublin Castle, to find that he and the others named in the Lord Deputy's document were to take ship with Sir Henry for England.

Had he, Hugh, not made obeisance enough?

"The queen of pirates, Grace O'Malley," Sir Henry told him in the midst of preparations to depart, "who has never lied to me, having no reason to, sent word that Shane would trouble the West no longer, and related how it came to be. It seems that she announced a banquet—if an Irish rout can be called so—to be held in the camp of the MacDonnells, to which Shane was called, to receive honors and submissions, as it was said."

The O'Malleys brought gold, he went on, and also gifts of French wine and Spanish sherris sack likely taken from Gráinne's prizes, all of which delighted Shane, who under the influence of it and white Irish whiskey, began to insult the O'Malleys and the others, and to put forward his claims again to the glens of Antrim, which no one but he accepted. At last, at the end of the night, five or seven Mac-Donnell esquires surrounded him and drew weapons, forbidden at the feast but carried anyway, and Shane, too drunk to fight them off, was done in: which took some time nonetheless.

Hugh briefly thanked the Lord Deputy for this news, and said nothing of his own part in it. The Lord Deputy was happy to have Shane as a guest of his, he said, on watch above the gate of the city, uncomplaining. Sir Henry was well aware that the silent young man before him had been hunted, as a boar or a stag is hunted, by that mad uncle of his; but he also knew that Hugh might not allow himself to rejoice publicly in the death of a relative who for all his vices was still the O'Neill. Sir Henry respected that, and said nothing about it.

What Hugh did not tell the Lord Deputy was that after the night when Shane went under the knives of the MacDonnells he had himself awakened early and walked out in the coming dawn as though summoned. Perturbed in his spirit and his mind, he went toward the high place where he had seen Gráinne's courier go away westward. As he walked he felt that a person walked with him there, like a detached part of himself, and when he turned to his left he saw her—a girl, but he could not say of what age or kind, and she seemed to be in light armor too, which was strange; and when she turned to smile at him he thought of that courier again, as though this person were he as well as she.

She seemed to speak, though he heard no words, not till he reached into his clothes and found the shard of flint that he carried always now. When he took it in his hand he heard her.

He was a big man, and a heavy one, she said.

Yes, Hugh said.

They complained of it, she said. The ones who must carry away his spirit, they asked to rest awhile in the doing of the task, but they could not be allowed to, lest he escape them, and return to his mortal body.

She turned then to point to the west, and Hugh saw the two she spoke of, struggling with the tall man his uncle, whom Hugh knew at once. The two were laughing as at a game but in earnest, one with two fingers hooked in Shane's cheek and tugging his head leftward while the other lifted Shane's right arm upward at his back. The three of them were sunk to their knees in the earth, wading this way and that as though in a pond of water.

You see? he heard the person beside him say. They are still at it.

He turned to her, but she was gone; and when he turned again to the place where Shane was drawn below the earth there was nothing there to see.

~

The Gaelic and old Norman captains who had chosen to come in to Dublin as demanded, rather than retreating into mountain fastnesses and fighting back, also passed through the city gate where Shane's head looked down and seemed to curse them. They knew that their best chance of keeping what was theirs would be to go and kneel before the Queen, beg forgiveness for whatever sins they were charged with, and take their chances that they'd be allowed to come home again. In somewhat better case, even, their lands and revenues safe at least for a year or two more.

The day was raw, strong wind and a small November rain; one or two of the suborned Irishmen had never taken ship before, though they'd lived their lives not far from the sea, and now clung to the rail in mute agony. The others talked in low voices, and in Irish; Sidney himself kept to the master's cabin writing his letters whenever the ship ceased to sway. None cheered when the ship entered the Thames estuary. They watched in surly wonderment the city pass. Hugh recognized with surprise the Privy Stair where he and Philip Sidney had taken the boat to Southwark: that had happened, there it was.

The delegation was marched through the arches of Hampton Court and up the stone way to the gates, where they were made to wait together in the rain at the Queen's pleasure. Hugh thought he saw her high up at a leaded window, looking down, touching a string of pearls at her breast. But more than that: he heard her speak, to Burghley or whoever it was that stood beside her, a shadow. *Who are these men?* she asked. The shadow whispered in her ear, no doubt explaining that they were Irish hostages brought before her by the Lord Deputy. *It is well*, he heard the Queen say. *He has two of the best offices in the kingdom. But this scuffle in Ulster was not worthy to be called a war. Shane O'Neill was nothing but a beggar and an outlaw.*

Hugh's heart filled. With rage: that his success in policy was scorned, with no acknowledgment that it was *he* who had brought low his uncle; Sir Henry Sidney had claimed the result of it for himself. And shame: that he and other men were made to stand in the cold amid the fallen leaves and await what would be permitted them.

And a warmth, too: a warmth that spoke of a certainty he felt, that he at least would be treated with kindness; for he had kept his word.

When at last they were admitted to the hall, passing among courtiers grinning and whispering behind their hands, two clanking armed men appeared as though conjured, took hold of two of the Irish barons, and marched them off. Hugh later learned they were rowed downriver to the Tower, where for years they'd go unheard of and unseen by family or friends. *Men whose reservations in their hearts made liars of their tongues,* the Queen said from her high seat at Court, looking on the remaining Irishmen one by one; and she scolded them in a language several did not understand. Her gaze from out the white face like a death-mask was clear enough. *She sees me always.* Into him alone that gaze entered through the black stone at his breast.

What was not told to him—not by Sidney at Penshurst where Hugh spent Christmas, nor when he returned to Ireland in the new year—was that the man the English had decided to back with all their subtle and also their more outright aid was not himself, not the Baron Dungannon now in the first flush of his powers and his reach, but old Turlough, Turlough Luineach O'Neill, his uncle: a man who had the ambitions of Shane but not Shane's wildness. The English officials at Dublin had been persuaded by the Ulster *flatha* to name Turlough as the O'Neill. Hugh remembered Turlough at Dungannon, in the beginning of his conscious life, how he spoke harshly of Sir Conn Bacach O'Neill, who had bent the knee to King Henry before Hugh was born: of Conn's velvet suit, his English cap with the white feather in it. Hugh had made himself more English than not; Turlough was more an Irishman than Hugh himself. Yet it was Turlough who'd pleased them more. Henry Sidney sent greetings to Turlough on his *ascension,* as he named it.

It was all to be done again: Turlough and the sons of Turlough, the sons of Shane as well, all stirring in the fastnesses of Ulster and its counties, each to be taken from the board before he could claim what he knew was his.

Who is on my side? he thought. Who stands behind me?

two

THE HALF OF MUG

VELLUM AND OLD INK

1574, and Gerald Fitzgerald, Earl of Desmond, has come home again.

He hadn't died of drink in London, nor of his other weaknesses; some of those had in time healed, and he'd grown a little stronger. Strong enough to dream of fleeing. After a long negotiation between their respective followers, he had met with the famed privateer Martin Frobisher at the Southwark inn where Hugh had once visited him, and in whispers they had talked of a ship that could take Desmond in secret to a port in Munster, to Smerwick or Cork city; Frobisher knew the Irish coast, he could sail whatever craft could be hired for the gold that Desmond's wife, Eleanor, had collected in Ireland. He'd be well rewarded, the Earl said, very well. The Queen had grown kinder, Desmond thought; she would not grant him his freedom outright, but she might not pursue him; she might even laugh at the trick, he and the old sea-dog slipping out on the tide and raising sail. *I am your only man,* Frobisher said to him, and raised his cup. They talked till dawn, of this obstacle and that sticking-point, but also of Gerald's hatred of the English colonials, the despoilers of his Munster lands, they would all be sent out of Ireland, he said, those who were not hanged or had their heads struck from their shoulders. Frobisher nodded, and went on nodding, saying nothing. A place and a time were named for the flight.

The chosen night was moonless, the wind set fair for the west; the Earl, disguised and armed, slipped from St. Leger House and set out for the docks with his aides and a lamp. He was arrested by the guard well before he reached the ship, if there ever was a ship. Frobisher's real employers, in Whitehall, had enjoyed the tale he had to tell: the inn, the ship, the vengeances, the planned escape by night. Desmond was brought before the Queen's secretary and questioned, and without much ado, charged with treason. Treason against this realm and its Queen, whose sworn subject he was. On his knees, with an armed man on each side of him to keep him from collapsing, he relinquished all his lands and all the castles, signories, and houses strewn across the hundred thousand acres of Munster that was the Desmond demesne. The Earl lowered his head, was commanded to read aloud what he had signed, and the Queen listened; and when he lifted his eyes to her eyes, he heard the Queen's decision spoken by a lawyer, the man Francis Bacon: he would be returned to Southwark and confinement in the city residence of Warham St. Leger for a further four years (the Earl gasped at this, and Sir Francis paused as though to relish it). The Queen's eyes did not leave the Earl as he was lifted up and taken away; they did not leave him ever.

There was an Englishman in Ireland then, Peter Carew, who professed to have papers from long ago that proved he owned large swathes of the Desmond lands. When the Earl of Desmond had gone to the Tower after the battle at Affane, Peter Carew, by then Sir Peter, had seen his opportunity. He sued in London for his rights in Munster, and though the documents themselves that he proffered were nearly illegible—altered, or perhaps only ancient—the Queen perceived in them a door into Ireland that she had not known could be opened. Families now in England that held such claims to Irish lands could do what this Carew fellow had done: exhibit in Irish courts their proofs, old or new-minted. The Crown would back them. Sir Peter, somewhat stunned by her encouragement, was sent off to found a new England in the Western isle. Like a purse-seine, he drew many after him: not only Warham St. Leger (the same whose house was Desmond's prison), but also Humphrey Gilbert, the famous seaman, Edmund Spenser, the little-known poet, and a crowd of landless knights and the younger sons of knights, dismissed Crown officers, outlaws, and bankrupts. Their various claims, presented to the Queen's Council in Dublin, were smiled upon. Carew in the van of this cavalcade was a cuckoo who has laid her egg in the warbler's nest: the cuckoo's egg is the bigger, and the warbler can't expel the parasite; the big nestling, once come forth, not only eats the most, it pushes the lawful offspring out of the nest to die, while the deceived parents stuff and stuff its wide-open mouth. When (as was common) no old Irish document attesting to a claim could be found, the hopeful claimant went off anyway to the South along with the many others who had no legal claim to make, following Sir Peter in hopes and in profound and fatal ignorance.

The incomers called their claims and their as-yet-unbuilt houses a Plantation, as though each of them would put green shoots into the rich ground with his own hands and tend to them every day, and the fruits thereof would be theirs. They wished—with native labor, not their own—to turn the unworked and idle Irish country into English shireland: fair mansions on the high places, metalled roads from town to town, deep harbors dug from which the fishing doggers, wide-beamed and bluff-bowed, could go out on the North Sea and come back with loads of fish, which the sea never tired of providing, whose sale would pay the Queen her just revenues. It was all there to be done. That the Irish had done none of this for themselves—hadn't divided the rolling plains into farms, drove their cattle anywhere and lived on the milk and meat—meant that the newcomers were justified, and Irish who rebelled must be suppressed. The Kavanaughs, an ancient and loyal family, could not show proof in court that the towns and lands that Sir Peter wanted were really theirs and had been for time out of mind, and so they lost them.

But there appeared at that juncture a Desmond who hadn't been accounted for: James Fitzmaurice Fitzgerald, a cousin of Gerald's. This cousin took the title Captain of Desmond, a title which hadn't before existed; he was contemptuous of his uncle the "pale Earl" in London, of his kissing the heretic Queen's satin shoe. For himself, he acknowledged no power higher than the Norman aristocracy except the Pope, and he signed his blazing letters to Henry Sidney and Peter Carew *Our hope is in Jesus and Mary*. With a selfless certainty he took up the rights that Gerald had surrendered and claimed them for himself, and through him for every Irish *flaith* and Old English baron. Before he rode out at the head of the Desmond forces to compel the New English to retreat, he sent the Catholic Archbishop of Cashel to seek military aid from Spain. At Fitzmaurice's furious command, Ireland was to be turned around like a galleon: the old religion restored, the Oath of Supremacy establishing the Church of England refuted, the long useless hostilities of the Munster earls annulled, and all made brothers of the new sword.

A strange passion swept the old earldoms. Everything good would be brought back, the thieving English planters would be laid dead in their own furrows and their flesh make for good harvests in the summers to come. Back in London, Gerald Fitzgerald, Earl of Desmond, wrote in haste to the Queen to insist that he had nothing to do with his relative, that he was no zealot himself, that if he were given the money and men he would chase away the Spaniards and the friars, restrain his kin, and sequester his mad nephew. He brought to the Court a letter that James Fitzmaurice had smuggled to him—*God forbid the day should ever come wherein it may be said that the Earl of Desmond has forsaken his kinsman, the banner of his merciful Savior, the safeguard of his noble house and posterity*—and tore it to pieces before them.

The only thing the Queen and her counselors could do—and the necessity bit at them like a vicious dog—was to return Desmond to Askeaton, the grand old castle he loved, his countess Eleanor with him, a good woman and a wise one, even the Queen knew it. His orders were to suppress the traitors, force obedience to the English laws that protected English settlers and their properties, and honor the Queen his liege. He was to know that not a single one of the legal burdens placed on him for his treachery in the past was to be lifted by this duty, if performed, and not distance nor obscurity would hide him from the consequences of failure. He again renounced every hereditary right he held in the vast palatinate of which he and his ancestors had been rulers for centuries: but the monarch to whom he surrendered them would herself have to keep them—if she could.

In Ulster, Hugh tugged at the lines of the *spiall* he had begun to establish: agents at the courts and offices of Dublin and London. *Desmond undertook to be answerable to the laws, ordinances and statutes of the realm*, one wrote to Hugh. Another wrote that Desmond had promised to put down Fitzmaurice's rebellion, *though the ways by which he might do so were not discussed*. More precious to Hugh, not alone for the knowledge it brought, was the Queen's own voice: it came, but more faintly, Hugh thought, than in earlier times. As though she were out-wearied, failing, uncertain. From the mirror she whispered to him: *The Earl of Desmond is a pile of paper, leaves that the mice have chewed for a hundred years. He smells of vellum and old ink.*

They sent Desmond home on a ship captained by Martin Frobisher, who laughed the whole way to Dublin harbor, though whether in mockery or mere delight at the turn of things Earl Desmond didn't know. A troop of Her Majesty's guard stood around him on board, and when a ship's boat had deposited him at Whitefriars landing they escorted him, marching in step, to the Dublin Castle gate. His brothers, all in arms, greeted him there, and he knew merely by their regard and their wide grins that they were sure he had returned to lead them into battle. Which was the last thing Desmond would want to do, and couldn't do if he would. Were they fools? Had Fitzmaurice and the Jesuits spoiled their brains? They clapped him on the back with their mailed hands and shouted aloud. They had brought him a horse, a horse sired (he was told) by the horse he'd ridden into battle at Affane. That was how long he had been gone.

Sir Henry Sidney, well informed of the Earl's movements, also came out from the castle to welcome him, to bring him within, and take him to the cell he was to occupy. The Lord Deputy had had no intention of setting Desmond free to go as he pleased, and the Earl was not surprised at it. He had not learned patience in the recent bad years, but he had learned to simulate patience. He was given the freedom of the town—kind Sir Henry!—and his beloved wife was there with him. He was allowed exercise in moderation—therefore, yes, he might join a stag-hunt in the city environs, though he could not bear any arms; very well, he forewent arms. But once beyond the Dublin gate he simply rode away from the hunting party and went south, entering the territory of his kinsman the Earl of Kildare without being sought for or hindered. He was met by old friends and rebel leaders, who escorted him safely through the midlands to the old Desmond island fortress of Lough Gur. Even before they reached it, the people had come in to see the Earl and his Countess and greet them, chieftains and their *bonnaght,* herders, beggars, women with children that they'd hold up to Gerald on the ramparts, his hand lifted as though in blessing. From Lough Gur he and his Countess went on progress to the great island-castle of Askeaton on the Deel; more people joined in the crowd following him, met him on the road and embraced him. By the time Askeaton was reached, a hundred fighters at least, more anyway than Gerald could count, had gathered in his train: his marshal, Maurice McSheehy, and the McSheehys, many O'Flahertys, the McSweeneys, the Ò Cruadhlaoich and his sept of the Burkes.

After long thought, Eleanor decided it would be best that *she* take the blame for her husband's flight to home, giving reasons that might be seen through—but since Gerald was home again, it hardly mattered. He would write that *he* had left Dublin and gone to Askeaton, sick with worry, concerned for his Countess: *the thought of whose care in mine absence, having nothing else to live upon, did prick so deeply that I came away, but with intent faithfully to serve Her Majesty as becometh a true subject.* Gerald, or was it Eleanor, thought to add that *yet if I thought my stay there in Dublin had been any way a further cause in your highness' service, I would be well contented to end my life there in captivity.* They laughed at their own daring.

PAPA ABÚ!

Even in the North of Ireland the English fever of land-taking was felt: the tug of shared blood, shared histories, the network of clan and family connections pulled taut. There was no reason to suppose that Englishmen desiring land on easy terms and urged on by their Queen and her lords would not in time break into Ulster and Tyrconnell, through the Gap of the North at Lough Neagh or the Gap of Erne in the lakes of the west; and if that were to happen, the lords of the North had better conduct themselves with *sassenach* deliberation and greater cooperation than they of the South had done. *Bind your friends to you with chains of iron:* Turlough Luineach had said that to the boy Hugh in the long-ago, before the world had changed. In their long galleys Gráinne O'Malley and the O'Malleys brought a thousand Scots redshank mercenaries to Clare Island and thence into Ulster. *Put them by,* Gráinne told the Lord of Tyrconnell, *their time will come.*

Hugh O'Neill had contracted a good marriage, with Siobhan O'Donnell of the Tyrconnell O'Donnells, to be consummated when she was of age, a year from then. The event when it came was grand and wild and lasted days, with no priest to read Latin, but a *brehon* binding the pair in the first degree of the ten degrees of marriage that could be applied. There were more O'Donnells than O'Neills present at the handfasting and then the days of feasting; everyone knew why, and looked upon the young man and his long-limbed wife with hope and trust. Still handfast—tied together at the wrist—they were taken to their chamber and the door shut on them, though the noise of revel and celebration below could still be heard. They lay together, nearly strangers still, and told each other tales of their childhoods; Siobhan had had brothers in plenty, to teach her to ride and shoot the crossbow.

"And you had none," she said, in pity.

"I had brothers," he answered, though he wished not to grieve her by an account of them, murdered by his uncle Shane. "Foster-brothers. O'Hagan boys, older than me."

"No brothers of your flesh," Siobhan said, pretending to ponder; she knew well enough what Hugh had not said. "Then you shall have sons instead." And with her free hand she reached within Hugh's wedding-garment and took hold.

Hugh wasn't called upon by the Queen to go to the South and fight Fitzmaurice's rebellion, though he feared he would be. He occupied himself not with Desmond or the wars of the Desmonds but with his new wife, soon pregnant and fat, and with . . . hunting. Into the glens of Antrim he brought men skilled with guns (*Fubún on the gray foreign gun*, O'Mahon had said long ago, but this was now, not then). He lived with his hunters out in shooting brakes, all sleeping out-doors in any weather, wrapped in their mantles; they brought home the skins of wolves and the carcasses of red deer, giving the meat to O'Neill followers or to anyone who asked. Wherever they went, Hugh would inquire of men and boys what weapons they were good at using, and after they named javelins and bows and the battle-axe he would bring out a long gun, and his hunters would explain the use of it, and let one or another of them take it and try it. The handiest of them Hugh would reward with a coin or other gift, and perhaps even the gun itself. *Keep it safe*, he'd say, smiling. Those who kept the guns knew well enough why they were given them, and if not, they would be instructed by others. Some learned themselves to make a coarse gunpowder from saltpeter, sulfur, and willow ash, and to cast round shot from molten lead. That was wisdom the mirror would never give Hugh and that the flint could not know: When the time came for *him* to lead men against English soldiery he would not lead hordes of screaming gallowglass against trained infantry with guns. His own shot would wheel on command, and march in step, and lay fire.

When the time came. If it came.

As soon as the winter rains were past and the green springing again, when men and horses could once more move, Dublin sent word to the O'Neills and the other Northern lords: intercepted letters showed that James Fitzmaurice Fitzgerald had been rousing Catholic support and seeking aid in Spain and France, and was expected to return, most likely putting ashore at Dingle Bay, bringing with him Papal and Spanish troops aboard Spanish great-ships, with Papal gold to pay them, and three thousand stand of arms, with powder and lead. Once a Spanish military government was established in Munster (so Fitzmaurice declared in his screeds), the Geraldines, the Butlers, the Burkes, all of them and their dependents, would be guaranteed in their ancient possession of their lands, and the *heretics*, which was the coming term now for any and all Englishmen in Ireland, would be uprooted and scattered. With this information in hand, reliable enough, the Council in London let the Earl of Tyrone and the Lord of Tyrconnell and chiefs of all clans know that every true liegeman of the Queen should be ready to oppose the Pope and Spain, their armies and their assassins, their lies and their tricks. A note in Henry Sidney's hand appended to Hugh's letter (how well Hugh O'Neill had come to know that hand) demanded that Hugh come to Dublin in all haste, bringing with him what forces he could muster, to go south and meet this threat.

Hugh folded the paper in his hands and folded it again. He was called upon to go down into Munster, where the world began (as O'Mahon the poet had taught him); tortured Munster, green and fruitful, land of death. The O'Neills were of the North, *Leath Cuinn,* the "half of Conn" in the division of the island by the sons of Mil in the beginning, as O'Mahon had sung; the South was the *Leath Mogha,* the "half of Mug." The North was the higher, the half of kings, of the head; the South of labor, of rich harvests, provision of all things. It was said that the Kindly Ones of Munster were all of the female sex; it was where Annan gave birth to gods, where Áine bore a leaping son to an Earl of Desmond. Desmond's wife, Eleanor, golden countess, who against all reckoning had made friends with the Queen, who had gathered the moneys that could redeem her husband when he was imprisoned in faraway London, and was now again mistress of the great square castle at Askeaton, where every young squire who came to serve Desmond fell in love with her. So it was said.

It wasn't true that Hugh O'Neill was afraid of women, though now at twenty-five years of age he knew they could make him reckless. He had been a boy not long returned from England when he married a first wife, a daughter of his uncle Phelim, but that marriage had been quickly dissolved—the *brehon* had ruled the marriage was within the forbidden degree of relationship. He'd not told Siobhan of that, but her relatives likely had. The girl would remain in Hugh's memory as a smiling sun-browned child gathering flowers on a mild spring day, following him and walking with him, talking of nothing or not talking at all, until they fell together in the shade of the rowans. Even now a fleeting image of her might wake him, erect and bereft beside his sturdy Siobhan of the O'Donnells, mother of strong sons.

Yes, he thought it best for him that he stay to the north of the Eiscir Riada, the low broken range of sandy eskers running from Dublin to Galway that marks the boundary dividing the halves of Ireland, of Conn and of Mug. But the obsidian mirror judged him and found him wanting. *You are a cold friend to her who loves you and will soon do you great good:* the Queen looked out at him, clearer now than she had lately been, her white face framed in a stiff ruff. How far away she was, to be so near. Why was he always made to feel shame at what he heard, like a child who'd done his work badly or skipped away? He hadn't done so. Were all her followers, the rich and proud men, young and old, were they all shamed by her as he was, and if not why was it different with him? For the first time he thought that no matter what the Doctor had told him, he could remove this thing from him in an instant, and with it her hand upon him.

He returned it to his breast.

That day he began to call in his *bonnaght* mercenaries and his gallowglass, to the smallest number he could bring that would meet the Lord Deputy's demand.

~

"I will tell you something of James Fitzmaurice, this Captain of Desmond," Henry Sidney said to Hugh as they rode together out of Dublin city. "Though perhaps you have heard all you need to know."

Hugh said nothing in reply; he had not been asked a question; he had lived long enough in Sir Henry's company to know when to keep his peace.

"He is a slight man," Sidney said thoughtfully, as though consulting an inward file. "But a brave one. A hero to every poor cottager and kern. Tireless, able to sit a saddle daylong. Mad with his own opinions, as being a Papist." He shifted in his seat, as though to make clear he was too old for this campaigning. "We had him once at sword's point, on his knees before us, in the rain, in a church burned for no reason we knew and smelling of wetted ashes—a foul odor. Sir John Perrot was the Lord President of Munster, which was then a new title. He held a sword to Fitzmaurice's bared breast, and might in a moment have ended his rebellion—a thing I myself could not have done. And he himself did not."

"Why did he not?" Hugh asked. He needn't ask why Sidney could not; he believed he knew the man.

"Fear of the Queen's judgment." He turned to smile at Hugh. "The wind in London was blowing from a new quarter. Pardon was bruited for the southern lords if the Captain of Desmond were shunned. Fitzmaurice confessed his crimes and his sins there and then, and in good English too. And Sir John lowered his sword. Fitzmaurice went to Dublin prison."

He laughed lightly then, shook his head as at a memory. "I will tell you a thing about Sir John, our Lord President of Munster." He cleared his throat and spat. "He is said—for the most part by himself, in confidence, a confidence that no one keeps—to be the bastard son of old King Harry."

"It may be that there are many of whom that has been said."

"He was then very fat, and still is," Sir Henry said. "Indeed, fatter than the old King. Horses fail beneath him; on long journeys he must have a string of them so that none go lame from long carrying of him. Sometime past, I believe, he began trusting to mules instead.

"Now, with Fitzmaurice in chains, Sir John—likely weary of the chase—bethought himself of a way to cancel rebellion at a stroke. What he did, Hugh, was to challenge Fitzmaurice *to a duel*—single combat. As knights did of old, or as our young men play at doing to please the Queen and her ladies at Hampton Court."

"And was the challenge accepted?" Hugh in fact had heard something of this weird event, though not the outcome. Uncelebrated in song.

"It was. Fitzmaurice took up the gauntlet, though I think none was thrown down but in words. Now, as I heard the tale—mark you, the tale has flourished as the green bay tree since it occurred—the two agreed to forego the steeds and the armor and the long lance of Sir Gawain and his like, for Irish horses and Irish broadswords."

"Ah," Hugh said thoughtfully. "By what you say, an Irish hob might have had some trouble bearing King Harry's son."

Sidney shrugged. "Well, the terms were set so."

"And they fought?"

"On the appointed day, the Geraldine was to be paroled from prison. Sir John appeared early in stout Irish breeches at the field of honor—a bare hilltop. There he waited for the Captain. It began to rain. Sir John grew weary, and—likely—hungry for his dinner. He was of a mind to cast away his cursed Irish short sword when a messenger appears. Not on horse but walking, hatless. And he gives the Lord President a letter, from Fitzmaurice, still in his cell. *Were I to kill him this day,* the letter read—I have heard Sir John himself recite it—*the Queen of England will send another Perrot or his like. But if he kill me there is none in Ireland that can succeed me or to command as I do, therefore I will not willingly fight with him, and so tell him from me.*

Hugh, still pondering what he had just been told (*a messenger appears, walking, hatless*), failed to respond to Sir Henry in amusement or amazement as he might have. "Yes," he said. "Strange." They had now reached the eskers marking the long border of North and South. He touched the gold-mounted mirror on its chain, and envisioned the flint he had in his leathers. He felt nothing of the fear he had expected here.

"The end of it," Sir Henry said, "was that not a week later, by means no one has discovered, Fitzmaurice escaped from Dublin prison and fled to France."

"From where he has now returned."

"Madder, fiercer, more bloody-minded."

They were silent a time, maneuvering their men and carts through the sandhills. The captains called a halt. "Tell me of your son Philip," Hugh said, one leg lifted to rest upon the saddle so that he could rub the sore calf. "Is he well?"

Sidney nodded with care, looking far off. "He is well. He has been sent by the Queen to the Netherlands, there to fight with the Dutch Protestant army against Spain. Gone with our prayers."

"Does he still write his poetry?"

Sir Henry Sidney was still, seeming not to have heard. Hugh raised his face to the clouded sky. "It is coming on to rain," he said.

Ten years before this day the Munster lords under Desmond leadership first rebelled against the Crown. The half of Mug is the land of farmers, and beneath farmers serfs, and though they alone grew the food that all classes ate, they were the ones who were most devastated in that war. Any Munster town or village that Sidney invested and would not surrender was put to the sword; Sidney had declared that any Irishman found in arms would be hanged, the leaders beheaded, and their heads impaled on stakes across the land. The great Earls and their followers issued from their strongholds to burn the English towns and houses, and the standing grain in the fields; they killed the animals to keep the Queen's army from taking them. Then in the spring the English soldiers burned the green crop as it sprung, to keep it from the Irish. The people ate cresses when there was nothing left, and when they had none they died, and others ate their flesh, and the flesh of their dead babes: so it was reported by the poet and landholder Edmund Spenser, though the Queen would not believe it could be so, that souls in her keeping (for she saw them as in her keeping) could do such things.

That had all happened when Hugh O'Neill was not long returned from England and Penshurst to Ireland and Ulster, before Shane's death. The land that Hugh O'Neill crossed now in Sir Henry's company—the land from which he had been told all good things come to be—was a wasteland still, from which nothing could come, no providing, no life; his horse stumbled over bones to which rags of cloth adhered, the bones of children, their mothers too. Death laid upon death. Hugh and his stolid gallowglass and his boys with heavy muskets they hardly knew how to use fell back from Sidney's fast-moving English pikemen and trained shot. Sir Henry had told him, without passion and without regret, as though recounting a long-ago tour, that at Castlemayer and Glanmire on the borders of Cork he had razed castles and burned fields, killed stock and left it to rot, and marked the land with hanging trees. In his tent that night the Queen spoke to O'Neill's lagging heart and said *Look not on their suffering but on me.*

For it was all to do again now: the pacifications, the uprootings of the ignorant and the immovable, like digging out boulders; the insult to true religion, the serpentine advancement of the Roman church. The hapless Earl of Desmond at Askeaton was worshipped as a god; rumors of two Spanish *tercios*, six thousand pike-and-halberd soldiers and mounted *arquebusiers* sailing from La Coruña inflamed the rebels and alarmed the settlers. Fitzmaurice had arrived from France as predicted, with a huge banner blessed by the Pope, picturing the bloodied head of Christ encircled in thorns, which could be unfolded and uplifted on stakes and then, before the sheriffs or the Lord President could confiscate it, would disappear and appear elsewhere, to cries of *Papa Abú:* Victory to the Pope. The Earl of Desmond, Fitzmaurice's elder, wrote to the English deputy in Cork city that *I and my own are ready to venture our lives in Her Majesty's quarrel, that we may prevent the traitorous attempts of the said James.* But what officer of the Crown could trust the Earl of Desmond?

Hugh O'Neill and his company were ordered to Smerwick harbor where the Spanish and Papal forces were said to be coming ashore. Hugh's force went that way at a run, but Earl Gerald had arrived sooner, and had seemingly done nothing to keep Fitzmaurice's rebels from taking the town and the *Dun an Oir,* the Golden Fort, high above it. Leaving his own fighters and captains outside the town walls, Hugh mounted to the fort and sought for the Earl. It was strange that he was surrounded as he went by Fitzmaurice's armed men, the very ones he had been ordered to put to flight, but who looked on him as a likely ally—an Irish lord, a child of the True Church. It was as though he had no substance, or was only substance and nothing else. He found Desmond on the battlements, seated cross-legged on a stone bench, face upward in the pale sunlight, seeming the same as he had been.

"What would you have me do, my lord?" Hugh asked.

Desmond looked up at him smiling, as at a stranger. "Nothing," he said.

"Nothing?"

"There were no *tercios* aboard any foreign ship," Desmond said, lifting a hand toward the harbor, a gesture Hugh O'Neill remembered from the night and Southwark. "Not any ones that came ashore. No horses neither. Priests and friars, in crowds. Cousin James has gone out to the country to find allies, to get horses too, and will take all those he finds. Farmers and wagoneers must give up their sole possession for their country's and their religion's sake, about which the poor men know little and care less. So I have been told."

Without other order, Hugh O'Neill waited, impatient and annoyed, and spent the length of the day seeking places for his troop and food and drink for them. He'd soon learn that the engagement would soon enough be over without his putting a hand in: a carter whose horse Fitzmaurice had commandeered had gone and complained to his lord, a Burke and a Protestant, who thereupon gathered armed followers and stopped James and his band at a ford: always a ford, men on either side opposed. *Give up my fellow's horse,* the Burke cried. *Papa Abú!* James answered. The blessed image was raised, and all his troop cried *Papa Abú!* The Burke called back *God save the Queen and the Devil take James Fitzmaurice!* At that James plunged into the river and one of Burke's men shot him midstream in the breast with a musket. It was said that James was still strong enough to ride for Burke, turning aside the reloading musketeer and driving his sword through Burke's neck. Then he tumbled from his horse and died. He had been in Ireland a hundred days and a day.

So Earl Desmond was right that there was nothing to do here now, though Sidney and the Court continually demanded that Desmond do *something;* why had he been given his freedom if he wouldn't keep his pledges? The crowd of James Fitzmaurice's people who had sequestered themselves in the Golden Fort at Smerwick remained there waiting for the promised Spanish forces to evade English pursuit and come in, seizing meantime what they could of provisions from the town, kneeling to hear the priests and the Jesuits declaim. *Enough,* the Earl of Desmond decided: he had done his duty as best he could. He gathered his own few fighters, bade farewell to Hugh, and went home to Askeaton and Eleanor.

Hugh O'Neill, wandering knight, and his companions later came very close to the ford where James was killed. Hugh had sought for the place, but the thick woods around kept him from it, and he turned his force for home. Later he was told that James's head, by his own instructions given to his chief men, was cut from his body and carried away by his followers, no one knew to where, nor knows now.

ON KNOCKAINEY HILL

I have been recalled," Sir Henry Sidney told Hugh O'Neill. "My service to the Queen and Council is no longer wanted." It was painful to Hugh that he had known this would come about, that a letter from the Queen would reach Sir Henry after Fitzmaurice was dead: he had been told of it.

"Three times has Her Majesty sent me as her Deputy to Ireland," he said to Hugh. "Each time I returned a thousand pounds to the worse than when I went, and this return is no different."

They parted at the port of Cork harbor: Hugh to return to Ulster with the small remaining force he had brought to face the Queen's Catholic enemies, Sir Henry to take ship for Dublin. When the Lord Deputy's affairs there were settled, he would travel to London and make his reports to the Council: admitting his failures, presenting his assessments, and putting before them all that he knew that might be of use to the next man who would be named Lord Deputy; hoping (he didn't say) that the man would be wealthy, and thus not come home a beggar. He'd accept from the Queen the quiet post of President of the Welsh Marches, lived at Ludlow Castle in Wales until he surrendered that post as well, and returned to Penshurst; he tended to his lands, he read, he saw his daughter married; he waited for Philip to return from fighting with the Protestant forces in the Netherlands, and died not long before his son, Hugh's childhood friend, poet and soldier, was killed on the field of battle at Zutphen, fighting for the Netherlandish Protestants.

⁓

Hugh chose to return from Munster a different way than the way he had come: it was becoming a custom of his, to return by a new route, and learn of things he had not before seen. Despite his travels his knowledge of the Irish island was meager, and whatever his place in the world, whether made by himself or granted by others, he should know what earth lay beneath his feet. Most of his remaining fighters, the O'Hagans, the gallowglass and their chiefs, would go home along the familiar roads to Dublin and then to Drogheda, Dundalk, and by the Gap of the North into Ulster; there would be some chance of provender that way, less the way Hugh would go. With a handful of men mounted and on foot, he set out toward the road to Limerick, then turned from it when another road seemed to take them a better way to the west and north; but that way was lost at the end of day, and at morning they chose a different way again, now riding in tight formation, looking this way and that. The road never ceased entirely, but there was hardly a farmstead where they might ask for direction. Desolation was everywhere. Every man or child they saw and hailed ran to hide. But then two boys astride one horse came near them, red-headed and fox-eyed, reminding Hugh of Siobhan's young brother. Could they guide the troop as far as the border of Roscommon? The boys clearly didn't know that name. North, said Hugh. And yes, they said they could, nodded grinning at each other and then at Hugh, and he understood that they were twins: a wonderful and strange thing.

The two went ahead on their old horse, with no saddle or bridle; the day seemed to last forever, the sun beclouded but unwilling to sink. Was it an omen? He couldn't tell. He asked the boys for the names of places, of old ruined towers and standing stones, rivers and fords, and some they knew; but names seemed of little interest to them. When darkness at last came, arising from the dark path more than falling, the boys began pointing to the west, and saying a name in their local speech. Hugh listened and made out a word, the name of a lake: *Lough Gur*. Desmond's castle on a lake island. He'd have liked to see it; was it far, he asked the boys, but he couldn't make sense of their answer. Earl Gerald was likely at Askeaton now, but Lough Gur was the more ancient place. He kept on, following the pale horse in the darkness. He'd have to stop soon, but the men with him wanted not to dismount; they didn't like this Munster land; they'd seen too much murder, and done enough themselves.

It was nearly dark now. The boys were far ahead, yet Hugh could sense that they were still leading them; his company followed, up a swell in the ground to the east, toward a black hill whose edge was drawn on the still-pale sky. A glow that way might be the rising of the Moon. The horsemen were silent. Then there appeared far off a sparkle of moving lights on the hillside, a few at first and then more, proceeding around the hill's bare top, a gold chain for its throat; but then more coming from high up, where a larger fire had been built, sparks rising. Ahead of Hugh the boys could be seen returning to him.

"What is it?" Hugh called to them. "What are the lights? Who carries them?" The boys laughed and pointed to the dancing fires that seemed held by no one. The men around Hugh tried to still their mounts, who didn't like the smell of smoke. *Faery*, one cried.

"No," said the twins, laughing. "Only folk! It is St. John's eve, did you not know?"

The hill was crowded now with torches of straw, and voices and song could be heard. The twins were singing, words whose meaning Hugh couldn't discern; the Moon now was half-risen in her fullness, and the songs ran through the people, one song lighting another. Hugh, as though granted the knowledge by the fires and the Moon, cried to the boys: "What is the name of this place? Is it Knockainey Hill?"

"Knock Áine!" they called. "Blessed Áine!" The mounted men around Hugh were laughing now, some of them, others crossing themselves and kissing the knuckle of their right-hand's long finger to ward off any evil. Still the Moon went on rising, Áine's Moon, and the songs turned to cries and ululations, and Hugh remembered the Earl of Desmond telling of his ancestor, Geároid Iarla, the first Geraldine earl that ever was, who stole the Goddess Áine's cloak where she bathed, and had a son borne to him by her, a leaping son who left the earth a gray goose. Hugh called to the boys, wanting to reward them, to learn more: but they only waved back as they rode their old horse away into the crowd of boys and girls bearing St. John's fire.

⁓

Many years later, in the Palazzo Salviati in Rome, Hugh O'Neill traversed those plains and woods of Munster again with Peter Lombard, Archbishop and Confessor, a Waterford boy and still a man of Munster in his mind and thought. It was cool in the palace; the two sat together as they had so many nights, Hugh talking, reluctantly now as the remembered years came near to the last. What was of interest to the cleric was as a thorn to the Earl, an unplucked thorn in his hand.

"Desmond," the Archbishop said. "How was it he came to the rescue of Mother Church in that island? He despised Fitzmaurice."

Hugh looked up to the dim angels on the ceiling. "I cannot tell," he said. "He had proved himself a Catholic by his failure to stop his cousin James, no matter that a Protestant, a Burke, had murdered James well before Desmond could act. The English commander Sidney and his soldiery roamed through Munster as wolves among the sheep, invading Desmond's towns and castles, and even though they surrendered, all those found within were killed. Catholic lords and chiefs of the clans were coming in to the English for pardons, renouncing their faith so that their lives at least might be spared."

"Was not his castle at Askeaton invested?" the Archbishop asked him. "And the Abbey there desecrated, the Mass vessels stolen, the pictured glass of the windows smashed?"

"All that," the Earl responded. "But also the graves of the Fitz-geralds were broken into, and the dead thrown out. The tomb of Joan Fitzgerald Butler too, the old Earl's wife, and her bones scattered as well."

"Unholy," Lombard said.

For some moments they sat silent, feeling the moving airs in the chamber.

"There was famine in the land then."

"There was, and it worsened. In time only soldiers could eat, and they had little enough."

"Wolves were seen in the streets of Dublin, seeking whom they may devour."

"I was told how Earl Desmond went out," Hugh said. "It was October, as it is now. The English, and Tom Butler too it was said, offered to Desmond that he might escape a proclamation of treason, already drawn up, if he would agree to come to England and live there peacefully. Think of that."

"England, land of heresy," Peter said. "Where so many Catholic saints were made by the headsman and the stake."

"Desmond could then barely stand. He was helped up upon a white horse, and the sword of the Desmonds put in his hand. I was told of this."

"I wonder," Peter asked the air, "was he perhaps spoken to by an angel?"

Again Hugh O'Neill raised his eyes to the darkening heaven of the ceiling, the gray angels vanishing. "I wouldn't think," he said, "that an angel would have spoken to Gerald Fitzgerald. It would have not been to that angel's profit then."

"Yet when at last Desmond went out, the West arose." The priest knew this history from letters and from the tales of exiles. The fear the New English colonials felt, which was felt by the English army too, was surely God-sent. "The four horsemen of the world's end rode the land," the Archbishop said. "The hanging-trees bore much fruit. The Spanish sent ships and men, but too few. Too-cautious Philip, may he rest in peace."

Hugh felt the priest's gaze on himself. Why had *he* not joined the cause, Peter asked, without asking. What had kept him from it? Why did they in the counties believe he would, that he would soon crown himself at Tara, a Catholic King, and so make the world new? Hugh O'Neill knew why he did not do those things—he knew, now, in what powerful hands he had been held, powers that he would escape from only long after that time of upheaval: and by then it was all too late to change the course of things, Time turning like a great-ship into a wind blowing from a wrong quarter.

"But at the end Desmond was alone, hidden in the Glanageenty woods in Kerry," said the Earl. "It's there that the clan Moriarty, never followers of Desmond, found him, in a mean cabin. Bound him, dragged him out to set him upon a horse to bring him in; when they found he was too weak even to walk or ride they cut his head off, and carried it away for the reward. All this I have heard from those who knew of it, who saw it, that head."

The Archbishop crossed himself. "Had it all so quickly come to nothing, then?"

The Earl arose, stiff with long sitting, lifting himself with the arms of the chair. "There is nothing that comes to nothing," he said. "Unless all things do."

He left the priest with an embrace and a blessing and went to his bed, followed by his ever-present pair of young servants, whom Hugh thought were twins. They helped him to undress, don his linen shirt, and recline on his couch; they put his old mantle around him, exchanging a look, perhaps of amusement. When he declared he was now comfortable, they backed away bowing and out his chamber door, which they shut soundlessly.

Toward morning he awoke, or perhaps he wasn't awake, but feeling himself to be not where he was. In darkness, but not a darkness here and now. A great black hill before him that rose sharply, one that he knew was not the one he'd seen, Knockainey, asleep and low. And yet this high crag *was* that hill, he had no doubt of that. And as his spirit observed it, he saw or had knowledge of a being climbing upward, swift, without effort, stepping from stone to stone. His lank gray hair streamed behind him like a nun's veil, his lean carven face pointed ahead. White as old bones. Hugh knew the man; he thought he *was* that man. Healed, or unhurt; all in one piece; holding, as a guide, a shard of flint that his thumb knew. The mountain regarded his ascent to a place where a gate or door appeared, two columns and a lintel of granite, deep dark within. And there were beings there, the Old Ones, the kings of Munster, Geároid Iarla, and beyond in the hill's heart, there was the Moon's child and mother, Áine Cli, Áine of the light, hastening to bring him in.

UNDER LOUGH NEAGH

hugh O'Neill had passed, almost without noticing, from his twenties to his thirties; one by one the endless line of enemies and false friends and mad fools that he faced in the claiming of his heritage were bought off, or befriended, or exiled, or hanged. The sons of Shane. His uncle Turlough Luineach. Whatever policy they formed in London, for him or against, the black mirror was his adviser and spy in the struggles. When he contested with the mirror itself, he might refuse its instruction, and later be sorry he had. Sometimes when he looked in, it would say *Strike now or lose all,* and sometimes it would only look upon him; sometimes it wept or smiled, or said *Power springs from the mind and the heart.* But never was any sound heard, and it was as though Hugh thought or said these things to himself in his own mind, which made them not the less true or potent. If he could discern the meaning of what was said and act on it, it was likely to come out as predicted, and he would win. And in the spring of 1587 he returned to London for what he imagined to be the last time, summoned finally to be invested by the Queen with the title Earl of Tyrone. He was thirty-seven years old.

The face Hugh saw in the black mirror had never changed—at least it would seem always unchanged to him, white and small and bejeweled—but the woman of flesh was not young. The paint couldn't cover the fine lines etched all around her eyes, nor the lines in the great bare skull above. He knelt before her, taking his hat from his head. "Cousin," the Queen said, and held out her ringed hand for him to kiss. Torn between love and shame Hugh put his lips near to the proffered hand without touching it, and when he raised his eyes she was for a moment young again and serenely lovely.

"My cousin. My lord of Tyrone."

The Council around him, bearded worthies, some white-headed now, nodded discreetly to one another and to the new Earl. Somehow—they knew not how—the Queen had conquered the heart of this rude Irishman. Those closest to him saw that there were tears in his eyes. He himself didn't know why he wept: he was not a knight, come home with trophies; he was not returned home; what had been his had been taken from him, and now was merely given back, and what glory was there for him in that? He knew for sure that the nobles around him did not count his name with theirs.

At the dock when he came home again, with more gifts and purchases in the hold of his English ship than twenty ox-carts could bear away, he saw, among the O'Neill and O'Hagan men-at-arms and their *brehons* and wives come to greet him, the poet O'Mahon, like a withered leaf, leaning on a staff. Hugh O'Neill went to him, knelt and kissed the pale hand the poet held out to him. O'Mahon raised him, felt his big face and broad shoulders, the figured steel breastplate upon him.

Streets that had been silent and empty when, some years before, a young Irishman came home from that other island to which he had been carried away—they were not empty now: from street to street and house to house the news went that Hugh O'Neill was home again, and they came around his horse to touch his boot and lift their babes to see him; and now and then he must acknowledge them, and doff the black velvet cap he wore, with the white owl's feather in its band.

"That promise given you was kept," said O'Mahon.

"How, cousin?"

"You are to be the O'Neill, inaugurated at Tullahogue as your ancestors have ever been. You are Earl of Tyrone too, by the grant of the English: you gave them rule over all your lands and they gave that rule back to you just as though the lands were theirs to give, and added on a title, Earl."

"How is that the keeping of a promise?" O'Neill asked.

"That is for them to know; yours to act and learn." He touched Hugh's arm and said, "Will you go on progress in this summer, cousin? The lands that owe you are wide."

"I may do so. The weather looks to be fine."

"I would be happy to go along with you, if I might. As far at least as to the long rath that rises beyond Dungannon."

"Well then you shall. You will have a litter to carry you, if you like."

"I can still ride," the poet said with a smile. "And my own horse knows the way there."

"What shall we do there?"

"I? Not a thing. But you: you might meet again your allies there, or perhaps their messenger or herald; and see what now they will say, not to a boy but to a man of years. And they may tell you of others, some greater than they, who are now waking from sleep, and their pale horses too."

The new Earl felt a shudder, of awe or fear or something with no name; it passed, overwhelmed by a resistance that was also nameless.

They carried O'Mahon in a litter after all; it was clear he was near his end, and might fall even from a horse who knew the way. From Dublin in the south, people followed the fire-new Earl and his train of soldiers the ninety miles to Dungannon, sleeping rough and eating what the householders along the way brought out, who came to see the Great Earl of Tir-Oen pass by them, cheering if he lifted his hand to them, cheering if he didn't. The company reached the tower in rain, and the old poet was cold and speechless when they lifted him from the litter and laid him on the couch from where often he had spoken his verses, sharp, potent, praiseful, witty. Everyone knew that more than one traitorous or worthless man had shrunk away and died from the force of young O'Mahon's satire. Now the poet could hardly whisper, couldn't cease shivering though wrapped in a heavy mantle. O'Neill brought him warmed wine with sugar, and meats that the old man turned away from. He lifted a hand to draw Hugh to him, so that his words faint almost as breath could be heard. Hugh put his hand beneath the poet's head and raised him a little, so that he might have ease to speak.

"Dying, cousin," was what he said.

"I forbid it," Hugh said. "We must have our poet."

"You will have," O'Mahon whispered. "A bard will arise from beyond this clan, and will defeat in song all others; that will be the one, and it may be the last one, that the septs of the O'Neills will know."

Saying all that had exhausted the man, and Hugh lowered his head again upon the couch. "The last?" he said.

"That may be." He moved his hand to again draw Hugh close. His breath had a faint sweetness. "But this is certain. That bard will be a woman."

"A woman?" He had not heard of any woman poet or bard in this land, though women sing the *caoine*, the keening for the dead, and would for O'Mahon.

"A woman. There have been such, though not for a long course of years now. Their song praised the kings who honored them, but they mocked those who refused them their right to sing."

"Who will she be, what will she sing?"

"She'll sing what she knows. She may be a bard fierce in satire, as Labercham, whose words could kill. Or like her who sang dying Diarmuid to sleep. And whether she sing long or not for long, whether she choose a successor or cannot, she will never be forgotten. I will be. She will not."

"*You* will not."

O'Mahon smiled then, as though pleased to be told this yet amused to hear it. He let go of Hugh's hand, the lids closed over his blind eyes. He spoke no words after that.

~~~

The women of the castle had washed O'Mahon's body and wrapped it in white linen. He was carried out then by Hugh O'Neill; his aged uncle Phelim; the O'Neill *brehon*, with whom the poet had often played chess though unable to see the pieces; and two men of the O'Hagans. They bore his litter the ten miles, following Hugh's piper, resting at each milestone, to the lake's shore at Machaire Grianáin, or Machery as the English called it, followed by the people of Dungannon Castle, the women keening without pause, passing the high cries from one group to another. There by the shore men had woven a narrow boat of thick willow withies. There was a priest of the clan to say words that O'Mahon would not have minded said, nor much cared to hear; his gods were before the priest's god. The bearers laid down the litter and lifted the body in their hands to place it in the boat, which was hardly a boat, and hardly needed to be one. This was near where the Blackwater River runs fast into the great lake, Lough Neagh, so the little boat once launched would be carried out over the lake by the current until it sank, which would not be long at all since large stones and dry tinder and hollow reeds filled with gunpowder had been placed around the last of O'Mahon, and were set afire as the boat was pushed out. It went out bravely, and for a time it kept on, and then it took on water; soon the fire was extinguished and the

boat began to go down beneath the gray surface. The men beat their
weapons on their shields, and the women sang the shrill descants of
the *caoine* as though their own sons had been taken from them.

The men and the women and the priest and the mounted fighters
returned to Dungannon at evening along the way they had come,
following Hugh. At a juncture of ways still a distance from the castle he stopped, and called forward his piper, who was also the chief
of the household kerne.

"Bring the people home," he said. "I have a thing I must do alone,
along this way."

The piper, walking backward a few steps so that the people could
see, began to play, drawing the line of folk with him. Hugh turned onto
the faint track and went through the heather and along a stream, until
near dark he could see from this new vantage the rath that O'Mahon
had twice led him to, where he had received the gift he carried. A
gift and a promise. Gifts have reasons for the giver and the receiver;
promises made are kept or broken, or they bring a thing different from
the thing promised. It was their promise to Hugh, O'Mahon said, that
had been kept; but Hugh did not know how to see that it was so.

The rath was pale, almost vanishing in the rising mist and the
evening. He rode closer to it than he had gone with O'Mahon,
not knowing what he meant by coming here now alone, without
interpretation. Though grass had grown over the sides and top of it,
it was clear now to him that the walls were scarped as straight and
high as dirt could be without falling into rubble. He saw now as
he had not before that it was set about in places with great stones,
uncut and lumpish, but remarkable—stones so large were uncom-
mon on the Ulster plain, and to move them to this place would
have been great labor. The being that he had first seen, the one like
a mounted prince, would not do such labor, nor the silvery warriors
he had seen gathered in the twilight. The black being from the
ground, though, who had lifted the stone that became a chest—he
and his like might do it. Doctor Dee in England had told him
that the Druids of Ireland had lifted and tossed across the sea the
great stones that stood on Salisbury plain. If they could do that it
would have been easy for them to make a dwelling-place of earth
and guardian stones, into which folk could go at need: folk not
like himself nor anyone now alive. They might long remain hidden

within it, they might change in nature there, and issue forth when they chose, or were called.

When he had come as close as he dared he dismounted. *The border of day and night,* O'Mahon had said. Hugh stood at the distance he had stood in childhood, and again when he'd returned from England at first. He searched within his coat for the flint, and for a moment thought he had lost it, but no, it was there as ever, and taking it he felt its eagerness to be held. He knew in his inmost soul that it could bring forth those hosts, but nothing on earth would cause him to use it so. Not now, perhaps never. If he awoke the island—how he would, or if he could, he knew no answers to that—and in that day called upon them, would they leave their feasting and dancing and come forth, would they agree to be commanded by him? He was descended from kings that, in the tales, once did command that folk, or dealt with them as comrades, at least for a time. Kings and heroes in that time could be brought down by an error, a little, little error. A stone kicked from the path, a stone that was not a stone; a flying bird pierced by an arrow-shot, a bird that was not a bird. The living folk in this day stayed indoors at night and smoored their fires, never threw their dirty foot-washing water out the door, never plucked the flower they knew not to pluck nor shot a javelin or flung a stone at a forbidden animal. When the Moon was full and golden in the night sky they knelt on the ground and prayed to her, prayed their prayers to Mary Ever Virgin, as they had for a thousand years. What error lay ahead for the Earl of Tyrone to make? A wrong word spoken; a wrong marriage made?

The bard to come, a woman—would she sing of him? What song? Would it kill him or give him life? She might not come for a hundred years, by which time he himself would be with O'Mahon and the so many others of his line whose bones lay on Lough Neagh's bottom. Or on a plain unburied, with men of flesh and bone and blood that he had led into death. He stood till darkness was full, but no persons appeared, no commandment was made or answered, no duties laid. He mounted, and turned for home.

～～

Some thousands of years before that day—no one can say for certain how long before—other warriors and leaders first came from

Spain into Ireland. They were people called Gaedhal or Gael because their ancestor in the days of Moses was Gaedhal Glas. When
this Gaedhal was a child Moses cured him of the bite of a serpent—
and he prophesied, look you, that no serpent or other poisonous
thing would infest the green western Island that his far-off posterity
would one day inhabit.

The Gael wandered for hundreds of years before they came into
Spain, following their leader Mil or Milesius, and after they had
long lived there they heard of the beautiful island to the north: the
Isle of Destiny, foretold by Moses. Mil's uncle Ith was first sent to
find that land, to return them a report upon it. But the Tuatha De
Danann, the great wizard-people of the island, suspecting his purpose, killed Ith. It was the first death of the wars of the Milesians
and the Tuatha De Danann.

When Mil was dead in Spain, his eight sons, with their mother,
Scota, and their families and followers, set out for that isle; but when
they attempted to land at a place in the South the Tuatha De raised
a great storm that drove them away, which they could do and have
done in other times. The Milesian poet Amergin prayed a prayer for
them: *I pray that they reach the land of Eirinn, those who ride upon the
vast and fruitful sea; that they come to live everywhere upon her plains,
her mountains, and her valleys, in her forests that drop nuts and all fruits,
upon her rivers and her cataracts, upon her lakes and her great waters and
her spring-abounding hills: and that kings may rise from them at Tara.*

In time they did reach Eirinn, and fought the Tuatha De Danann
until at last a peace was made whereby the Milesians took the land
under the sky and the stars for their part, and the Tuatha the land beneath the earth and in the hollow hills for theirs. And the lands of the
children of Mil under the sky were divided into fourths, north, east,
south, and west: and a fifth part lay in their hearts always, wherever
they went, no matter how far away.

Everyone knows these things. Fathers taught their children the
tale, with many details of weapons and combats, trials and riddles.
But Hugh O'Neill had had no father to teach him: not tales of the
Other Lands, not his prayers, not how to fight nor how to die. He
didn't grieve for his father, but he grieved for his father's absence from
him. Alone, he had felt doubled, torn in two by himself; but on this
day he felt himself a Fachen: sad warrior of one eye, one leg to run on,
one withered arm to fight with, a half-person who learned to seem a

whole man to others, while knowing always that he was not. In his thirty-seventh year Hugh, Earl of Tyrone, remained as afraid within as when he was a boy in England. He never dreamed: but within him, before and behind, a kind of night was always present, darkness visible: each day he woke to it, and each night retired knowing he would meet it again: perhaps, on one future night, to meet at last himself.

STEGANOGRAPHIA

In the year Hugh O'Neill was vested with the earldom of Tyrone, Doctor John Dee and his wife, Jane, and their many children left their house and the isle of Britain for the Continent with trunk-loads of books, an astronomer's staff, bottles of remedy for every ill, a cradleboard for the newest, and in a velvet bag a small orb of quartz crystal with a flaw like a lost star not quite at its center. In a cold room in a high tower in the golden city in the middle of the Emperor's land of Bohemia he placed the stone in its frame carved with the names and sigilla that his angelic informants had given to him.

There was war in heaven, he had been told, and therefore war under the earth, and soon enough on the lands and seas of all the kingdoms of men.

It would engulf the States and Empires of Europe; even the Sultan might be drawn in. Spain had overcome the Portingale king and attached his nation and its empire in Great Atlantis to herself, and so Atlantis too would be in play, and Francis Drake's license as a privateer would be traded for the chain of an Admiral of the Ocean Sea, and Walter Raleigh given one too. The heavenly powers, the armed angelic hosts that must aid the true Christian faith, would go into battle, opposed by other powers great and small. The creatures of the middle realm, of earth and water, hills and trees, shy and self-protective, would surely fight with the old religion: not because they loved the Pope or even knew of him, but only because they hated change. There was little harm they could do, Doctor Dee was sure, though much annoyance. But in the contested Irish Isle where Spain would be welcomed, there were still other powers: warriors who appeared and disappeared after sudden slaughter, bright swords and spears that made no sound. Were they men, had they once been men, were they but empty casques and breastplates? They could be captured, sometimes, imprisoned if you knew the spells, but never for long. *It is useless to hang us*, they would say to their jailers, *we cannot die*.

Look now: there was a swirl of winds within the stone, the sense (not the sound) of heavenly laughter, and the clouds parted to show the ocean as though from a sea-bird's eye, and on the sea small dots that Doctor Dee, bending closer, perceived to be big-bellied ships, or the signs of such ships, the red Spanish crosses just visible or guessable on their sails. In the stone the tiny ships rocked on the main like mock ships in a masque or a children's show. An angel finger pointed to them, and John Dee heard a whisper: *That is not far off from now.*

A flotilla in the North Sea, and then in St. George's Channel, come to throw down Elizabeth and put Catholic Mary Stuart on the throne, with a Catholic consort beside her. It was known that the Spanish Duke of Parma had built a bridge of ships around Antwerp with which to subdue the Dutch; King Philip, fattened on gold and silver from the ransacked empires of dark-peopled Atlantis, had wealth aplenty to begin, and to begin again if his schemes were frustrated. What Doctor Dee had seen in the glass confirmed it: *Not far off from now.* He must learn more, know more; if he could, he must look into the heart and soul of that cold, crippled king.

The lesser legions of heaven, those assigned to the earth's business, are gatherers and bearers of messages and news, passing all that they learn here below to the ranks above, where it is transmitted to the highest places, the seats of judgment and foreknowledge. No active interference in earthly things issues from those seats; the will of God had in the beginning made it a law that the children of Adam and of Eve must be free in the choices and elections they make, no matter the consequences: for the singular soul of each one, but also for the life of all in the time to come. The pious could believe that their prayers and appeals to the saints, the Virgin, and God could change the course of things for the better, or bring about the destruction of their enemies and the supposed enemies of God, but the actual calculus of heaven is simple and easily understood: every earthly alteration produced by Man is at the same time and equally a work of God; every appeal to the powers of darkness or of light is fulfilled by the actions of human souls and hands. The Emperor Maximilian once asked a holy abbot why it was that wicked sorcerers and witches could contract for whatever they desired from the devils of Hell, but a pious man could receive nothing of worth from an angel. The Abbot knew—but he didn't say it to the Emperor—that what the angels gave was knowledge, and a good man could get that for nothing.

The Abbot's invention of a hundred years ago had in fact been for eliciting that knowledge from the angels, who granted it to anyone who had learned how to ask. From the Abbot's rare and precious books, suppressed and condemned by orthodoxy but still findable, books that meant twice as much as they seemed to mean, John Dee had learned the art of angelic petitioning; after years of study he had been rewarded, too. Books of common phrases with fixed hidden meanings: every court possessed them, all differing from the books of other courts. The counting of the lines, the numbers of the letters, the variation of typefaces—anyone could do the arithmetic that revealed the meanings. But none of the tricks and devices common to earthly cyphers were of use in angelic communion: the face message might be cast in the most recondite language the writer possesses, only to baffle mere human investigators and spycatchers; the more urgent message beneath or behind the face message is directed to the angels, who flock to the writings of men, which they can never have enough of, because they cannot themselves create such things; even their consumption of them can be said to be more like eating and drinking than the human activity of reading. But the message they alone can carry and deliver, the message merely *embodied* in the outward paper and ink, is produced like the orderly web of a spider from the writer's own body and soul, and is transmitted to the angel bearers by the writer's hope and need as much as by his letters red and black.

All this John Dee knew. And though the cost in toil and waste of substance in the process was great, he was seated now in Prague before his table of practice to bring forth (in the midnight, under a shaded light, with the soft breathing of his wife and children in their beds in the next chamber) a message that the angels might take. He felt them pluck at the meanings even as he put them down, like naughty pupils snatching their teacher's notes and quill from behind his back. He had no assurances that the answer he required, the answer that would help to save his Queen and nation, would be returned to him: if it came it would come on no paper, but in the opening of his breast and the placing of the answer there where his spirit, like a mirror, could reflect it to his mind and his senses.

He knew by now that each messenger angel can bear a message only as far as to the border of her demesne. There she waits to pass the message to another—Doctor Dee imagined the one reading the letter to the other, who hears and then bears it on, like couriers changing horses at an inn. Of course it isn't words that are passed but scraps of possibility, futures and presents: and the answers that are returned at the angelic borders are liable to change as they are brought down through the upper air. Though they can only be true, and the angel messengers know them to be true, the truth they hold is a form of knowledge that human persons alone can possess: knowledge that is labile, that bears conviction without proof, that is always shadowed by a different and opposite knowledge, tempting or terrifying.

The Moon was waning gibbous on the night the Doctor cast his message and felt it taken up; it was in its last quarter when he understood he had been answered. He fasted for a day, and when morning was full and his wife had shooed the children to their tasks and their schoolwork, and after he had prayed at his faldstool for a quarter of an hour, asking God and His angels that nothing in the letter that had come for him would harm him or his immortal soul, he opened it.

A windowless hall, arched like an immense tunnel, painted on all sides with scenes of battle. Hundreds of warriors in each of many panels, on the ceiling as well as the walls—they seemed to pass beside the Doctor one after another while he himself put one foot before the other without moving forward. In some panels, commanders accompanied by priests and bishops made obeisance, or knelt in surrender to other commanders; in some, horses and men and weapons, cannon firing, clusters of pikes like aspen groves.

There were also living persons in this hall he walked, Augustinian friars in black, secretaries carrying letter-boxes; but they seemed not to arrive and pass by but to occur and vanish, then occur again a little farther off and vanish again. Though many spoke together, and the booted feet of soldiers struck the stone floor, no sound came that the Doctor could hear. That was not surprising. What was surprising was how he, as message and messenger, was carried along by the people who passed by him: like a leaf on a stream carried backward as the stream goes forward. He was drawn up before a small door, guarded by helmeted men in extravagant attire; he was for a time becalmed there, until the door was knocked upon within and opened by the guards, and men in dark robes, arms full of papers, came out and swept around the place where the Doctor stood. Then, without having taken steps, he was inside.

A spare, low room, holding a long wooden table of no magnificence; no carpet upon the stone floor, no curtains at the small deep windows. Only wide shelves where great folders of papers were held, some leaning on others, some fallen flat and with others stacked upon them. More were piled on each end of the wooden table. As Doctor Dee stood unseen, a monk took away a folder from before the man, all in black, seated at the table. A monk at the table's other end opened an identical folder and placed it before the man. There was no doubt who the man at the table was; his habits and his dress were known to the world, half of which was his to command. He wore no coronet, no chain. He dipped a pen and began to study and to annotate the pages of the folder before him. John Dee thought of the tales in which a wise child or a hero begs to be transformed into a fly, to spy upon his enemies and their doings. And though he could not himself ask for that, in his state now he thought he could by will alone cause his being to take the form of that insect eye, unnoticeable. For a few moments. Now.

There on the papers where the King scribbled his orders, names came to be, not as though drawn by a pen but rising like bubbles from a pond. The names were of ships, and the ships' captains: *San Felipe, Florencia, San Francesco, Santa Anna, Gran Grifon.* Urcas, great-ships, galleons, galleasses, down to small *fregatas, zabras, pataches.* All presented to the King for his study, the names to be checked off with his pen: the duke of Medina Sidonia, the duke of Parma, the count-duke Olivares. And the names also of angelic hosts whom his friars had identified with this or that fleet or squadron, who would need to be praised in hymns and Masses every day for success to follow.

It was to be: the notes that John Dee perceived on the King's table named May as the month the vast fleet would be launched. From the lowlands of Holland the great rafts or barges would be filled with soldiers and sent off; that was Parma's charge. Dee sensed what the man in black perceived, what he himself had imagined: the English Queen imprisoned or dead, Catholic Mary on the throne, Philip's son her husband. He shuddered, or the free soul that looked on these future things shuddered. So did the King, his hand beginning to tremble, his pen dropping, spoiling his page. A figure in doctor's robes appeared, placed a thick shawl around the King's shoulders, and a servant placed a cup before him, heated wine.

Doctor Dee couldn't tell, and no being could tell him, if the King would live till England was conquered, or if conquest was unavoidable, or was impossible. In that moment the letter that he had opened in his bosom came to an end: it folded itself up small, and he was once more in his study in Prague. It was evening now here, as it had been morning in Spain. A church-bell in the city was pealing slowly, as for one dead; in the house a dinner-bell rang. He began a letter—ordinary paper, a quill and ink—for Walsingham in London, in a simple code they shared. *This is to be,* the decoded letters would spell. *These are the names, these the numbers. It is not far off from now.*

AEODH RUE

*T*he country of the O'Donnells of Tyrconnell lay to the west and north of Hugh O'Neill's Ulster strongholds, reaching from Malin Head, the northernmost point of the Irish island, and down to Donegal Bay. South of the bay lay the lands of the O'Connors of Sligo and the O'Malleys of Clew Bay; toward Galway Bay were the vast lands of the Burkes, and even farther south the lands of the O'Brien earls of Thomond. There were few fixed borders between these fiefdoms, and claims made on this or that stretch of ground or stand of forest had to be backed up with force until a settlement was made, sometimes after years of merry battling had passed, only to be challenged again later.

The present head of the clan was *Aeodh Duvh* O'Donnell—"Black Hugh," Sir Hugh: his knighthood granted him by the Queen, to whom he had made obeisance; it was a fine honor to have got, but his real power was as the O'Donnell. The only one as great as himself now in the lands of the O'Donnells was another of high name: Fionnula MacDonnell of the Scots MacDonnells over the water, the daughter of a Scots laird and his Campbell wife, and called by all *Ineen Duvh*, "the dark girl"—wife to O'Donnell, mother of nine of his children, some of whom she loved, and some she didn't, which could at times be fatal to them or their offspring if they claimed honors or titles that Ineen Duvh thought should go to another of the crowd, a daughter's or a son's son. The child of her own that she loved the best was *Aeodh Rue*, "Red Hugh": red for his brilliant head of Scots red hair, red for the scatter of freckles across his open face—for the red of his sword, too, it would be said later, when he joined the Earl of Tyrone in the last war against the English colonials and the Queen's armies.

He was a boy of fifteen when Hugh O'Neill, on a politic journey to Tyrconnell—a marriage agreement, to strengthen an alliance— became aware of him: watching him leap aboard a dappled pony without saddle or stirrups, ride against four of his younger brothers, tapping each with a slim wand that stood for a weapon, laughing and dodging away from them, only to turn the pony on them and with a piercing cry charge them again.

"A wraith," O'Neill said. "Hardly he seems to be there. Yet he's iron."

"A fine son he'll be to you," said O'Donnell, gripping O'Neill's shoulder. It had been agreed, with the assent of Ineen Duvh, that this Red Hugh would be married to a natural daughter of O'Neill's, a child now being cared for by his elder sister, Siobhan, the Earl's wife, alongside her own small sons.

"Siobhan," Hugh O'Donnell said. "She's happy with you?"

"I believe she is."

"She's well?"

"She is, and now with child again."

"Pray for a son," O'Donnell said, teasing. "If you pray."

Hugh O'Neill didn't think that a son of dark Siobhan needed praying for; he thought she had the power to decide, son or daughter, or both at once, and have it come to be. But he might pray, if he could, to have a son like that red-head, now lifted in triumph by his brothers like a king aloft.

The O'Donnells didn't know, and the new-made Earl of Tyrone didn't know, that the boy was just then being thought about in Dublin.

Sir John Perrot, the Lord Deputy, amid his council, had been asked what was to be done with the restive O'Donnells and their Ulster ally, the new Earl of Tyrone. Should an English army be sent to settle the matter? In response Sir John gazed at the ceiling, as though awaiting a thought to form in his mind, though in truth the thought had already been thought, only not yet spoken. "Perhaps there is another way," he averred. "If your Honors will give me leave, I may have a spider's trick to play, that might suppress clan O'Donnell's stirrings."

What sort of trick, the Council wanted to know, but Sir John would only ask that he be allowed to try what he had conceived, and if it failed, as was perhaps likely, the Council might then turn to military force, "and see what might be invented." The Council voted to suspend the hearing *sine die,* and the Lord Deputy smiled upon them, hands across his great middle.

On an evening not long after, Sir John walked the Dublin wharves making inquiries, and settled upon a sea-captain named Skinner for his plan. A heavy purse persuaded Skinner to take some fifty soldiers up the coast and around by the west to Donegal, with a cargo of sherris sack and white wines of Spain, as though he had just come from that country.

With good winds and a following sea Skinner's ship turned Malin Head in a day and a night, and on the next day drew into the deep cut of Lough Swilly, not a lake but a long inlet of the sea, and tied up at the O'Donnell fortress of Rathmullan. It might have happened that on this day the young Red Hugh had gone off with his cousins of the McSweeney clan to hunt or run races; but no, he was at the fortress with the McSweeney boys, and the mate called from the deck that they were welcome to come up. They were invited into the captain's cabin, and given a taste of the sack, which was fine, and a glass of the Spanish wine too, and then a wine from a different bottle. A nor'wester was blowing up; the generous captain excused himself to see to his ship, and invited the boys to stay and drink; and by the time they had put their dizzy heads down upon the table, that nor'wester was pushing Skinner's ship out of Swilly at twelve knots by the sand-glass, and the hatch, when they tried it, they found to be locked.

Two days later the ship came again into Dublin harbor. Under guard the young men were brought out, marched to Dublin Castle, and put in chains, condemned and talked at by judges in a language few of them knew at all. *Your father shall keep the peace and aid the appointed officers of the Crown as instructed, or you, you here, will answer for it.* They were taken to cells, the same that the Earl of Desmond had occupied: there was his sign, cut with a fragment of slate into a three-legged stool. They were shut up with a crowd of others, all children of one age or another, all of them offered up by their families as pledges to assure the Crown that their parents would do no evil, all of them in irons that were checked every day by a jailer.

The North was enraged by this trick, aggrieved, afraid. Tyrone sent appeals to every person of rank and power he could think of. He offered the government in Dublin a thousand pounds as ransom for the prisoners, to which Perrot responded that if offered two thousand he'd reject it. The boys were not to be ransomed; they were themselves ransom, did the Earl not understand this? At length Perrot released the McSweeney boys into the care of Ineen

Duvh, who'd knelt before him on her old stiff knees and wept; the
McSweeneys were of no value to him. But the O'Donnell boy was
a treasure. Perrot wrote to the Queen that *the having of Master
O'Donnell, in respect he is come of the Scots and matched in marriage
with the greatest in Ulster, will serve you of good purpose.*

Sore at heart, Hugh O'Neill set out for the O'Donnell stronghold
to give what comfort and make what plans he could, but he had
hardly reached the old fort at Castlederg before he stopped. What
good could he do in Donegal? He sent his guard to seek food and
shelter, and sat in the pale sun on the fallen stones. He thought
of Desmond, how he had lain immured in the Tower, and then in
the damp precincts of Southwark. How many years had that been?
Would Red Hugh spend his youth in chains?

There was only one person who could decide.

The obsidian mirror was blank in the sun; it was sometimes hard
to tell if what he saw there was the familiar face, or merely lights
chasing over the black surface. But he knew when he was spoken to:
or perhaps he overheard words that were not spoken to him but to
herself, Elizabeth, to which he could only listen. *The wife of O'Donnell,
the black witch of the Isles, she hates me.* It was like a whistle in his ear,
faint and vanishing. *She has hated, ever hated me since the reiver Sorley
Boye MacDonnell was defeated on Rathlin Island and every pirate child
and mother, all of them her kin, were slain. And in justice too.*

All that O'Neill knew of the happenings at Rathlin Island he had
heard from Ineen Duvh.

She, the Queen's whisper came again. *She is a beast and a witch,
and her issue, her brat, she will never see again. Who will say me nay.*

He rose from the warm stone. He saw, not far off, his guard returning. He let the mirror on its chain fall within his shirt, where
it lay against his breast. What was the value of his elevation by her
hand, his nobilitation, his being *charmed,* if he had less power than
some she hated? No: that boy and his brethren would not die in
prison. She might see into Hugh O'Neill, his heart even, but she
didn't know all of him. No one did. He mounted, lifted a gloved
hand, and pointed east, back toward Dungannon.

Then there came an end to all business and all matters high and lov
an end to the reading of petitions and the bargaining over ransom

the unresolvable disputes of clans at enmity, the knighting of eldest sons of English settlers with the Lord Deputy's permission. Word from sources in Portugal and the Netherlands was that the Spanish fleet was on the seas, and in a week or a month from now England might no longer be England. A kind of stasis fell over Ireland, or at least over the minds and hearts of those who knew what turn the world was taking. Summoned to Dublin to face the charge that he was plotting with the MacMahons in Monaghan, Hugh O'Neill did not respond. What in this fast-turning world did MacMahon count for? Would Spain in victory return the island to its saints and its kings? Let Dublin wait to see who would be master before they insulted him with their demands.

It was the great action that John Dee in Prague had seen coming to be, the thing that his angel informants had shown in play, now real and at hand. A century ago a mathematician and astronomer calling himself Regiomontanus had constructed a chart of the heavens for this year of Our Lord 1588: all the conjunctions, the oppositions, the occupants of the twelve houses throughout that year. Two eclipses of the Moon seemed certain, foreboding: one in March, one more in August. Jupiter, Saturn, and Mars would hang for weeks poisonously conjoined in Jupiter's own domicile, the sign of Leo. *Post mille exactos a partu virginis,* Regiomontanus wrote in a lengthy Latin poem to accompany his chart: *A thousand years after the birth of the Virgin, then five hundred eighty-eight more.* Why had the German mathematician chosen 1588 for his investigations? What angel had whispered in his ear that states would totter, mountains tumble, stars fall from their circuits in that future year, which had now become *this* year? John Dee had studied the hundred-year-old accounts, redone the arithmetic, drawn his own charts: as to the stars he found no flaw. But what consequences might come from the heavens thus arrayed, so disordered and queer, was impossible to say. Rather: it was easy to say, and impossible to know.

Doctor Dee served two royal masters. Neither the Queen of England nor the Holy Roman Emperor disbelieved in the warnings of the stars and planets; both were sure that if the stars did prognosticate, it was the fates of princes that they foretold. Both rulers supposed that Doctor John Dee had ways to learn what was to come, whether by study or some other means. Of the two rulers, it was the Queen who was the braver—she whose fortunes were governed by

the inconstant Moon, the Moon that would suffer its second eclipse in the first degrees of her own sign of Virgo. "We defy augury," she said, a phrase that the court and the City repeated for years. Everyone knew it was treason to predict the death of a monarch, whether on good grounds or none. Pamphlet-writers who could learnedly dispute or dismiss the dire oncoming events were put to work by the Queen's Council even as weird evidence mounted up.

"You have heard of the stone that came out of the ground in England," the Holy Roman Emperor, Rudolf II, said to John Dee.

He had sent for the Englishman, whom he was sure knew many things he had yet to reveal. For weeks the Emperor had not issued from the royal apartments in his vast Hradschin palace, not even so far as the offices of state, where great decisions awaited him. He had decided not to decide. It was safest, given what loomed ahead, to sit still, and take no steps of any gravity at all.

"That information has reached me, Your Imperial Majesty." From the clutch of papers in the Emperor's hands, it was clear to the Doctor that he intended to read the news to him anyway.

"A slab of marble," the Emperor said. "Buried for centuries in the foundation of an ancient abbey."

Glastonbury, the Doctor wanted to say, but he had not been asked.

"The ground heaved, as in a spasm, an earthquake. This stone was thrown up, brought forth."

The Doctor nodded.

"On that never-before-seen marble," the Emperor continued, "as though cut or burned upon it, were words: *Post mille exactos a partu virginis annos.* The very words of Regiomontanus." The Emperor's sad-dog eyes were wide. "The *very words.*" He flourished the papers at the Doctor, who took it as a sign that he was now to speak. He knew every square yard of Glastonbury. He was not afraid of a stone.

"The stars speak," he said. "We cannot always hear their converse. And we do not know their language. Like a man in the market or court of a foreign city, the wisest can only make suppositions: What is this? What that?"

The Emperor goggled at him for a moment. "Well? What *does* it mean?"

The first wind bears in the time, a golden angel child had said to

John Dee, with careless certainty. *And the second bears it away again.* "Your Imperial Highness. It is well known that the movements of the stars have long been your study. If permitted I will take up this prophecy that has swept the world, and, with Your Grace, show where it is certain and where not."

The Emperor turned away, letting fall his papers, and went to Mercator's great globe on its stand. His finger traced the path from Lisbon and the Spanish ports to the English isles. "Spain's warships are on the sea. The Spanish Ambassador has revealed it to me. The English Queen can fall. The Catholic Church could be restored."

"She is ruled by the Moon," Doctor Dee said. "The Moon may suffer, but she cannot die."

The Emperor Rudolf was the grandson of Emperor Charles, once sovereign over half the world. "He says there will come *the fall of empires.* Certain, or not?"

John Dee thought of England, of his Queen, who might be in chains by the next full Moon. Empires contain kingdoms, kingdoms contain lands, lands contain duchies, duchies cities towns and houses. Empires are many: there are the great and the small, the visible and the invisible. "It may be that our Regiomontanus, Master Kingsmount, was certain," he said to Rudolf. "But he doesn't then say which empires, or how many."

three

ON STREEDAGH'S STRAND

COMMINATION

When she turned away from the seaward windows and looked through the window that faced the rocky way leading down to the village, Ineen Fitzgerald could see that someone was coming up toward the house. He was having some difficulty; at times the rainy wind seemed to snatch away his cloak entirely and to be on the point of taking flight, but he hauled it in and wrapped it around himself again; and by pulling himself up the stones and planting his feet heavily he made progress toward her. The rippled diamond panes of the window, streaked with the rain, made the little figure seem to shift size and nature continually; sometimes, when the wind threw a mighty slew of rain across the glass, he disappeared from view entirely, as though he had been drowned.

Cormac, she thought. He was coming all the way up from the strand to tell her what she already knew: that was like him. She, who always knew first whatever happened in the surrounding country and on the sea, for her house stood above the village and oversaw not only the road that wound under great Ben Bulben from the east, but the sea-road and the long stony spit as well: what had she to do but watch? Yet he would always come up to her with cold news. That a curragh which had gone out with four brothers in it had come back on the tide stove in and empty, and lay overturned on the beach. That a line of English soldiery was coming from the east with pieces of ordnance and a man in armor at its head. "Yes, Cormac," she would say patiently, for she had seen them already at dawn, counted their cannon, and seen the glint of armor in the sun. It was only that he loved her, not that he was an idle gossip; the fiction that he was bringing her news was understood by both of them for what it was and she didn't dislike him for it. Yet she did feel, as she turned away from the window, a small irritation. Why hadn't he more sense than to climb up here uselessly in a storm?

Out the seaward windows she could see that the huge ships were coming, helplessly, nearer the shore. The black, white-fringed waves rose so high that now and then the ships were lost to sight entirely, as though swamped and sunk already, but then they would appear again: one, a fleck of white sail only, far off; the other westerly and straining to keep to the open sea; and the third, seeming to have surrendered to its awful fate, nearest the land, near enough for her to see the red cross on its sails, its shrouds torn away and waving rhythmically—or was that only the spray of rain cast off its spars as it creased the storm? The waves that bore it landward seemed to rise with an unreal slowness, like the great crushing waves that rose in her dreams: seemed to rise endlessly, black glass hung with froth, each one falling against the tormented strand only at the last moment before its movement upward would become unceasing and it would rise up and drown the world.

She, who had watched the sea most of her life, had never seen a catastrophe anything like this one, had never seen the sea attempt to destroy men on such a scale. She had seen storms as bad, and worse, but they spent themselves against the land, which she knew could always bear it. And the sea even in a mood of mild petulance could kill fishermen of the village, singly or in pairs, and send their curraghs to the bottom; and then she would feel a sickening anger at the unfairness. But she had never seen ships the size of these galleons, like mansions put to sea. There would be dozens of men aboard them, hundreds; she could see now, with a thrill of terror, that tiny men actually clung to the masts and rigging of the nearest ship, trying to cut loose the luffing sails as large as meadows, and as the sea canted the ship over suddenly, one man was flung into the sea.

What should she feel? Pity for them? She couldn't. For the destruction of the floating castles? The pride of them, even in destruction, forbade it. She could only watch fascinated the two monstrosities, sea and galleon, contend.

The same winds that carried the ships toward shore tormented the house, hooting in the chimney and rattling the windows in their frames. Small winds, wet and salt, were in the house, couldn't be kept out. In the silences which came momentarily when the wind turned round she could hear her father, in the loft praying. *Ave Maria gratia plena Dominus tecum.* If her father died this night, that would be right; she, caught up in the vast wasting of human life by the sea and somehow fiercely indifferent, unable to feel pity or shock, wouldn't feel then at her father's death all the guilty anguish she had long expected to feel when at last his strong, mad ghost gave up its body. She almost, wrapped in a sudden draft of cold sea air, almost wished for it.

The nearest galleon had begun to break up on the drowned stones of the causeway that ran out beyond the spit. Farther off, the seaward ship had lost its battle, and, a loose sail flapping with slow grace like a handkerchief, swept down toward the cliffy places to the south. The third she could no longer see. The sea had thrown it away.

At the other end of the house the unbarred door was opened, and shut again. She felt a gust of wind that made her shiver.

"Bar the door, Cormac," she said. She turned with reluctance from the window and went into the narrow tangle of hallway that led to the door. "You're a fool, Cormac Burke," she said, not quite as gently as she had intended to, "to come up all the way here in this weather, and to tell me about the ships, who is it?"

She stopped then, because the man turned to face her from barring the door wasn't Cormac Burke. She didn't know him. The water coursing down his mantle and the brim of his hat spattered rapidly on the floor; there was a puddle around his booted feet, and when he stepped toward her the boots made a sodden sound.

"Who are you?" she said, stepping back.

"Not the one you named. One very wet."

They stood facing each other for a long moment. In the darkness of the hall she couldn't well see his face. His Irish had a Scots intonation, and sounded wet as well, as though the water had got into his throat.

"Might I," he said at last, "claim the hospitality of this house? A seat by the fire, if you have such a thing? I wouldn't trouble you at all." He held out both hands, slowly, as though to show he wasn't armed. His two hands seemed to glow faintly in the dark hall, as silver objects and certain sea-shells do in dimness.

She came to herself. "Yes, come in," she said. "Warm yourself. I didn't mean to refuse the house."

He stripped off his mantle heavy with water, and followed her into the comparative warmth and light of the main room of the house. He stood a moment looking about himself, seeming to take inventory of the place, or as though trying to remember if he had ever been in it before. Then he went to the chimney corner and hung his mantle and hat on a peg there.

"We get few guests," she said.

"I think that's odd," he said. His hair was thin and gray, and his face was white like his hands, though now in the light of the fire and the rush-lights they seemed to glow as they had in the hall. His eyes were large and pale and with some humorous melancholy in them that was disconcerting.

"Odd? We're far off the travelled roads."

"But it's the finest house hereabouts. A traveller who put out the effort might be likely to find more than a cup of water for himself."

She ought to have resented this calculation, but she couldn't, he said it so frankly. "You are a stranger here."

"Oh, I am."

"And from where?"

He said a mouth-filling Scots place-name she didn't recognize, and said that he was called Sorley.

"Like Sorley Boye?"

"Not of that clan or name," he said, with a slight smile that made Ineen wonder if he was lying, and then wonder why she wondered. "And what might your name be called?"

"Ineen," she said, and looked away.

"And right, too," he said; for *ineen* is only *girl* in Irish.

"Ineen Fitzgerald," she said. To another that might have stopped further inquiry. She felt it wouldn't with this Sorley, and in fact he right away asked her what one with such a name did living in this northern place.

"There's a tale in that," she said, and turned away to the window again. The near Spanish ship was stove in now, the breach in its side was evident, it was shipping water and seemed to pant like a dying bull as it rose and fell on the heaving surf. There was flotsam, boards, barrels. Did men cling to them? With a sudden fear she realized that the sea might not take them all, not all those dozens. Some might live, and gain the strand. Spanish men. Spanish soldiers. What would happen then?

"They are only men after all," said Sorley.

So intent was she, had she been all that day, on the ships that she didn't find it odd that he seemed to have read her thoughts.

"All up and down the coast," he said, "from Donegal down to Kerry, they've been putting in, or trying to; coming to grief, many of them. Most of the men drowning."

"Why have they come? Why so many?"

"No reason of their own. They never wanted to. They were meant to sail and conquer England. The sea and the wind drove them here."

She turned to him. "How do you come to know so much of it?" she asked.

"Travel with eyes and ears open."

"You came up from the south, then."

He answered nothing to this. The wind rose to a sudden shriek, and the rain made a fierce hissing in the thatch of the roof. Outside, something loose, a bucket, a rake, went blown across the yard, making a noise that startled her. In the loft her father groaned, and began murmuring the Commination: *Cursed be he who putteth his trust in Man, who taketh Man for his salvation* . . .

Sorley looked up toward the dimness of the loft. "What others are in the house?"

"My father. Ill." Mad and dying the word meant. "A serving-girl. Gone down now to the strand, to watch the ships."

"When the Spanish come on the strand," he said, "they will be murdered. Half-drowned they'll come out of the sea and each be struck by a mattock or an axe, or be stoned or sworded to death, till all those not drowned will be just as dead." He spoke all this calmly, as though it had already happened, perhaps years ago. "Ill luck, to come up out of the sea, alive, and speak no Irish."

"They never would!" She—a Geraldine, a Norman, however she might have fallen—had no illusions about the villagers below her. But to murder the Spanish, their true friends, only because they are foreign to them—that was too absurdly savage. Sorley only smiled his thin fixed smile; she had begun to think he smiled only as hawks frown, out of his nature somehow and not his mood.

"Would you have anything to eat?" he said. "I seem to have come a long way on yesterday's dinner." Called to herself again, reminded of how inhospitable she'd grown in her long exile, she blushed, and went to see what might be in the house. On an impulse she drew a jug of red wine from one of the remaining tuns. When she returned with this, and some herring and a loaf, he was sitting on a stool by the fire, looking at his long pale hands. "You see how much sea has blown in today," he said. She looked more closely, and saw that his hands were dusted with a fine white glowing powder. "Salt," he said. His face was dusty the same way. She accepted his reason for this without thinking that while stones and driftwood left long in the sea may become salt-encrusted like that, her hands and face had never been, though she often spent whole days walking in sea spray. She brought him a bowl of water, and he dipped his hands into it. When he withdrew them wet, they had again become glistening and faintly opalescent.

"Now it's sea-water in the bowl," he said. "Look into it, Ineen Fitzgerald."

She did look in, apprehensive and not knowing why. The bowl was old dark crockery, thick and cracked. For a strange moment she did seem to see the whole sea, as though she were a gull, or God, looking down on it; the ripples Sorley's hands had made in it lapped its edge as tides lap the edges of the world. She saw something moving over the face of the waters, indistinct and multiform, as though the creatures might be rising to look up at her as she looked down; then she saw it was only a faint reflection of her own face. She laughed, and looked at Sorley, who was smiling more broadly. Her apprehension was gone. She felt as if she had been playing a children's game with him, and it seemed to make an intimacy between them; an elation almost, the same fierce indifferent elation she had felt watching the ships. She was then aware that a charm had been worked on her, like the charm in fast sea-breezes and scudding cloud, a charm to make her free. *Stop it now, mad girl*, she told herself, too much alone, *stop all that*. She pulled her shawl around her. Sorley ate herring and bread, delicately, as though he didn't need it for sustenance. He poured wine into a battered cup and tasted it. "Canary," he said. "And fine, too." Without really considering it, she took a cup for herself and filled it. "What do you do abroad, Sorley?" she said.

"Looking for a wife, Ineen Fitzgerald," he said.

～✲

On the strand, Cormac Burke stared helplessly at the oblique lines of waves folding together and dashing against the stony beach with a noise like a rising but never climaxing peal of thunder. His voice was raw from shouting against it. A few shards and pieces were still coming in on the tide: a window frame, a barrel stave. Strung out across the strand in tight, self-defensive knots, the villagers ran from one to another of these treasures and exclaimed over them. He had tried to organize them into a troop of sorts, armed men in front, then other men, the women to salvage, a priest for the dying. Hopeless. He had tried to explain to them that there were three things that must be done: aid should be given to the hurt; the goods should be rounded up and put in piles; the soldiers must be disarmed and, for the moment, made prisoner, for the English would certainly see them as invaders, and any Irish who helped them as rebels. Their arms could be taken from them and hidden; later . . . But it was useless. The sea was mad; and there was no schooling these men. On the strand, now nearly covered in sand, lay three—four—bodies. If he had not known them to be Spaniards he wouldn't, as darkness came on, have known they were men. But he knew; he had rushed toward them with the others when they came tumbling from the sea, staggering away from the withdrawing water. They had reached out hands to him: *Auxilio. Succoro, Señores.* And the Irishmen with him, crying out like animals, their faces distended so that he seemed not to know them at all, had murdered them; had almost murdered Cormac when he tried to stop them. Now he stood farther off, afraid to watch any longer to see more Spaniards come ashore, knowing he would not again try to interfere in the villagers' madness, unable to leave, yet with no way to stop them.

If he had a gun.

He turned away from the sea and looked up to where, just raising itself above a coign of sea-wall, the roof of the Fitzgerald house could be seen. Was there a light burning? He thought there was. *And what did you do when they came ashore, Cormac? I could do nothing, and the Spanish were murdered, Ineen.* He pulled his feet from the muddy sand and began to work his way down the shingle, watching the sea and the knots of men, and, far off, the ship, whose masts were now aslant to the slabs of sea that bore it up.

It wasn't the wine, not entirely: though when she went to draw another jug she noticed that her lips and nose itched a little, growing numb, and that filling the jug she was slapdash; she spoke aloud to herself, saying she shouldn't have babbled on to this stranger, and laughed.

She had told him about her father, who had been a priest, and was a cousin of the Fitzgerald Earl of Kildare, and how the English had persuaded him to come into the new dispensation and he would soon be made a bishop by the Queen; how despite all his kin's despising him for it he did so; how he renounced his vows and the True Church, and married the frail daughter of an English colonial. His family rejected him, his wife despised him and lived in a continual state of loathing at Irish ways and the Irish until she departed for her father's house—which was soon after Ineen was born to a serving-girl in the house, a Gael. And after their promises, and in spite of a hundred letters her father sent to London, and twenty visits to Dublin, the English never began raising her father toward the promised bishopric, not so much as a wardenship—apparently satisfied that promises had been enough to draw him out of his church. In the end he had lost even the empty parish the English had given him, where he preached to nearly nobody, because Desmond—his distant cousin too—rose up then against the English and heresy, and her father had to be taken off by sea lest he be hanged by his flock. Was it that terrible story, or was it God's vengeance at his defection, that had made him mad? The English, as though tossing him away, had placed him in this western isolation and given him a piece of the wine trade—wine! that with his breath he had once altered in its red heart to the blood of Christ!—and let him live on a tariff he collected, a useless middleman. Was all that enough to make him mad? Or was God's vengeance needed?

"It hasn't made you mad, Ineen," Sorley said, and she saw that the story had washed over him without altering his features. "And the Captain of Desmond is dead, who fought for Mother Church. Whose vengeance was that, then?" She lifted the jug, and filled the cups; two drops splashed out and stained the linen of her sleeve as quick as blood. She dipped the sleeve in the bowl of water, pressing water through it absently. "I wouldn't like to drown," she said. "Not of any way."

"Avoid the sea."

"They say men drowning can see treasures lost in the sea—ships sunk, gold, jewels."

"Do they? And do they have candles with them to light up the darkness?"

She laughed, wiping her mouth. Her father cried out, dreaming; a sob, as though someone were stifling him with a pillow. Another cry, louder. He called her name; he was awake. She waited a moment, feeling vaguely ashamed. Maybe he would sleep again. But again he called her name, his voice edged now with that piteous panic she knew well, which worked on her senses like a rasp.

"Yes, Father," she said gently, and went to the press in the corner, from which she took a jar of powder; some of this she mixed into a cup of wine, and, having lit a rush-light at the fire, carried the wine and the light carefully up into the loft. Her father's white face looked out from the bed curtains, his white cap and large pinkish eyes making him look like a terrified rabbit looking out from its burrow. "Who is it in the house?" he whispered urgently. "Cormac?"

"Yes," she said, "only Cormac." She had him drink the wine, and kissed him, and said a prayer with him; then when he groaned again she laid him firmly down, speaking calmly but with authority, as she might to a child. He lay back on the pillows, his stricken eyes still searching her face. She smiled, and drew his curtains.

Sorley sat unchanged by the fire, turning his cup in his fingers.

Why had she lied to her father?

"They say too," she said, taking a gulp of wine, "that there's a bishop under the sea. A fish bishop." She had seen a picture in a bestiary of her father's.

"Certainly," Sorley said. "To marry and bury."

"What rites does he use, do you think?"

"And the mackerel is the fish's bawd. Men!" He shook his head, smiling. "They think even the fish live by the laws they live by. A little handful of folk, huddled up on the dry land that's not a tenth part the size of the seas, and dreaming of bishops for the fish."

"How is it, then, in the sea?" she said, for some reason not doubting he knew.

"Come with me and see," he said.

Where they went that night was not seaward. Cold as his touch was, it was strong, and she would not have been able to resist it even if she'd chosen to do so, which she did not choose. She thought to press her hand against his mouth so that he would not cry aloud, but he was not the one who cried aloud. She slept then like one dead, and he was gone when she awoke, and her father was awake too, calling from the loft, but she paid no mind, and got up; felt run down the inside of her thigh a dribble of slime she thought might be blood, but no, she hadn't bled.

He would not have gone far. How she knew it she could not have said. She wrapped herself in a long black shawl and went out into the day, where the storm-wrack still filled the sky and the sea. The ship she had watched could still be seen, dis-masted now and smashed in the rocks like unswallowed fragments in a mastiff's mouth. She went down along the way to the strand, and it wasn't long before she saw him striding ahead of her, holding his hat on his head for the off-shore breeze. She passed the place where last night the men from the Spanish ship had come up onto the beach; their bodies lay dark and shapeless as seals, half-buried in sand: no place a human soul could rest. They must be buried as Christian men, whatever. She would ask Cormac Burke to help.

He, Sorley, had not turned at all to look at the bodies of the men on the strand, kept on till the turn of the cove. He was after tossing away his hat, and then his cloak, and when he came to the rocky place he was as naked as he had been in her bed in the night. And when he bent to reach into the sea-weed and the crusted stones wedged in a great split of the rocks and found something there to don, she knew whom she had had in her. She thought that she had in some way known it all along, but now she knew it to see, and to think: to think what would come of this, now and in the months and years to come.

EL GRAN-GRIN

the news had reached Dungannon days before that the Spanish fleet had been driven into the North Sea, with the English ships in pursuit; they seemed to be in process to round Scotland and make for open ocean, to return that way to Spain. Before they could make away, the storm arose that drove them relentlessly onto the western coast of Ireland, to be battered to pieces on the Donegal shore in heavy seas. O'Neill and old Hugh O'Donnell sent as many as they could of their followers to the coast and set out themselves with a force of gallowglass, knowing now they would not reach the coast themselves in time to stop the killing. *Rescue who can be rescued,* they commanded those who went ahead. *If the guns can be saved hide them, if they cannot be saved, then delay the English who come to kill the Spanish as best you can, to the limit of your strength.* And yet they were soon to hear from those who returned that Gráinne O'Malley and her crews had gone down to the beaches of Clare Island and pulled Spanish crewmen washed half-dead ashore from the wreck of the *Gran-Grin*, and that the Dowdary O'Malleys, for no reason O'Neill could fathom, had beaten many of them to death with clubs—*like seals,* his messengers said.

"They can't be saved," O'Donnell cried into the wind. "It's too late."

"Some can," O'Neill said. "We must."

They had ridden farther west a ways and O'Donnell had fallen behind. Hugh turned back to where the older man had stopped.

"My lord," O'Donnell said. "If a few can be gathered up. I wish to offer some of them, to the number thirty or more, to the Lord Deputy Perrot at Dublin."

"Hostages in exchange for your son's freedom."

"Yes."

"You know that if the Lord Deputy agrees, he will take your hostages and then kill them all. *If* he agrees. Or pretends to."

"No, no," O'Donnell cried, a plea.

O'Neill took the older man's bridle. "Those Spanish men. What would we do if one day, we, like they, had to seek refuge in a land not our own? If we betray them to the English and to Bingham and Perrot to hang them or knock their brains out we will in our turn go down into the darkness forever."

The two stood side by side looking each into the other's face. Then O'Donnell turned his horse to the way they had been going. They rode on together through the slackening storm, their horses seeking purchase on the mud-slick way, their gallowglass on ahead carrying sputtering torches. Hopeless. Not long thereafter they called a halt, signaled to the men ahead to turn back; there was nothing they could do, they would come too late. O'Neill felt his heart fill with rage, at the English, at his fellow Irishmen. What would it mean to win their land for them, what would it mean to lead such ones, where would it end? The English murdered for policy; they cared nothing for those they slew, but they knew why they did it. Was he himself one of them, was he like his folk, or was he himself alone? Rabbit or hunter, pursuer or pursued? *Look not on their suffering but on me.* It might be that in youth he had been made one of them, the English, and he should deal in Spanish heads as markers in the game, the one game, and get what he could for them. Yet he could not.

"We'll free your son," he cried. "He and all of them. I pledge my life on it. What's begun now will not end, no not when you and I are dead—not ever, if that is what's to be. Stay with me, sir, and we will go together."

Torches came toward them as they stood there. Running men, the torchbearers they had sent on ahead now returning, crying out: *Men approaching, men marching together, Spanish men.* Dawn had begun to break, gray and cloaked in storm, but when O'Neill and O'Donnell rode forward they began to see the Spanish sailors and soldiers coming toward them, some holding up others, some signaling for help or to plead for mercy—what did they know of what would become of them? Hugh O'Neill raised his hand, calling for his bodyguards to slow to a walk, not to terrify the Spanish.

"Where have they come from?" O'Donnell asked of no one. "They cannot have come from Donegal. All those were killed, we've had the news."

"They're alive, for all that," O'Neill said, and in a gesture he rarely used, he crossed himself: Could they be dead after all, and walking the night away? No: for now he saw among them, with long strides making his way ahead of the stumbling sailors and soldiers, that courier of Gráinne's, the one who years ago had carried to Gráinne Hugh O'Neill's plan to end the life of Shane.

"The walking man!" he cried aloud. "Who are these?"

The courier reached Hugh's horse, and stood by its head, one hand curled against his hip, looking up: that faint smile that told nothing. "These are all that were rescued from the great-ship *Gran-Grin*," he said. "My lady sent out galleys, sent men to the beaches from Killybegs inlet to Clew Bay, to bring in every one that escaped drowning."

O'Donnell leaned from his saddle. "We had news that they were all killed by the O'Malleys. Sworded and flung into the sea, clubbed to death like seals."

The courier acknowledged O'Donnell, nodding as though to confirm what he said. "Yes. So it is said, and so it will be said. Now and hereafter. And likely no one will go to seek for them in the sands or in the bay waters; if they do, only a few will be found. These are the many remaining."

"She lied," Hugh O'Neill said, laughing. "Queen Gráinne lied!"

"She would have you know that you must get these out of sight and sound, and not speak of them even to your own people, so far as you can. These are men that do not exist."

"Does she mean us to return them to Spain?"

The courier only shook his head slightly, as though he had no answer to make to that; but then he said: "This number of them are yours to care for, my lord." He tilted his head a degree sidewise with the same absence of deference that Hugh O'Neill remembered. Then he backed away courteously from the riders, turned, and started along the track they had come. In a moment he couldn't be seen.

"How did that fellow know which way to take through Ulster?" O'Donnell said. "The best way is not the shortest."

Hugh O'Neill, Earl of Tyrone, felt without touching it the small flint, safe in his clothes. "He was guided, perhaps. Or told."

"Guided? Or told? By whom was he?"

Hugh laughed. "Day's come," he said, and turned his horse.

O'Neill had spoken truth: of the men from the Spanish ships who came ashore and were rounded up by the English forces sent out for the purpose, the nobles were saved to be ransomed, the rest were delivered to Dublin to be killed, or were killed on the spot by the easiest means. The sailors and soldiers that the Earl of Tyrone preserved were later said to have come, in all, to some two thousand, but in stories of war the numbers of the defeated, or of the victorious, will multiply with each telling. Most of those he took in charge he got to safety in Scotland, others to the northern peninsula of Inishowen, to which he brought a great herd of cattle for their sustenance, because he could. Still others would become men of Ulster, and few knew of their presence in the highlands and mountains; they tended sheep, they fished in the lakes, they drove cattle. One, neither soldier nor sailor, would serve Hugh O'Neill for years as secretary, trainer of his soldiers, translator, and adviser: Pedro Blanco.

That the Spanish were darker-complexioned than those around them, that some few were darker even than that, were *blackamoors* to the Irish, seemed not to rouse any great scorn or laughter or fear; in ten years' time they had become as unremarkable as stones. Soldiers now weaponless, sailors who'd never again go on the sea, they learned a new tongue; some married, and some who married and some who didn't fathered children in numbers. They prayed at Mass in their old language and in a Latin not like their neighbors', but at Easter Irish priests placed the Communion wafer on their tongues the same. Only when they were called to war at last, given arms and armor from the hidden stores of the Earl of Ulster and the Lord of Tyrconnell and ordered to the south for the last battle, did they inspire fear as they went: dressed in white, as they had when they were seamen, *daghaidhe duvh*, dark of face, they would seem as they moved over the land to be of that black tribe of the O'Donahues that cast no shadow. Yet they went in hope to join their old ships, that were sailing again for Ireland from Spain: to join the fight against the English on Ireland's behalf, and on the side of those who had saved them.

MONSTROUS

he had climbed to the wrinkled rocks where she stood often, where anyone could see her, red hair free, her long body wrapped tight in her black shawl.

"Ineen," he called to her. She didn't turn to him. When he was close enough that the wind could not snatch away his words he said again: "Ineen."

"Cormac," she said, but not as though *to* him. He was accustomed to this, but on this day he would not assent to being dismissed.

"Ineen, you must not go about as you do. Not as you are."

"How is it that I am, Cormac?"

"Great with child, Ineen. You know what I meant."

"The women hereabouts go about the roads and walk the strand with their babes showing."

"You aren't one of them, Ineen. Not a common woman."

"I am Gael, though you don't know it. My mother was a Gael, beloved of my father. She died in birthing me. I am *common*. I was."

They both looked out to the sea—because she would not look at him, and if she would not, he would not look at her—to the places where the Spanish ships had been embayed and broken up. Quiet now. White clouds moved overhead as though in haste. They spoke in English.

"What should I do then, Cormac? Stay alone in my house with my old mad father, and batten the shutters?"

Cormac clasped his hands behind his back, as though to keep them from taking actions he would not have them do. "Tell me now, Ineen. Who is it? Who got you with child? You must tell me."

"I *must* tell you nothing."

"Who?"

"No man." He turned to her then, to draw her face to him. "No one you know of or can name," she said. With her small finger she drew from her lips a wisp of hair that had blown across them. "A

Scot," she said, and then laughed at his bewildered face. "Why does it trouble you so, my state?"

"For one reason. If I knew him or where to find him, I would revenge you upon him. I swear. And for another . . ." He looked away sharply, and spoke almost as to himself alone. "Before this. I would have asked for your hand. You know that, Ineen. And I still would."

She lowered her head then, and her mocking smile went away. "You have been a good friend to me, Cormac Burke."

"I could be a better one. I could be father to this child."

"No."

"The Scots child."

She made to put her hand on his sleeve, then did not quite touch it. "Cormac. As you have been my friend, I beg this of you. Ask me no more about this child. I will not answer. There is no answer."

~~~

Her father died in the coming of winter, and was carried to the old church by men and women bundled in their mantles and facing a close wind. It mattered nothing to them that he had been of the new faith; they knew him for a true priest, and from his place there beneath the stones of the floor he could be an aid to them, if he were properly supplicated; and the doing of this burial was the first of those supplications.

Then she was entirely alone. And she knew what she must do.

He insisted that it be done in the chapel of the little friary where, when he had come into this country, he had been taken in and given a bed and work to do, but she would not agree. She would go only to the old church, which passers-by might well suppose was nothing but a pile of stones. In that church, open to the sky through the rents in the roof, without a priest, without witnesses except the women of the place who had begun to watch over her, perceiving a thing about her that was *unseelie,* she vowed the vows that joined her to Cormac Burke, outcast son of the Earl of Clanricarde. He ringed her finger with his dead mother's ring. She gave to him a tiny book of psalms her father had cherished, that locked up with a clasp and a key. That night in the house on the hill she told him that she would not have him in her bed, not now in her condition, not ever after either. Their marriage was to be white, if it was a marriage at all. *I am monstrous,* she told him, eyes huge and fiery, *and the being within me is more*

monstrous, and if it don't consume me from within it will kill me in its
coming forth.

⁓

At five months she walked the strand, her feet bare, the shawl held
tight around her and the child. When the tide was low, the rocky
bar a distance out was revealed, and the seals came up into the sun
to heat their cold bodies, a great mass of them flopping and rising,
lifting their heads and then lying low again. The fisher-folk said that
when they took to the rocks in bands this way the females were with
young, and before winter they would calve.

And so would she.

They sang: it's what the fisher-folk called it, but it wasn't song.
A single seal or a few together on the strand could make a horrid
croaking or a grunting, sounds a drunk man makes expelling his
wine; but when they were gathered out there on their stone beds on
the spit's end, when they sounded all at once or in answer to others,
the tone and pitch of it was different: it was good. She hated that it
was good, that it was song. She wanted it not to wind around her, to
compel her. She would cry out into the wind *Fubún! Fubún* on the
traitorous legless beasts, on the spotted faces, the shameless cou-
pling, *fubún* on the ones who come ashore and walk upright as men.
Fubún on their taking, *fubún* on their giving. St. Ciwa was suckled
by a wolf, and had a long black nail on her left hand's great finger
to show the kinship she held with her godmother. What would her
own suckling bestow, if she could give suck, upon this thing within
her? *Fubún.* It was curious to feel herself going mad.

She was seven months gone when Cormac Burke departed. For
many days he had followed behind her where she walked staring at
the sea, but at a distance, not wanting to be closer, nor did she want
him close. He was unable to hear what curses she cried into the wind,
only that she cried them. In the nights in her small house she lay
alone on her old bed; one or another of the women who watched over
her slept on the floor or at the doorstep. There were days when he and
she would sit companionably together but mostly in silence; she wove
on a small loom, he read in a book of Latin lessons the brothers at
the friary had given him. When she went to her bed he might climb
to the loft where her father had died, or if the place and its presences
and her bitter recalcitrance left him feeling flensed and unbodied, he

would walk away the night, or return to the friary and ring the bell to be allowed in. And at length his heart shrank within him.

When the seal-wives had calved, the curraghs went out to try to take the pups—bash their soft heads in with long clubs, or catch them in thrown nets—but it was dangerous work, the big males could overturn a skin boat easily. She watched the boats and the sea and the seals contend, and didn't turn back to Cormac and see him go.

In the priest's house there above the sea there was a wise-woman to attend at the birth of the child, if a child it was: a woman who brought oils to anoint her, herbs to burn whose ash she spread with her thumb over Ineen's stomach and her breast, who could say the words of the Mass that the priest used, but also other words that had no meaning for Ineen except as a thing to hold her up from sinking into blackness, like the straw a drowning man is said to clutch at, hopeless hope. The other women, mostly mothers of many children, took their turns at being with her, unalarmed, talking and singing, knowing everything and nothing. A hundred dreams she'd had of this coming-forth, dreams that sometimes woke her in loathing and horror, others merely ordinary, of a child somehow having come to be without needing to be born; on other nights, of that child melting slowly or fast into a ghastly thing. Never a seal pup: not that at least. The women told of the selkies: how they were *ròin* upon the sea but men upon the land, who came out to woo young women: and somehow it comforted her to hear them, because the telling of them turned her and her child into story, so that she and it and Sorley and the seal-people might all leave the world and vanish into air, just as the words of the tales vanished even as they were spoken.

Then it was simple struggle and pain, no different from any mother's, no different from her own mother's, who had died of it, as she hoped to do on that day, in that night, which was endless, the chat of the women passing from one to another, exchanging knowledge, pressing in to take hold of the bloody head emerging. She supposed they would strangle it when whatever it was came forth, and she closed tight her eyes. *It is but a boy,* they said to her, *just a slip of a boy.* They washed it and wrapped it in soft cloth and brought it to place on her bosom. Then it was *he,* not *it:* strange, maculated, purplish and blind—oh yes, the women said, yes so it is always. Soon he will suck, and by that milk become a real boy. She saw then that they had never believed the tales they'd told her. If they had believed them, they would not have told them.

~

A year passed when he came to her again. He did not come up out of the sea; he came as the people came, by the rocky way from the village, along the inlet to the strand, and she had not seen him before he was there by her, when she sensed him and turned. Unsurprised. He wore the same battered hat, or its descendant; the long mantle; a shirt of coarse linen. Trews of wool, belted with a plaited band. He stood not speaking, his face expressing nothing, his hands clasped before him.

The boy, nameless still and still unchristened, opened his eyes. For months, since his birth, they had been a watery blue; she had thought at first he might be blind, for the eyes would not follow her finger as she moved it before him. That seemed wondrous to her. But the women said no, it happened so: as though eyes were born unfinished, and the blue would be lost and their true color come in as the child grew, and yes they had then begun to change, and were now green, like her own; she could watch them move as he looked at this or that, at her face too, in deep indifference.

His hands, though: they had not shed strangeness. They had grown to be hands no child born of woman could have. She grasped one hand at the wrist and showed it to Sorley. "The web grows between the fingers," she said. "When it grows and thickens I cut it away with my sharpest knife."

He regarded her, the child, the hand. "Why do you do that?"

"So he will not be monstrous," she said. "So he may live on the land."

Sorley's still face didn't change at this. It was as though no time or events had passed between the dawn when he left her bed and now.

"It causes him no pain," she said. "No more than the cutting of a nail." The boy was staring at Sorley, that was clear. She spread his fingers to show where she'd done the cutting, and how still a dark line of tissue remained along the fingers. "It grows back," she said. "Always grows back."

"Leave it," Sorley said mildly. "When he's grown he will need it in the sea. When he is on the land it will not show." Smiling, he lifted his own hand, fingers spread for her to see. "But all that change is to come. If it comes at all."

Nothing he had said to her on the night of the Spanish ships made her think he would return to her, and he hadn't; yet she'd known that, one day, he would. And when he did return it would not be to take her with him to the sea, as the stories told it; no, not her. He had come closer, and though she wanted to draw away she couldn't. When he came close enough to touch the two of them, the boy reached for him, and grasped the long bony finger Sorley held out. "Strong," he said. "And fat with milk."

"He has teeth," she said. "Sharp ones."

"Let me hold him in my hands. Let me know him."

The child was wrapped up so that the fine gray hair or wool of his back, which had begun to appear only in this month, would not be seen by the curious. There was nothing now to hide. She pulled the wrapping away and let it fall, where it crawled over the stones at the wind's tugging. Sorley took the boy in his hands, looked him up and down as though to measure him.

"You have done well."

"What would you have thought I'd do? Smother him at his birth?"

For a time he merely regarded the boy, who studied him in turn. He took the child in the crook of his left arm and with his free hand pulled his rough cloak partly over him. He untied from his waist a purse and held it out.

"Take this," he said to Ineen. "For all this good that you did instead." When he saw she would not accept it he bent and tossed it lightly at her feet. "Gold," he said. "It's not easy for one like me to gather. It's all I could get."

"It's not enough," she said, holding his regard, not looking down. She would no more touch that purse in his sight than she would grasp thorns. She felt the fierceness in her face, the sting in her words. "What will you do with him, then, Sorley?"

"Take him to my home. Teach him."

She could think of no more cold or cruel thing that could be said to her. "I teach him," she said.

He spoke softly: "Can you teach him to swim, to catch his dinner in the dark water? To sing? To avoid men?"

For a time the three of them stood motionless; her son had a quality of stillness like no babe she'd ever seen. She'd taught him nothing. "Will he be like you?" she said at last. "How will he not drown, under the sea?"

He was a long time in answering. "He is my son," he said. "Ineen, I may not live long. It's a thing I have been told. But perhaps at least until he is grown." He seemed then on the point of saying more; she watched the stone of his throat move as though to allow words to pass out.

"Told?"

"Well. It might not be so. We aren't long-lived, our kind. When I am gone he will be grown, and it may be that though you will see me no more you will see him again."

"I pray not," she said. "Not to see him ever. Nor you."

They stood, the three, for a length of time neither long nor short, or in a time that did not pass. He turned away from her then, not to go toward the sea but to the land; she saw the face of her son, he looked back for a moment and away again. She had come to feel as though made of glass or some brittle hard matter, and had held herself that way so long that she could not now call or move: only when Sorley and the child were gone on past the piled stones of the beach did the hardness splinter, break, crumble. She fell to earth, mouth open wide, hands and knees on the sand like a beast. She felt what she was made of, the stuff of her, come out from her as though she were torn or ripped down her front, like a calf strung up and butchered. A high, thin cry reached her then that she did not at first know was her own, nor where it came from. At the sea's edge a curragh was being brought ashore, the fishermen lifting it so that its leather hide would not be torn by the shingle. It could not be that they heard her cry, so far off; yet they paused there with their hands on the boat's rails, the surf pouring around their legs, and as though they were called out to, they looked up to where she lay huddled.

CANNON ANGELS

he carried nothing away with him but what little he had brought to that place, and the little that he had got there: among that little was the book of psalms she had given him. There was no reason for him to go in one direction or another, except that he would not go south or west into the lands where his brothers contested for the legacy of Earl Richard, their father: the Sassenach Earl he'd come to be called for his services to the English—the *sassenach*—in the Desmond wars. His father had had three wives and a number of concubines, all producing sons and daughters who almost all hated Earl Richard; the three eldest of the legitimate sons took the side of Fitzmaurice, the Jesuits, and Catholic Spain, and the father the side of the English, the Queen, and the new religion. Cormac would have despised his father if he had had the courage to despise. He was a small man who doubted his own bravery, tongue-tied in the few times he'd been alone in the Earl's presence: the man seemed to him as hard and weathered as a standing stone, and as cold. How then could Cormac have thought that he could kill him?

It may be that his brothers were as afraid of their father as Cormac was, at least the ones who had joined together to fight him: John of the Shamrocks, Richard, Ulick. Cormac was the youngest, a bastard child raised among women, almost unknown to his father, and had not been part of their rebellion. When they brought him the gun, they praised him for qualities he did not see in himself—courage, steadfastness. He took their attentions and swallowed them down like sweetened wine, but he was more captivated by the weapon they put before him. *Learn to use this, brother.* He had seen hand-cannons fired, had heard brass culverins sound from Galway Castle on the Queen's birthday, remembered the shiver of delight and terror it brought. This *pistolet*, as brother Richard named it, was a wheel lock gun, and the brothers argued over the use of it, but Cormac quickly saw what made it work, how the ridged wheel turned with the pulling of the trigger and scraped the flint that caused a spark that fired the powder. He stroked the long barrel, the silver chasing on it; held the curved handle that ended in a knob of ivory. It was he alone, the brothers said, who could go unsuspected before their father, holding this, and shoot him dead, for which all would be glad. He knew that he would go down to Hell if he did as he had been told to do, but he could not muster whatever strength it would have taken to deny his brothers, and for certain his father's soul would go into the darkness farther and faster than his own; he would have time for penance, for rites of remorse, years of them if needed. Perhaps he would turn friar; safe then.

He learned the weapon in secret, his brother John bringing powder and lead; his father, gone off to Galway to treat with the English sheriff, couldn't hear the hiss and bang of it in the yard though Cormac felt he might have, far away though he was. It was like possessing a being, a small animal of great power but no will; the will was his, Cormac's, the gun the only dangerous thing he had ever tamed. When news came that his father was near home, Cormac went to the forecourt, the pistolet charged and primed, and stood to wait: exalted, huge with purpose, terrified. Outside, the Earl was cheered, the horses snorted, weapons were stacked, drink called for. Cormac raised the gun, holding it with both hands.

His father with his captains strode laughing through the door. The Earl, seeing Cormac, flung out his arms to stop the men around him, and without a moment's pause he walked steadily toward his son as though to his dinner. With no word spoken he took the pistolet by the barrel and pulled it from his son's hand. *Fool*, he said then. *Begone out of my house. Go to the women. Never dare to look on me again.*

By the end of that day he had set out for the north, out of the Burke lands: north, for no reason he knew. He had a purse of money that his disgusted brothers threw at him, a bag of clothes, a rosary, the ring that had been his mother's. Past Maam Cross he turned to the sea, and when he reached it he kept it on his left, around Clew Bay and Achill Island and past Sligo, and so in a year's time he came at last to Ben Bulben and to the friary where he was cared for, thence to Streedagh's strand; and wherever he went from there, from Ineen Fitzgerald's house and name, he would never turn back.

Now without his brothers' purse—he'd doled the money out to himself with niggardly care, and it had sustained him a long while and was now all spent—he must beg, or at religious houses appeal for work, food, a pallet; his book of psalms and the one of Latin lessons were like licenses to beg at those doors, and he would spend as long as he could in an abbey or chapter-house. When winter came he summoned the courage to enter an Augustinian monastery at Murrisk and ask to be received into the order, as a novice. Admitted at least, he tended goats and cut peat and carried water in leather buckets to wash the flags of the church floor. He'd pray with the friars in Irish and in Latin, listen to the soft and tedious chant they wove all together; sometimes he wept.

The new Irish Protestants of Mayo complained that the Augustinians were spies, fractious, rebellious, and should be suppressed; instead the Crown leased the abbey and lands to an adventurer, naming a large figure of money for it. The friars were let to stay on, in quiet, but they dared not take in postulants. In winter Cormac knelt before the aged abbot and begged an exception be made for him; he wept; he had nothing, nowhere to go. The abbot gently elicited his history: that he had been pressed by his brothers to murder his father, and had agreed to do it, though he had failed; that he had been married, though the marriage had not been sanctified and was never consummated; that he had seen the Spanish come ashore at Streedagh beach and had not saved them, not one: all of which sounded now like lies to his own ears. The abbot lifted him to his feet, kissed his cheeks, blessed him. He told Cormac that when he had returned to his father's house and begged his pardon, and received it; when he had comforted the wife he had abandoned; when he had done penance for these things, then he might come again, and ask again for entrance.

He set out again down the ragged coast, half-wondering what would happen if he reached his father's house; or if he turned the other way, and sought out Ineen Fitzgerald and the unblessed child. Hardly noticing which way he did go or where he went, he came again to Clew Bay. Spring was yielding to summer: that he had apprehended. Even this stony earth put out hidden blossoms; Solomon in all his glory was not arrayed as one of these. He sat amid the new grasses, turned his face away from the giant mountain to the east whose name he did not know, as oppressive to his spirit as Ben Bulben had been, and looked out across the bay waters, a blessed blue now. He hadn't eaten in two days. Perhaps on a day like this it would not be terrible to die.

Out on the bay then, in the humid air, he could see but not recognize a thing that seemed to rise up out of the water, huge and dragonish. It came closer and grew larger until Cormac could see that it was a man-made thing, was a sea-going vessel, a galley: the long oars rose, and in perfect accord reached back, went into the water, were pulled forward, and the ship moved ahead. Its single square sail bellied in an offshore breeze; now Cormac could perceive a red boar on it, seeming alive in the luffing of the sail. The craft passed amid the small islands of the shallow bay waters, the tall mast inclining a little this way then that, as though changing partners in a dance. What skill that must take, he thought. It wasn't far from shore when it made a sharp turn, came about, seemingly intending to sail out of the harbor again, but instead it began to slide stern-forward toward land. And now ashore men were running toward where it would run up on the beach, and from the high decks of the galley others were preparing to heave coils of tarred rope out to them. He could see that a large board of strange shape had been pulled up with great effort and care out of the ship's behind and laid down, even as the men on the beach ran into the water and made for the ropes that were thrown to them, which they put over their shoulders, turning again to the land. It seemed impossible, but they were pulling the galley up onto the beach, and men on the ship were calling and urging them on, the luffing sail too. Cormac, up on the meadow, could hear the grind of the ship's bottom on the sand as it was beached. The oars had been shipped, and now the sail was furled.

Rope ladders were lowered from the ship, and a few men went down them with swift assurance, dropped into the water, and strode through the surf. Cormac had been so caught up in the spectacle of all this labor and skill he hadn't noticed that beyond where he sat, ox-carts were coming through the witchgrass toward the beach. He stood, alarmed. The big creaking wagons were likely unable to stop in their plodding progress downward to the shore, the oxen goaded by men and women; Cormac went ahead of them to avoid being stepped on and trampled. On the beach the men from the boat hola'd and waved their hats to the carters.

One of the boatmen pointed to Cormac. After a moment's conference, two were sent in his direction. He wondered if he should
flee, if he might be suborned, or killed, though for no reason he
could think of. He turned away, and when the two men came running he tried to run as well, but he was so weak that he soon fell and
for a time lay panting, trying to get up. He felt arms take his arms;
he was pulled to his feet.

"Who are you, fellow?"

"No one."

"Of what name, what people?"

"None." Could he say to them that he didn't know who he was?
It was so.

"Why do you sit here, watching the harbor, why did you run?"

"Why should I not? And I ran because I was threatened."

"Spy?"

He couldn't answer that; to say he was not a spy would make him
one.

Those who had hold of him pushed him toward the beach and the
ship, where the carts were drawn up now and being unloaded. What
had they brought? Big hide pouches, laced with thongs at the tops,
but leaking, darkening the leather.

Water. They were bringing water to the ship. Which stood
upon the sea, with water for infinite miles. Staggering in the sand,
propelled by his captors, he laughed. One of those handling him
slapped his head. He was forced into the sea, colder than he had
thought it would be, and made to take hold of the rope ladder that
went up to the deck, which seemed as high up as a castle tower. He
understood he was to climb but he could not; the disused cassock,
too large and ragged at the hem, nearly all the clothing he owned,
was now soaked and heavy as stone. The men pushing him from
behind called up to the ship, in a language Cormac didn't know;
someone looked over the rail, then disappeared; reappeared with a
rope, whose end he threw down. The men quickly and neatly tied it
around Cormac's breast under his arms, and when it was tight, they
cried out to the one on the rail. So he went up: in part climbing, in
part pulled, clinging in desperation to the ladder, until men above
could take hold of him and drag him aboard, throw him down on
the deck. He thought, looking up at the beards around him, red,
brown, black, that perhaps he had alarmed them because his hair

had been cut short and his beard shaved off when he served the monks. Then he knew nothing.

Gráinne O'Malley in her tiny cabin at the stern—more tent than cabin, an arched frame of bent wood covered with hides—sorted through the pitiful things in the woven bag that the sailors had taken from the young man they had dragged aboard. One coarse linen shirt, once fine. Four English pence. Two books, one of psalms, the other Latin lessons. Her watchful crew called him a spy; but a spy who carried nothing but these few things would be a very poor one. Where was his short knife, his pistol, his lockpicks? His papers in secret writing, and his tools for making them?

She rose slowly. Her hips had begun to ache when she went to sea these days. She forgot the ache when she sat, only to feel it again when she stood. She called from her cabin—heard the length of the ship, it was always said of her commands—to bring the fellow before her. She sat again, and picked up her long clay pipe, to fill it. When the flap of hide was pulled aside and the fellow was pushed in, she shuddered, for no reason; he was slight, frightened, all alone. She beckoned him to come in. He took two steps within. The curtain was let fall behind him, and he started at that.

"Sit," she said, and pointed to a stool. It was an odd thing, but in the time since he had appeared in the doorway he had not blinked once. But he didn't seem afraid. "Do you know me?" she said.

"I know who you are. All on this coast know your name."

"I don't know yours," she said. "Will you tell it me?"

"I am called Cormac."

She waited a moment. "Cormacs are many." She watched him look around himself, as if help were somewhere near, or escape. With a small tongs she took a bright coal from a burner near her, and with it lit the tobacco in her pipe. She laughed to see this Cormac's face at what he saw. She drew strongly and exhaled a blue cloud.

"That land-taker Raleigh," she said, "thinks he was the first to use a pipe, with leaves of America. But the Turks had it long ago, from the Portingales, sailing from Brazil."

"I am of the Burkes of Galway," Cormac said. "Cormac Burke my name."

"A Burke you are! Why, of what family, what sept?"

Cormac's throat seized at this question, which the woman before him—it was clear—thought would be easy to answer. "Of Clanricarde," he said at last.

"A child of that Earl," she said, her eyes wide. She set aside her pipe.

He could hide no more. "Yes," he said. "A child of Earl Richard, but not of his wedded wife."

She said nothing to this, though her look had altered. She studied him head to foot.

"You are a priest, by your clothing," she said then. "And a lettered man."

"Not a priest. I was an abbey servant."

"What abbey?"

"An Augustinian house, at Murrisk, or Murrask, I don't know which; I did not need to know."

The Queen softened at that, grinned widely, clapped her hands together. "Why that is a house supported by our own family," she said. "Yes, for centuries!" She'd stood by now, taller than himself, her heavy skirts making her huge around as well. A little cry or moan of pity came from her, she lifted him from the stool where he sat, and wrapped her long arms around him. Smothered in her bosom he heard her say *You are of our family, now and to come.* When she released him she still held him by the shoulders. "Do you not know that my husband, and my son by him, are of the Burkes?" She drew from within her bosom a chain with a medal, lifted it to his face. A miniature painting of a man, too dim to tell much. "Richard," she said. "My beloved husband. Richard-an-Ihrain Burke. Here on the reverse our son Tibbott-ne-Long. Mayo Burkes, but as good as Burkes anywhere."

She turned and sat again, seeming to Cormac to be in some pain. That he was here before this person seemed to be impossible, and though anyone might say *It can't be, it's but a dream,* it wasn't and he didn't think it was; *he* didn't dream a dream, the world and the day did, and he was in it.

The Queen's eyes—so deep, changeful, hungry—were wet, he thought. "Your father," she said at last, "poor man, is dead. Did you know that?"

He could make no answer. He lived again the moment when his father had come into the house, had seen his bastard son with the gun lifted. "I," he said, "I . . ."

"Dead these several years. Poor man."

He couldn't tell if the *poor man* she meant was he, or his father, or both of them. "Who then is the Earl now?" he asked.

"His sons battled a year for the name and title," Gráinne said, "and Ulick won. How is it you know nothing of these things?"

At last, from hunger, shame, ignorance, and deprivation, he lifted his head and wept. Not for his father, as Gráinne would think, but for himself, who knew nothing and no one, had long lived in a foul dream not his own, unable to wake. The Queen folded her hands in her lap and waited for the tears to cease.

Galleys like those of the O'Malley concern were moved over the sea by the labor of thirty or fifty oarsmen (the great galleys of Venice and the Turk carried a hundred or more). They were stuffed with armed men, who when the galley slid up alongside a merchantman or other sail, would throw grappling-irons on ropes over the rail, board and overwhelm the crews and sea-soldiers. The oarsmen, laboring daylong, required great amounts of two things: bread and water. The bread was biscuit, hard, dry, and (unless seas came in and wetted it) deathless: just the same after a year's storage, and no better. Oarsmen consumed it and whatever else could be carried that wouldn't spoil: salt herring, hake, salt cod, early apples, onions, ling, turbot, salmon smoked, but herring above all. And they drank water, in whatever amounts they needed and called for.

"Why bring on so much water?" Cormac asked. Queen Gráinne had brought him out to stand on the high deck. "When water is all around."

"You don't know?" Gráinne asked in amazement. "What, have you never been at sea? Never been *in* the sea?"

He chose not to answer.

"Sea water can't be drunk. It's salty. It will kill you to drink much of it, kill you dead and in great anguish."

The crew came and went around them where they stood; beneath the deck the oarsmen on their benches could be glimpsed, their oars now lifted, at rest. The tide had turned; the master and the navigator watched the rising water gently lift the *Richard* from the sands. The lateen sail with the sign of the red boar—heraldic beast of the Burkes—was raised again, and an offshore wind filled it, and the *rudder*—that strange board—was let down. Because of its shallow draft and thin keel, it rode out onto the bay waters as though by itself. Once out in wider water the master called for the oars to be unshipped, and to the pounding of a great drum and a piper's shriek, the *Richard* made for open sea, skirting Clare Island, the lady that guarded the entrance to the bay. The fisher-people of the island in their boats waved and called but they couldn't be heard. Cormac Burke, elated and terrified, his soul ventilated by the wind of the galley's passage, could almost not resist taking Gráinne O'Malley's hand where they stood together at the rail. He now wore old clothes of her son's she had found. He had been fed what the crew had been fed. He was not meant to die.

For self-defense, and to overawe the defenses of a harbor or a round-ship, the *Richard* carried a small array of long guns in the bow (tall ships could set their guns on a deck below, but a galley had no room for that). Here was a black wrought-iron *verso* bound in iron rings, two small cast-bronze Spanish *morteretes* that flung scattershot, and a long half-cannon also of bronze, the biggest of the four and set in the center, like a tall man with smaller friends around him. They were mounted on swivels, to raise and lower them and swing port to starboard when needed. The bronze half-cannon was covered with raised decoration, twisting dragons and sea-monsters, coats of arms, asterisks. Cormac, rushing back and forth along the crowded gangway between the oarsmen's benches on Queen Gráinne's errands, couldn't help stopping to regard them, all asleep, awaiting their time to be awakened. The cannoneer and his gunners tended to them as to favored children, wiping them with oiled rags for the salt, counting over the stone balls and the iron balls in their different stacks. The kegs of powder that would bring them to life were brought up only when an encounter was imminent.

Cormac's fascination with the guns was clear to the gunners, who allowed him up to watch. He kept his hands clasped behind him, unworthy to touch them. He listened, trying to pierce the gunners' thick language by mere attention, watching their gestures. He knew—the Queen had told him—that the guns were of most use to overawe and threaten, and out of many voyages the *Richard* had only fired at a ship twice. Three times. Maybe it had been four, but always and only when it appeared that the roundship they planned to board and

discuss terms with had flung open its gun-deck portals and like the
snouts of black pigs the guns had poked out. Then the *Richard* would
fall back, allow the prey to fly ahead: but only till the groaning oars-
man brought the galley up to the roundship's unarmed stern, and the
cannoneer let fly, one, three, five, and the bronze-man last with the
largest ball, splintering timbers. Rather than take the chance of being
sent to the bottom, the ship would cease to run, and when the galley
came up alongside her again and the armed pirates had clambered
over the rails, then Queen Gráinne with two pistols in her belt would
be heaved up and on board the ship, to call a halt to murdering, and
invite the captain to a conference.

How Cormac longed to see it.

The *Richard* and other ships of the O'Malleys rarely went far out;
high seas could swamp a low-lying galley, the storms of the open
Atlantic were fierce, the necessity of more provisions left less room
for anything else. The masters and navigators were skilled and wise
enough in home waters, but lacked the seamanship that could take
a galley out to India or to Atlantis in the west, and safe home again.
They knew the tides and could read the age of the Moon, they could
calculate to a fine degree the currents at harbors they knew well—
but unlike the broad, smooth, nearly tideless Mediterranean where
the great galleys of Venice and the Ottoman Empire could range and
hunt at will, the Atlantic galleys stayed close to the known world: the
Channel and the Isles, the Irish Sea, down the Bay of Biscay and the
coast of Brittany.

Ships of any sort in the Channel were considered by the O'Malleys
to be theirs to stop and search, as though they possessed the badges
of Crown servants or tax-collectors who could seal a cargo and ex-
tract a payment before graciously allowing the ship to pass on. They
knew well enough not to interfere with the great-ships of the Han-
seatic League bearing grain and timber to London, but small trade
was stopped or pursued if convenient. Almost every ship that was
stopped made its payment; they were aware of what would happen if
they didn't; they knew not to say the word "pirate" in any language
they knew, for honor was as precious to the boarders as gold, or
almost.

But the two ships that the *Richard* encountered that spring were
in no category known to the O'Malleys. They were galleys, like
Queen Gráinne's, though they differed in details; when the *Richard*

slid with its smooth grace around one of them, Gráinne herself was at the bow to study them, salute them too if she thought good. A white puff appeared at the other's bow, and then came a noise, and then a ball whizzing overhead: not aimed to harm, only to warn, and to state a distance to be kept. But Gráinne was outraged, and the only thing for it was to respond. The gunners and the cannoneer called for the stone balls, thirty pounds apiece, and the powder and the breech chambers; the chambers—looking to Cormac much like beer-mugs—had already been filled with powder, and now placed with care in the breeches of the five guns. Cormac, almost mad with excitement, helped bring up the shot, saw it loaded into the muzzles. The great sweeps of the oars swung the *Richard* around even as the foreign ship also maneuvered to fire again, or evade fire, and Cormac, leaning the way the ship leaned, didn't see the first of the *Richard*'s guns fired—the iron *verso*—but the sound shook and deafened him. The stone ball could be seen, flying in a long arc, but falling short: a thousand yards was the farthest such a gun could throw.

The two foreign ships were closing now, and the sun was setting. The second galley sent a ball at the *Richard*, and Cormac stood frozen at the rail watching it come near: but what he saw as it came on was not a black Moon, or a hole in the sky, or his own death: it was a face. A cloud of white-gray hair around it, eyes huge and mouth open to shriek. A woman's face. And as it flew over his head he saw—he thought he saw, he *knew* he saw the face change from fierce rage to laughter, to joy.

The gunners beside him had seen it too, raised their hands to it as it came, and cried out, even as it tore a rent in their sail, flew on and fell into the sea.

Now the faster of the foreign galleys was so near that the sailors aboard it could be clearly seen. *Moors!* the cannoneer cried. *Barbary men! What do they do here?* A powder chamber went into the half-cannon, the bronze-man. The hissing fuse reached the powder and the ball was flung out with a sound so vast that Cormac felt blown apart, though he remained at the rail clinging on. The sailors on the Barbary pirates' ship could be seen pointing to the oncoming ball, their dark faces open, their white teeth. Did they now see what the *Richard* had seen? The ball struck amidships, and gilded wood and armed men flew into the air, oars were dropped and entangled with those still deployed.

The second, farther-off galley turned neatly, leaning half-over in its hurry, and made away. The first, damaged, sat still for a time, but then turned as best it could and was off as well. Should they follow, the master wanted to know. But the Queen raised a hand: they would not follow. When she turned to face them she seemed stunned and delighted. "Did you see?" she cried out. And the gunners and the master each flung up a hand. They had all seen. She put a hand on Cormac's shoulder, and he went with her, aiding her, down the gangway toward the tent in the stern.

"What was it?" he asked. "What did we see?"

"A cannon angel," Gráinne said. "They in the other ship saw one too, and today the one *they* saw was the stronger one."

~~~~~

"They ride the cannon-balls," she said to Cormac seated again on his stool beside her. "Or they impel them, no one knows which."

"Why do they?"

"No one knows that at all. Sailors believe that they seek out the faithless, the unbelievers, and guide the balls they ride toward them, to sink their ships. But the faithful bearing Christ's cross on the bow see them coming too. It may be that they do it as children ride down hillsides in a cart, as fast as ever they can, and sometimes tip over and all fall out and laugh." She lifted her clay pipe from the bowl where it resided. "For the joy of it only," she said smiling. "Children of God, His firstborn, and they are let to do as they like."

Cormac thought: *demons*. For the first time in weeks he saw in his mind Ineen Fitzgerald's face and furious eyes, saying *monstrous*.

"They will ride the stone balls," the Queen mused. "But they love the iron ones better. I know not why."

four

THOSE AWAKE

A BOLT OF SARSANET

On Epiphany morning in Dublin, the turnkey of the prison went on his rounds about the cells of criminals and hostages, to be certain of their chains. Some of the more honorable or highly valued prisoners had had their shackles removed on the night before so that they might have rest and attend to their prayers on the holy-day, which in Gaelic is called *Nottlaic Stell* or the Christmas of the Stars. He opened the thick door of the cell where the O'Donnell boy, Red Hugh, was kept, along with two sons of Shane O'Neill, Henry and Art, who had been put in with him as further pledges for good behavior on the part of Shane's people.

The cell was empty. A thick rope of twisted silk had been tied to the bars of a window, but the bars were in place, as they had been; the turnkey's eye followed the rope to where it went down into the privy and disappeared; baffled, he knelt to peer down into the shithole, but dawn had just broken and he could see nothing. But he knew now what had been done; he rose, ran or stumbled (an old man, he was) out and down to the guardroom, shouting that his prisoners had escaped.

Some guardsmen went back up to the cell, which was still empty; others went out and walked the walls to where the windows of the empty cell could be seen high up, and also the stone privy attached to the castle wall. The privy stuck out far enough so that what was voided there would not slime the wall, but it was after all nothing but a large pot without a bottom, and the wall was filthy; and now as day grew they could see the silk rope hanging out the hole, reaching toward the ditch or dry-moat around the castle. Nothing else.

The week before, on the third day of Christmas, a secretary of the Earl of Tyrone's had come to the castle, and begged permission to bring to the Earl's imprisoned kin some food and drink for the holy-day, and was allowed. The guard and the turnkey remembered now, that here was a bolt of white sarsanet silk among the gifts, and though the silk was famously light and strong they didn't think about it then. There was no point, now, in cursing the Earl, or themselves, or the prisoners: it was the master of the prison, white-bearded and in his red coat, who had himself admitted the gifts of the jolly season. Soon he'd have to be told the result.

The boys were miles gone by then, out of the gates of the city, which were left open on the sacred night, and where a few of that O'Hagan sept who had fostered Hugh O'Neill in the long-ago waited in the snow to take the boys, two to a horse, toward the Wicklow Mountains. Laughing. Art O'Neill was not laughing: an eternally hungry young man, he'd managed to grow fat in prison, and could not get himself out of that privy once he'd got in it, and despite the desperate whisper-cries from the others below he could hardly move. When at last he squirmed down out of the loathsome hole and began to descend on the silk rope he lost his grip and fell to the ditch, hurting his leg, and had to helped out by the others and almost carried to the gate. His brother Henry, as soon as the O'Hagans appeared, kissed Art, bade farewell to Red Hugh, and went his own way.

Hugh O'Neill's greatest friend among the English then resident in Ulster was Sir Garrett Moore, Viscount Moore, a wise and an honest man. From Dublin it was some forty miles to safety in the Moore stronghold, the ancient abbey of Mellifont. There was no road to follow in the deepening snow, not a goat-track or by-road. They were close to the way leading to the house—down a steep way into the cleft of Glenmalure, now impassable—when they gave up. They had hauled weeping Art along with them this far, but could take him no farther. They laid themselves down in the snow and a couple of the O'Hagans lay with them, wrapping their mantles around them, while another went on to get help. When men arrived at dawn the boys in their thin prison gowns were nearly dead; they tried to shake Art awake, make him drink warmed beer, but could not. The O'Donnell boy—wraith and iron—lived. He would be carried into Ulster when the roads opened; till then Hugh O'Neill saw to it that he was kept at Mellifont, to evade the searchers sent out from Dublin. He came from Dungannon to see the boy there, bringing warm clothes and a doctor, and found him still abed, though grinning in triumph; the Earl stayed the day, and held Red Hugh tight in his arms while the doctor prepared to amputate his two great-toes, frozen and black. "You won't need them on horseback," he said, and the young man buried his face in Hugh's doublet and made not a sound while the doctor cut.

~

Strong as he was, the young O'Donnell was severely weakened; the Earl took him no farther than his castle at Dungannon, where Siobhan would feed him and cheer him: his oldest sibling, more the age of a mother to him than a sister. She embraced them both, and in her arms Hugh O'Neill felt the weakness that had nearly killed her in giving birth to a daughter in the fall: the midwives shaking their heads over her, something gone wrong they couldn't heal. As soon as the men were seated and food and drink put before them she slipped away to her bed.

"She's not well," Red Hugh said, a whisper.

"She is not. No doctor seems able to lift the weakness from her. Nor lift her sorrow neither."

The boy watched the door that Siobhan had gone out by. "Will she die?" he asked.

O'Neill covered the younger man's hand with his own. "We will all die," he said. "Which is no comfort. Sons and daughters, they are comfort." O'Neill supposed the boy knew of the plan that old O'Donnell (and more importantly his wife) had agreed to—that he should in time marry O'Neill's natural daughter Rose, a child without a mother, beloved of all and raised by Siobhan. Such a match would seal again the pact between the families. Old Hugh was unwell; it seemed certain that he'd yield his place to his son, who would then be named the O'Donnell, no matter his youth. Every O'Donnell knew of the prophecy that when two men named Hugh ruled in turn the house of O'Donnell, the second will be a god-like prince who will rule for nine years, and pass into the Other Lands a savior of his country and people. Hugh O'Neill did not believe in prophecy—he thought he did not—but it was hard not to hope that this one had some truth. Red Hugh was asleep now; for a time O'Neill watched him, how his restless eyes moved beneath the thin lids (what did he watch, while O'Neill watched him?), and now and again his arms trembled slightly. Never at rest, not even now. O'Neill felt for the gold chain within his leathers and drew it out.

She was there.

I have been told a foolish story of a bolt of sarsenet, he heard. *A trick in a poor play that no one believes.* There was no answering her; there never had been and would not be till the end of all. *Think you I know not the escape was by practice of money? I know there was a corruption made, a jewel worth five hundred pounds to the Lord Deputy, who loves lucre more than he loves his Queen. Take your boy where you may, it will end soon enough for him.*

No, there was no reason to think the Queen did not know what she spoke of. But the Queen could die, and would; he himself could die, surely. *We will all die,* he had said to Red Hugh. But he was beginning to think that Red Hugh could never die.

From the far part of the house the women had raised a moan, a keening.

◈

Hugh O'Neill was widely known for his fits of weeping. When he felt wronged, misunderstood, challenged unfairly, tears might begin to spring from his eyes; it never stopped the flow of his words. He wept in pleading for his rights and his ancient privileges, for his clan and for allies threatened or arrested or sent to be hanged, while those he bargained with watched in embarrassment or contempt. He wept when he was in the right, and wept when in the wrong. He had not wept often as a child, faced with wonders that he could only accept, threats that he didn't know how to meet: a fierce courage was the response. And young or old he never wept at hearing of deaths: for tears had no power over death, and could win no reprieve. Yet he wept beside Siobhan, whom he'd thought nothing could conquer.

While she could still speak, she begged him that when she was gone he would take no other wife: and what could he say to her but promise he would not? She took his hands and put her face in his palms and he felt the heat of her skin. Daylong he watched. When she wept, or tried to, he wept too. And all through the last of her days the pain would arise in his heart: not alone for her dying, not for the promise he had made to her, but because he knew that when she was in her grave and gone to the country of the fathers, the time would come, and not long, when he would marry again. He knew who that new wife would be, if she could be won. He knew, but only he; Siobhan would never know of it, not unless her spirit were to return to haunt and harry him for his faithlessness.

In May in Tyrconnell, with the approval of Ineen Duvh, old O'Donnell at last resigned his title in favor of his son. By then that son was steady enough on his damaged feet; he'd always be happier, though, astride one or another of his beautiful horses, roan and black, who seemed to love him just as his young kinsmen loved him. No one laughed or grinned at Red Hugh, walking as unsteadily as a tipsy man. Who'd have thought that the thumbs of the feet mattered so much?

Even before he was fully accepted as the O'Donnell, in his own name he had sent messengers to the families of Tyrconnell, calling them to an assembly, which without much talk—talk being unprofitable now—elected Red Hugh to the leadership his father had held.

That wasn't all that the young man did. As soon as he could stand and ride, he gathered his brothers and a number of his followers, and in arms they confronted the English garrison at Donegal city, and ordered the troops to leave the North for Connaught, where if anywhere they belonged. It might have been the cock-sureness with which Red Hugh stood before the officers of the garrison, or the troubles it seemed certain would be heaped on them if they defied these youths, but they did order a departure soon enough, to the cheers of the town. Not long after, Red Hugh repaid his uncle O'Neill by going on the offensive with his crew against old Turlough Luineach O'Neill. They raided Turlough's people and their holdings, overran Turlough's ramshackle fort at Strabane and burned it down, and then the old man had had enough: he wrote a shaky letter to Dublin, stating his retirement from all his claims to the O'Neill titles, and his plan to seek balm for his soul at a house of religion. This last he did not do, but the way was open now for the Earl of Tyrone to be named the O'Neill at the Stone of the Kings at Tullahogue. It was Red Hugh's gift to the man who had brought him out of prison, so that he would not die there of despair. The day of the election would be the day that began at sunset on the summer solstice.

From Dungannon to Tullahogue was but a morning's ride, but in the days before his naming Hugh O'Neill had ordered a shelter for himself put up amid the others raised in the fields around the great stone throne all but buried in the mound of earth on which it stood or sat in the center of the encircling raths. There Hugh lay awake all that short night. When the morning-star arose in the green sky he had the chip of flint in his hand, held so tight it had marked his palm. Would the Kindly Ones approve him, would the souls of the old Ulster heroes not groan at his presumption? He thought of Shane, who had usurped the name and rights, and how he'd died. Where now were the gallowglass who would in time come around him in a closed place, and remove him from this office forever? He started then, and reached for a weapon: the tent-flap was softly drawn aside.

Red Hugh. Without a greeting he came and sat upon the couch's end. The sleeping armed men around O'Neill didn't stir. Red Hugh put his hand on the hand that held the flint. "Tell me," he said. "How long has it been since there was a High King in Ireland?"

O'Neill put down the short sword he had seized. "I cannot tell. When the Norman English came, half a thousand years ago? Some called themselves kings."

"None was *ard Rí*."

"None commanded all the others. None was called High King." He wondered if that was so; the tales he was told in his childhood, the songs of the bards and the genealogies of the *brehons*, were somewhere in his memory, not to be sought for but returning to him at odd times as though by their own choosing.

Red Hugh released O'Neill's hand. "I am glad to be with you on this day," he said, with his big grin. "And will be glad on other and greater days." He rose then and, like a servant, backed bowing away and out of the dew-damp tent. Sounds of piping and drums, coming closer.

When O'Neill appeared, having drunk herbed wine and had the saffron robe put around him by his closest relatives, and an ancient sword of the O'Neills put in his wide belt, he came forth to the cheers of the O'Hagans and the clashing of weapons that would follow him on the way to the Stone. Some were already a bit drunk. These were the men, or the sons of the men, who had fostered him in the beginning of his conscious life; his own two sons were now in houses of the O'Hagans. In ancient times the clan O'Hagan had produced the *brehons* that gave laws to the O'Neill's, and on this day they had tasks to do that by right they alone could do, and had always done, in the making of *an Ò Neill*. When Hugh stepped up to the stone seat, to the crying of the pipes and the dueling genealogies shouted out by ancient men who never forgot a word, he saw that among the O'Hagans were men and women he had known when they were young and he a child, now with hair turning white, beards long. He would not weep, could not laugh, with the great love he felt for them all. The talking done, the eldest of these elder O'Hagans came before him with the slim white wand that signified, in its little-ness and weakness, the great power of the O'Neill: the same wand that had been given before to Hugh's uncle Shane, and before him to Conn his grandfather. Hugh O'Neill, descendant of Niall of the Nine Hostages, took the wand and raised it, and the people gathered around made a soft high moan of wonder and assent. And in the blaze of noon Hugh O'Neill saw that, beyond the ranks of his kinsmen and his fighters, others were there, vague in the shimmer of the sun: some old and crowned, some young and armed with long lances as though of silver sunlight; and white-haired children, naked or clothed in pale nothing: all looking on him in calm assess-ment, without judgment.

PALE MAN, DARK MAN

The Earl of Tyrone was a divided man. A man who desired to be one and whole, who believed that in some way he *was* whole, though more often he felt himself not to be. He felt division, or complication, in himself, within every part of him: his mind, his spirit, his language, his hopes and fears and ambitions, his love and his hate. He knew who, or what, had divided him, and he sought within for the singular self he believed he was: but like a ship tacking to avoid the rocks on one side, then the shallows on the other, seeking a harbor, he remained cleft in two.

Once as a young man, not yet an earl, not yet the O'Neill, he had watched two men wrestling in a London market, both powerful, neither the stronger; one a pale-skinned hairless man, the other a black man from Atlantis or Africa, his muscles rolling like a horse's beneath his gleaming skin, the other's reddened where he had been gripped. Hugh felt his own muscles tense as the wrestlers tensed theirs, their bare feet stamping in the blood-flecked sawdust. They seemed one beast in the intensity of their bonding, but at length one threw down the other and held him down to a count, then leapt up victorious, arms high, and those watching cheered and tossed pennies toward him. All this Hugh remembered. What was odd was that he couldn't recall which man, the pale red man or the heavy-limbed dark man, was the one who outlasted.

The English knights who had first come to the Irish island with King Henry the Second, the founders of the families of Burke and Desmond and Thomond and Kildare, had never settled and remade the North as they had the South; in Ulster there were no Old English earls whose ancestors had come from what John Dee called the Isles Britannicæ. Hugh, despite his English title, was not of them; he had come from this soil he stood on. Yet though an Ulsterman, he was in other ways more English than they. Few of the Irishmen he knew best, and almost none of the women, could speak or understand English; he could speak English well, and read it to a degree; he dictated his letters to Pedro Blanco, but the sentences were his own. His childhood friend Philip Sidney had considered him to be English, a gracious knight like Philip himself; his father Sir Henry had attributed Hugh's rebellious spasms to the old Irish Adam coming forth.

Hugh loved them both, but neither knew him: not in full.

Late in that summer, the summer when he became the O'Neill by the acclamation of the people to whom he belonged, and in full knowledge of his sin against the spirit of his dead wife, he set out to wed again. The woman who'd captivated him was the daughter of the Englishman Nicholas Bagenal, who had been Marshal of the Queen's army in Ireland for decades. Henry, son of Nicholas and now his successor as Marshal, was the brother of the woman Hugh set out to win. Henry Bagenal despised the Irish, and O'Neills in particular. Not so long before, old Turlough Luineach O'Neill, then still abroad and claiming titles he had no right to, had sued for the hand of this young woman. The young Marshal was said to have answered *I would rather see her burned.*

Her name was Mabel. Just twenty in this year, old for marriages among the Gael but not the English. Her brother Henry had arranged the marriages of her four older sisters to English colonials: two Plunketts, a Loftus, a Barnewall. Hugh was forty-two years old; there was gray in his red beard. It was an impossible match.

He had first seen her at Dublin Castle, a meeting of the Queen's Council to which he had been once again summoned, a summons that he had often postponed or refused: Henry Bagenal being the summoner. On this occasion, afraid he might be clapped in irons (as his Dublin *spiall* or circle of informers warned him he might be, English patience tried), he had come in at the head of a band of mounted armed men, lancers and musketeers, *bonnaght* running at the stirrups, enough to inspire caution but not alarm.

Looking up from the courtyard of the castle on that day, he could see a woman leaning on the sill of a window above, long loose hair, red-gold like her complexion. Amused, he thought she looked; or interested somehow. He lifted his hat to her, as he ought, and she might have smiled. He turned to his followers, gave orders, and when he looked back she was gone.

He'd learn that it was unusual for her to come to the Court at Dublin with her brother, that she mostly remained in the Bagenal houses in Newry—strong but fine places in English style, furnished and decorated from London—or in the houses of her sisters, chiefly Mary Barnewall's; Mary was her closest friend among them. He learned these things in bits from among Henry's associates whom he spoke with, and put them together as best he could when (as he was, though rarely) invited to the Bagenals' house at Newry. She'd appear at these meetings, usually with her mother, bringing news or household questions to her brother; only then did he begin to know her. And hear her speak. And speak to her: rising from his seat at the Marshal's round table to bow to the mother, take her hand and bring it to his lips, and again bow, but less deeply, to the daughter, and ask her name: Mabel.

"My brother has spoken of your Lordship," she said, her first words to him alone. Henry in his tall chair was motionless and unsmiling.

"I am certain that he has," Hugh said. "I hope not in such terms as would make you my enemy."

"I am no one's enemy," she said back to him, her look returning his. "But for those who think me theirs."

"I could not be one of them."

She dipped a slight curtsy and then turned away from him, body first and eyes last (he thought) and went from the room; he was careful not to watch her go; he returned immediately to the topic that was before the Marshal and the men, which he had momentarily forgot. How was he to speak to her again, and alone?

But it was she who next spoke to him, she who met him when alone.

Sir Patrick Barnewall, husband of sister Mary, was well known to Hugh O'Neill. A firm Catholic, unlike the Bagenals, but the English tolerated the fault if the man were steady and did not take the Irish side entirely. In his house was a freedom that Mabel's house didn't provide. When Hugh came to the house—having learned from Sir Patrick when she'd be visiting—he dismounted and stood at the door, and it was she who opened it.

"You ride well, sir," she said. "I saw you on the road, from the window there." She stepped out, and came to where he stood. "Sir Patrick is at his dinner."

"But not yourself."

"I live on air and the scent of roses." She said it with calm conviction, then laughed lightly—at his own baffled look, he supposed. "No, no. I rose late and will dine late. It's my constant habit." Still

smiling, a teasing smile. She walked away along the pebbled walk.
Small trees, their trunks bare of branches and their tops barbered
into perfect rounds, walked beside her. He followed at a small distance. When she stopped, and bent to a stand of flowers that might
be roses of a kind, he came beside her. "How does it happen," he
said, "that no man has claimed your hand?"

"Oh, several have," she said. "I denied the claims."

He looked upward at the rosy brick of the wall, the window-glass
that caught the sun. "It's a fine house, Sir Patrick's."

"But it has no name," she said. "That's a flaw." She looked then directly at him—he was no taller than she. "I know you have a castle to
live in," she said. "And I know its name." They were face-to-face now,
and Hugh was out of words. Pale man; dark man. They were hailed
from the porch: Lady Mary, her children behind her, peeking out to
see the Irish earl.

"Castle Dungannon," Mabel said.

❦

She was absent for the rest of that day at Sir Patrick's, and didn't
appear at the late supper served him. But it had taken no more than
the conversation on the path for Hugh to bear a petition to Henry
Bagenal at his court in Newry, to ask for Mabel's hand.

Hugh O'Neill knew very well what reply Sir Henry had given
Turlough Luineach when Turlough sued for that hand; the story
had been widely reported. But Hugh O'Neill, as Henry Bagenal
knew, was the great force now in the North, an Earl created by
the Queen, yet a man who could easily spoil English plans and
send royal officials back to Dublin afraid for their lives. Sir Henry
must perforce listen, and nod, and name a date for a decision—a
date he intended to let go by. He knew what all the English knew,
or thought they knew: that the Earl was easily angered, and when
angered could be murderous. Shane's fate had not been forgotten.
In any case, the Marshal noted to the Earl—glancing upward as if
in thought or speculation—that a marriage between a colonist and
a Gael might require a royal benefice; the Marshal did not know
for sure; he must put the matter before the Privy Council. The two
parted with cold compliments.

❦

Sir Henry thought it would better secure his sister if she were moved closer to Dublin, to the Barnewall house; he hadn't learned that O'Neill had already visited there, and conversed with the child in the garden. Nor would he know that she had entered the room where the Earl slept that night, and waked him. They'd talked softly and long there, the Earl in his *léine*, a long linen nightshirt, she in a *robe de chambre* of great luxury, whose price the Earl couldn't guess; but for his part he took from his satchel a glittering snake of gold (whose worth he knew): the links of the chain were the heads of beasts that each bit the next, in a long circle. She said nothing when he brought it forth, nothing when he passed it to her, but she poured it back and forth between one hand and the other, entranced, watching the faces come alive in the candlelight.

"Yours," he said.

She let it fall into his lap. "There can be but one reason you should give such a thing to me."

"That's true," he said. "One reason."

She knelt on the floor by his bed. "My brother despises you, and will never consent."

"If you consent, his consent doesn't weigh. If you will have me, you will, in whatever manner you choose, and Sir Henry may not say you nay."

She rose then and went away to the fire, mere gray ash now and glowing coals. He thought he had offended; perhaps she thought he had belittled her love for her brother. But when she faced him again her smile was sly.

"It can't be," she said.

"It can."

"What—would you steal me away?"

"Could you be stolen? If you could, yes."

She prettily pretended fear. "You would not reive me from my house and family," she said. "Would not, against my will."

"I never would," he said. "Never against your will."

"Irish men in times past," she said, "commonly took a wife in that way. So I am told."

"Times past are times past."

She returned to him in three long steps and knelt again by him where he sat, and put her clasped hands in his lap where the gold chain still lay. She wasn't teasing now. "Find me a way to go with you and he will not dare come to take me back," she said. "He may hate you but he is an abider of rules. He is in love with rules. Marry me in good form and there will be naught he can say."

~

It happened in this way: the Earl paid another visit to Sir Patrick Barnewall some weeks later, bringing with him a few longstanding English friends he knew would entertain the family gathered at dinner there, and so they did. Mabel absented herself early on, complaining of headache, and went to her room, or seemed to. Outside in the dark, Sir William Warren, a man who (like Garrett Moore) was one among the few Englishmen in Ireland the young O' Neill had come to trust as he found his feet in the swift currents of those years. Patiently Sir William curry-combed the fine horse he'd ridden here, and cleaned the glistening hide with a dandy-brush. Stable-hands came to offer help but he sent them away curtly, almost unkindly. He kept it up until he heard a door from the house opened and gently closed, and stowed his tools.

She was dressed sensibly in a warm hooded cape and good boots, and carried only a small satchel, as she'd known to do. Only a word or two passed between them, a smile and a nod in the dark, and Sir William mounted up, and leaned down to take her arm and lift her to the horse's back. She gave a small sob—he heard it—and then took hold of his belt with both gloved hands. He walked the horse to the road, and then kicked him into a gallop; Mabel looked back once to see the glow of firelight in the windows of the house.

Inside, the wine and brandy—Hugh's gifts—had the company telling tales true and not, handing off the japes one to another. *It is just as though I was at an English table*, Mary said, and though her husband hinted with his eyes that she depart, she stayed, and kept him there as well. The Earl—who had, as he said, the longest ride to home, where he was obliged this night to stay—rose, thanked his hosts, his friends, Lady Mary, and with no hurry went to the stables for his own horse, a tall roan that could run for hours. Spurring the horse toward the northward road and the meeting place at the gates of Drogheda town, Hugh O'Neill felt himself for this night to be one person, one being, and not two. He would not feel so again for many years.

~~~

He was careful of her in Dungannon, knowing that he could consign her to oblivion and shame in the Bagenals' houses if he took her to his bed, to which she made clear in her witty sidewise speech she wanted to go, and now. No: they must be wed, and wed directly—as she had said herself, in proper form, with the proof of it in hand. Beside her he watched the nights come on, played at chess with her, rode with her, kissed and embraced—no more. He told her stories of famous elopements, translating as best he could the Irish in his head into the English of his mouth: of jealous King Conchobar pursuing Derdriu and her lover Noísiu, for Derdriu was raised to be Conchobar's wife; of Diarmaid and Gráinne, who ran away from King Cormac, and slept together many nights in the greenwood, a sword between them so that there was no sin in it. "I don't like these kings of yours," Mabel said, head on his shoulder.

It was Mabel who instructed Hugh in how their flight might be proven sinless, like Diarmaid and Gráinne's, and how a marriage in proper form might be done, and Sir Henry not know until too late. Hugh laughed in delight when he heard, watched her walk up and down the room tapping a forefinger of one hand into the palm of the other, explaining. She was right, and he said to her that the story of Hugh and Mabel would one day be as often told as that of Derdriu and her Noísiu. And since she had been ready to flee her house and family to ride with him, had urged Hugh to be quick, then leapt from the back of William Warren's fast horse and thence onto Hugh's roan, her arms tight around him, her cheek against his back, skirts pulled up to sit astride, then perhaps he had not broken his vow to Siobhan: he had not sought a new wife, only taken a woman who had first taken him, and to whom he'd played the maid's part.

In Rome, years after, when his long confessions to Peter Lombard had reached this time and these events, the Archbishop had called it *casuistical*, the way Hugh had persuaded himself that a wrong (the breaking of the vow he had made to Siobhan) was not a wrong. But in any event—Peter told him—you did marry; and though that was indeed a breaking of your former vow, it was not a sin. What *was* perhaps a sin, or an offense to God, was that Mabel and her Hugh were married by the Protestant bishop of Meath, a man named Jones who was known to Hugh O'Neill and beloved by Mabel and the sisters, in his episcopal palace at Drumcondra; but then again, that bishop was a wise man and later explained to Henry Bagenal—who was furious with him for what he'd consented to do—that he had fully examined Mabel and her motives, and her chastity, before acceding. *She told me that unless she had agreed to that device and the manner of her escape (as she termed it), it would never have been attempted.* That Protestant marriage was uncanonical and void, of course, but Mabel whispered to him as though it were a secret never to be told, that she was, herself, a Catholic, and had become a Catholic in childhood, and no one in her family knew of it but she and her favorite lady's maid, an Irish girl who prayed with her. Hugh O'Neill, his cheek in his hand where he lay beside her, smiled upon her in wonder.

The morning after their wedding night Mabel discovered on her husband's breast a strange thing on a chain that in the darkness she hadn't seen. She tried to lift it off, but he wouldn't let her; he only turned it to her and asked her what she saw. The third soul ever to look in. She studied it, brow knit, and said she saw herself, but dimly.

Himself was never what Hugh O'Neill saw there, not since he first looked in. He turned it back again to himself. "It was a gift," he said. "From a wise man in England. To keep me safe, he said."

Mabel looked into her husband's face, which seemed to seek itself in the black mirror, though she was wrong about that; and she said, "May God will that it do so."

In that winter Hugh O'Neill, room by room, floor by floor, rebuilt his house. It was no longer the place he had come to as a boy; what had been timber was now stone; fireplaces were masoned and real chimneys built to draw off the smoke. For the cold flags of his floors, Queen Gráinne O'Malley got him carpets from faraway places that had somehow never reached their markets in the English isles, and rich hangings for his walls as well, all at a cost he was glad to pay. It was the fine house in the English style he had long imagined, which he believed Mabel needed and wanted, where wardrobes of glossy wood held his velvet English suits and hats, Mabel's dresses and coats; where wax candles glowed in the place of pine torches, where good wine was drunk from vessels of glass and silver, where dead persons near-related to Mabel looked out from gilded frames as though they spied through curtained windows. When he could get no lead for the leaking wooden roofs, he appealed to his friends at the Court in London; Lord Burghley saw to it that a shipment of some tons of sheet lead were sent to him, a wedding gift; some was laid on Dungannon's roofs, and the rest lay for years in the pine woods until a different use was found for it, in the different world to come. Each morning before his lie-abed wife awakened, Hugh walked out to the place where Siobhan lay buried, and sat by her awhile. He was given no word, felt no reproach; but (though less and less often) he continued to sit by her there; pluck the grasses at his feet; speak in his mind to her, about her sons, about the horses, about the folk.

Hugh believed that Mabel would soon be with child, and Mabel believed so too; but as winter deepened there were none of the signs that she knew to look for. Their night-times were intense and gratifying, but nothing came of them, which saddened both. He wanted sons: his sons with Siobhan would be men in time, but in the world now coming to be, more sons would be needed. Mabel applied dutifully the prayers and helps that her sister Mary had offered, and (out of her husband's hearing) other advice from the women of the castle: but still she didn't conceive. When spring was born out of winter's dark womb the whole world began producing young: the women, the horses and the cattle, the dogs, even the trees and the grasses. Mabel looked out at the burgeoning land and felt herself the only one empty.

She told her husband that she must return to Newry, to her mother and her sisters, to tell them of her happiness, and reluctantly he got her a good horse and a companion; and she did go to Newry, but not at first to the Bagenal house. She turned away from the main way and took a short road to the Killeavy Old Churches—two ancient piles joined in times past to make one long edifice, too little visited to be worth the stripping of its great altars, yet never closed. Mabel had sent for her beloved servant Niamh, to meet her here, to wait in the churchyard, where flowering bushes gave off their May odor. She kissed the girl and went in through the big door, never locked, and down the wide corridor that led through one church and into another, seeking the figure of Mary, Mother and Child, fearful that it might have been removed or shattered by Protestant fanatics, but it was there, just as it was when Mabel had first come here as a child with Niamh, in secret, wrapped in black like a spy.

She knelt there. *Ave Maria gratia plena:* all she knew of the prayer in Latin. In English she entreated: *The fruit of thy womb. Bless me, Mother of God, so that I may not be left barren.* She began a rosary, beads that her father had never discovered in his searches of her room and clothes when he sought to purge her of her mad choice of the old faith over his new faith. *Why have you chosen this?* he'd cry. But it was not what she had chosen but what had chosen her.

After a time in silence, words rising to her lips but not spoken, cheeks wet, she rose from the stone floor. She was level with the Child in Mary's arms, the Child reaching outward to whomever came near, impatient perhaps; his mother, eyes lowered, smiled down upon him. Both mother and child had suffered wounds long before Mabel had first come here: bits of the plaster had fallen off, the blue and white paint was crackled and flaking; Jesus's finger raised in blessing or forgiveness was broken at the knuckle. It didn't matter. The love and power flowed unhampered through these human things. When a child, she hadn't known this; the plaster child *was* the Child, and when she dared to touch it she had felt a touch in return.

She'd told her family, calmly but with certainty, that she intended to join the Augustinian nunnery that was then still attached to Killeavy church, and a storm of objection and hilarity broke over her. Did she not know that the Irish who followed that religion sought the deaths or expulsion of her family? Was she aware that as a nun she could never marry or bear children? And have to wear those absurd wrappings and not the pretty clothes she loved? She mustn't ever go there again; the devil, or something more human, could surprise her there. And Mabel in peace withstood it all: she knew by then the stories of the martyrs; she rejoiced in her brother's beatings. The sweetness she had felt when the Host was first placed on her tongue was so great as to make her family as good as invisible, though she prayed for them each by name and for Niamh every day.

She thought now on this May afternoon, wrapping her light shawl around her shoulders and spying the face of her servant at the open door, that in that wondrous and fearsome time they'd both been eleven or twelve years old. She crossed herself, and genuflected at the altar as she passed it, thinking that if she could she would pray for that long-ago child she had been. She didn't wish to be a nun; she hadn't wanted to for long and she no longer thought of it, she wished to ride and laugh and lie with her husband, and be a mother: that was her prayer.

FOX AND DOG

*t*he Catholic Primate of Ireland in that year 1593 was Edmund Magauran, Archbishop of Armagh, who didn't reside in Ireland, had been educated abroad, mostly in Spain, and been awarded his bishopric *in absentia* by the Pope. Spanish lords had financed Magauran's return to Ireland to prepare the native Irish leaders for a new Spanish invasion. Rather than send him on a Spanish ship, from which he'd likely be extracted by the English Queen's privateers before he ever landed, King Philip brought Magauran with him on progress into France, where his daughter Isabella was to be married to the young Duc de Guise.

The King of Spain's daughter! She could be all the daughters of all the kings of Spain, for the King of Spain's Daughter was a great figure in Gaelic legend, a distant and angelic beauty, virgin savior and goddess: awaited, ever-rumored to be just now borne on her way over the sea, to be wedded to an Irish king or hero, to rule gently and justly over the island, and in the end never arriving. Nevertheless, the fact that Archbishop Magauran had actually *travelled in her company* gave him a share in her sacred glamour. Did he ever really think he might indeed be able to bring Isabella to Ireland, see her crowned, the earls and the chieftains at her feet? No one ever claimed to have heard him say it. From the tiny obsidian hiding-place where the Queen of England sat as though weaving, she murmured to Hugh O'Neill about the warp and weft of royal connections on the continent, the marriages and the heirs: *Isabella is a horse-faced clumsy girl, taller than any husband proposed to her, likely to die a nun.* There could be no Queen of Ireland: no *other* queen.

Magauran reached Ulster by the usual secret routes and was made welcome at the house of the young Maguire lord of Fermanagh, a firm Catholic. Good angels had guided him through the dangers of the journey, he said, but in fact he knew no angels, not at least to speak to. What he wanted of the Maguire and all his kin was a holy war: they couldn't win it alone, surely, but merely to begin it in the certainty of divine grace, with the promise of Spanish soldiers, would draw others to Maguire and his fellows as a lodestone draws iron filings.

Hugh O'Neill would have nothing to do with him.

He had done his best to keep this fiery Maguire chief and his fighters in the North, and to see that Red Hugh O'Donnell didn't fall under Maguire's spell, which could bind any young man in search of adventure and a companion. But Hugh O'Neill stood at the center of a balance beam, and couldn't take even a baby's step toward one end or the other, toward the old clans like the Maguires or toward the men of power in Dublin and their bonds with London. Dublin wanted Maguire to stop hiding Jesuits and raiding English fields; and they wanted the young O'Donnell to cease confronting English garrisons and scattering them like doves in a dovecote. Hugh wrote to Dublin on their behalf: they were fine young men, he averred, they would be under his wing till they had learned modern ways.

At midwinter he took them, red-haired Hugh O'Donnell and black Maguire, like unwilling schoolboys to Dundalk church, there to kneel and swear fealty to the Queen. The Marshal, Henry Bagenal, now Hugh's brother-in-law, had given assurances that the two young leaders wouldn't be arrested or bound over, much as he might have wished it. The Lord Deputy, the Marshal's superior, took Hugh O'Neill aside to whisper: *Were the young chieftains sincere?* O'Neill assured him that they were. He had got them to speak their oaths to keep the peace, and on their knees too. It gave him no pleasure; he felt soiled and doubted, even as the officials had taken his hand and nodded their hatted heads to him. The Lord Deputy then demanded O'Neill send his elder son and namesake to Dublin as a pledge on that assurance. No, he responded, he would not—indeed *could* not—yield up the boy, nor his brother Henry: their O'Hagan fosterers, he asserted, had made away with them, and who knew now where they might be? Marshal and Lord Deputy looked coldly on this assertion, and on Hugh's open hands and honest face.

The three Irishmen rode north from the meeting at Dundalk church. The day was mild, but the clouded sun was cold, deep in the molt like an aged hawk. They passed, on the western side, the long mound that was Newgrange, like a great brown loaf, and didn't see the sun's dim fingers reach in the one opening still unblocked by ancient rubble, seeking those asleep a thousand years, waking those who could awaken.

Maguire, restless and still in great annoyance at what he had had to do in Dundalk, bade the other two farewell and sped away: his followers, he said, awaited him at Dungannon.

"Maguire's a brute," O'Neill said thoughtfully to Red Hugh. "He knows nothing of policy. Nothing of accommodation." Maguire was married to a daughter of Hugh O'Neill's by Siobhan, her last child: which had not endeared him to the Earl. He disliked the man's visage, like a bad dog's, and the way he shaved off his chin-beard but let the black moustaches grow absurdly long. "He is a man of the old times; he has no insides, he can only respond, he can't consider, can only bite. He can't be trusted."

"He is a brute," Red Hugh said cheerfully. "But he is a brute *for us.*"

They rode in companionable silence for a mile. The wind sharpened.

"They would have me make war on Maguire," O'Neill said, who'd brooded on it as he rode. "The Lord Deputy. To no benefit to me."

"Then join with him, Uncle," Red Hugh said.

Red Hugh slept that night at Dungannon, woke early and dressed to ride. O'Neill found the young man up before him, at the Dungannon portal open to the weak sun, watching Maguire ready his horse. Maguire took hold of the horse's jaw and looked it in the eye as though to challenge it. A dog he was, a black dog. Though a fine horseman; there was no doubt of that.

Young Red Hugh, unmindful of the cold, arms crossed, his usual expression of gay insolence: O'Neill studied him too. If Maguire was a black dog, Red Hugh was a fox: golden-whiskered, red-headed, dark-eyed, sly and quick. The Earl hoped to keep them, both of them, with him: yet doubted he had as much power over them as they held over each other. Dog and Fox: they should not be friends, nature would not permit it, yet their love was as complete as any he knew or had heard of in song. He watched Maguire mount, walk his horse left, then right, then by a tug at the reins that the Earl didn't perceive, make the great gray animal step backward, hindquarters quivering, delicate as a maid at a country dance.

The comedy of Dublin and Ulster went on. Hugh O'Neill, double-souled man, was like an actor in a theater playing two parts, changing clothes and beard and voice all in a moment and then back again. He'd demand of the Marshal Sir Henry Bagenal, his brother-in-law, the thousand pounds he was owed as Mabel's dowry, and by the week's end wrote that he cared nothing for it. Of course he wasn't *trusted*; there were good reasons for that; but he thought he should be trusted anyway, and not constantly suspected and challenged. The English pursuivant-at-arms came with summonses weekly, twice weekly, until Hugh cried out in Irish that *by the Son of God I'd rather be dead than be looking at your running to me every second day in your accursed little jacketeen of red!*

The two younger men couldn't fathom why O'Neill tried so hard to please the Lord Deputy and the rest. He could rouse an entire kingdom in the North with a word, but instead he wrote his endless letters, begging pardon, swearing fealty, telling again all the tales of how he had served the Queen faithfully and done battle against her enemies in her name and taken wounds for her—which indeed he sometimes had done, to some small extent. What was he afraid of, they wanted to know. Was he hagridden, had the old Queen some-how climbed upon the Earl's back and now rode him as a steed? They laughed at that together, Dog and Fox, but they couldn't be sure it wasn't so.

"Ride with me," Dog says to Fox. "Before they crush us. Before Tyrone changes his mind and becomes an Englishman."

"He saved my life."

"Then spend it wisely. The time is now."

It was good weather. They went with a force of raiders into Sligo county, stealing cattle from their neighbors' fields and driving them north as their ancestors had done for time out of mind: a bit ashamed, a bit proud. Dublin would care nothing for this reiving, Irish de-spoiling Irish. Well, they'd soon send those beeves back, they told themselves, and perhaps they did.

When spring came, and in the elation of having done *something*, something at last, they turned their most tested forces south into Connacht, where the great clan of the O'Rourkes was severely pressed by the English government and its forces under Sir Richard Bingham, lately dubbed Governor of Connacht. The Earl of Tyrone cautioned them about this violation of the vows the two had so lately made to the English, demanding to know what value could be got out of flouting those promises. Yet they went, and the Earl had no choice but to order Pedro Blanco, his *major domo* as he styled himself in his own language, to select a force of O'Neill fighters to send after them and make up their number.

"This O'Rourke," Maguire said to Red Hugh as they rode south, "now chief of his clan, is the son of that O'Rourke who went to Scotland to beg the help of King James on his throne. He brought a gift of Irish wolfhounds, never seen in Scotland before. The King loved him and promised him the help that he begged for . . ."

"Until the Queen demanded he be taken prisoner."

"Yes. And though the Scots tried their best to keep him safe, he was brought in chains to England, and, look you, he was hanged in London for a crime the English imputed to him *that was committed in Ireland,* though there was no precedent in English law that permitted that."

"Long ago," said Red Hugh. The Fox had little sense of the great reaches of time that lay behind each passing day. What histories impinged on him he knew in the form of tales: it was all he needed. Evening and morning are the Fox's day.

"*Not,*" growled the Dog. "*Not* long ago. Then and also now. If O'Rourke can't stand, none of us can."

They camped in the low hills there, waiting for young Brian O'Rourke and his family's fighters to gather and for Richard Bingham to appear with his English army. Riders sent east to mark his coming-on returned without news. Then boys who'd come on foot up from Roscommon in the south told them that the English had turned their way, and a large force was gathering at the plain of Machery, by the gate of Tulsk, not a day's ride from where they now stood. Maguire sent his captains through the camp to get their men mounted and armed; he wouldn't wait to be attacked.

"Who is that, then," Red Hugh asked, "coming on at a run?"

Maguire looked where he pointed. "Ah," Maguire said. "My archbishop. Come with a blessing, certainly."

The Titular Archbishop of Armagh, in partial armor and a

borrowed headpiece, came through the mounted men on a long-backed black gelding. He'd offered Maguire, his host in Fermanagh, to accompany the force as Chaplain, and here he was.

"You ride like a Spaniard, my lord Bishop," Maguire said.

"It is a fine mount for a light rider," said the priest. "I will keep pace with you."

Red Hugh grinned, rose a little in his saddle, fixed the hang of his sword. "Then let us ride."

How fine it was to thunder over the swells of the June-green land, and then down into the plain of Machery in Roscommon under the Moon, their forces spreading ghost-like behind and to either side of their chiefs. The great joy of *striking back*.

When next morning came it was white with thick fog, blanketing their camps. They could hear the English forces, the rattle of arms, the calling of sentries, whinnying of horses. But they could *see* nothing. Red Hugh and Maguire rode out to find a place above the great pale body prone over the plain, and when they did get clear of it, and looked over it to where the English must be, they could actually *see* Sir Richard Bingham on his horse, standing on a high place that rose above the fog. Mist swirled around his horse's fetlocks. He could no more see the field than they could.

They trusted to the horses' noses to bring them back to where their fighters were arming and cheering for officers they couldn't see. They found Bishop Magauran at a camp table, saying Mass; he'd brought silver Mass vessels in a leather case. To the men who approached and knelt in the wet grass he gave a consecrated Host, murmuring to each the *Corpus Dei*. Fox and Dog knelt there too before the priest and felt the thin circle of unleavened bread melt on their tongues. When no more communicants appeared, when horse and foot began to move forward to the sounding of the pipers and drummers, none able to see anyone but those next to them, the Archbishop got to his horse. "He despiseth fear, he turneth not his back to the sword!" he cried into the air, in a voice not his own, kicking his steed into a walk.

"Who says this, Father?" Maguire turned to ask.

"God," Magauran called out. "God, telling Job of His wondrous creations, look you!" He had pulled almost abreast of Maguire. "When he heareth the trumpet he saith: *Ha, ha!*" the prelate shouted. "He smelleth the battle afar off, the encouraging of the captains, and the shouting of the army!" Maguire laughed with him. And then with an awful suddenness they were colliding with the enemy, a multitude of ghosts coming out of the white glare of fog brightened by the sun, shouting.

~

The fog had only begun to shred when Sir Richard ordered his forces to withdraw, nothing accomplished. The Irish kerne and gallowglass tried to hold them where they stood so that more could be brought down, now that friend could be told from enemy, but Bingham got his forces away. The Irish retired, to search the clouded field for dead and wounded. Hugh Maguire and Red Hugh were called to a place where a dead man lay, one that they should see and acknowledge: Edmund Magauran, Primate of Ireland. He lay facedown on the wet ground, his horse standing by him. Red Hugh knelt there and crossed himself. A sword lay near the horse, its grip bloodied, as though it had dropped from the priest's hand. Where had he got that? Or was it an English blade, the one that had struck him down? *In Paradisum deducant te Angeli,* if angels chose to notice the one anointed man among the many dead, who all needed guidance toward what lay beyond.

As Red Hugh arose from where he knelt, he saw a man coming toward them, as though materializing out of rising wraiths of mist. He stepped around dead men and horses, seeming hardly to see them, and stopped before Red Hugh and Maguire. He made no obeisance, did not remove his hat—he had no hat—and he looked on the chiefs with a frankness that suggested rank, though his slight smile was that of a servant.

"I bear a message for your honors," he said, and waited for a nod of permission to proceed. "You are wanted at a place near here, named Cruachain. Those waiting there invite you."

"And who are you to urge us to this?" Red Hugh asked.

"One who knows," said the walker. "Who knows the need."

"I know of the place," Maguire said. "It's a place where the ancestors of the old kings of the West were buried, and before that, they ruled from there."

"Long ago. And also now."

Men who had been wrapping the body of the Archbishop in a mantle now lifted him to their shoulders. Where *he* would be carried to burial was still to be told them.

"You should know I am a Catholic," Maguire said, "and I avoid such things as the souls of dead kings."

"There are not such things at Cruachain." The messenger clasped his hands behind his back. "I will accompany you, if a guide is wanted."

"None is."

The walker inclined his head, that gesture just short of insolence; he stepped away from the chiefs, the kerne, the body of the Archbishop, turned and was gone.

"Why should we go there?" says Fox.

"We won't learn," says Dog, "until we do."

First there were duties for both of them to do: fighters to be buried, or put onto carts to be borne home for burial; honors to be distributed for the victory, wounded men seen to, the dying comforted without their priest; riders sent out to make certain that the enemy was withdrawing and not regrouping to fight again. The sun was still high when the two set out alone; it was an hour till the place was reached, northwest of the village called Tulsk. They had no certainty where it was, how it would appear, but when they came near to it they knew it. At the crest of a wide low hill was a sort of crown, if a hill could wear one; a thing that only living persons could have made and kept. A fort, a castle, a high house, a habitation where once towers and walls had stood, now earth alone and the grasses covering it. Newgrange was far greater, but they had been summoned to here, and to here they had come.

Cottages crowded the slope of the hill as though for shelter, though it offered none; dogs and bony cattle wandered, children were called in by their mothers as the two riders came near. They chose a lane to go up by, and followed it until it dwindled away, but that was no matter, it was evident how to reach whatever it was that circled the hilltop, ramparts or walls or great stones or nothing. Perhaps they made light of it all, as young men do, men with little in them of awe; but soon they were silent, looking around themselves, seeking something by which to grasp the meanings here, if there were meanings. As they began to circle widdershins around it, not minding the ill omen of that direction, they caught sight of a man seated on a rock, wrapped in a mantle and a blanket as well. He stood as they came near, raising himself with a long staff, but didn't turn to them. "Who comes here?" he called out to the air.

"Two who would learn of this place," Red Hugh responded. "Sent to be taught." It had only then occurred to him that he had come here to be taught, to learn. They dismounted, throwing their reins over a narrow standing stone—perhaps it had always been used for that. The man with the staff had begun to speak, but he was too far off still to be heard, and also—it was now evident—blind.

"Father," Maguire said. "Show us what we should see here."

"Follow," said the old man. He set out walking, taking long strides, planting his staff at each step. "It is the palace of Queen Medb," he cried out, as though the men following him were far away. "The warrior queen that the foreigner calls Maeve. Around are the raths that formed her city, greatest in Ireland." He stopped. Puzzled, Dog and Fox look around for what the old one sees, or knows without seeing.

"Of pine the house was made," he sang out. "Were there not sixteen windows in the house, and a frame of brass to each of them, a tie of brass across the roof-light? Four beams of brass made the room where Ailill lay with Medb, adorned all with bronze, and it in the center of the house."

There was nothing of this where they stood. An opening almost too low to enter by, like a beast's den. They teased each other about who would creep first into that dark place, but when they were within, the dim slant sunlight showed them little. Down a cracked stair into a room larger than seemed quite possible. Rubble and animal bones. Cold silence. They could just perceive, by where a spiral sign was chiseled in the stone, a way further in; but neither made any motion to enter there: a spiral way is fearsome.

They sat until a motion of the spirit came over both at once, but neither could speak of it, then or after: as though the light hand of an ancient was put on Red Hugh's shoulder, in friendship or command, then upon Maguire's, then gone from both. Together they hurried to crawl out, each thinking that what had been felt in the cave had been his alone, not wanting to speak of it, for fear it would make a difference between them. The relentless blind man was still talking. "Two rails of silver around it all gilded," he sang, throwing out an arm as though it were all before them. "In the front a wand of silver that reached the middle rafters of the house, and all round from one door to the other."

"That is a hard thing to imagine," Maguire said.

"Perhaps not to one blind," Red Hugh said.

"Strange that your honors have no eyes to see," the old one said.

"We have seen that there is no one and nothing here." They had come around the great pile to where they had started, and where their horses stood flicking their tails.

"Yet they are waiting," the old man of the rath said softly. "They are here."

"If they are," said Red Hugh, "are they friends to us?"

The old one chewed at nothing for a time. "They are both powerful and powerless," he said. "Powerful in striking fear, in giving heart to the faint. They can never be defeated, but they cannot triumph."

"But are they for us?"

"They are not one people. They are many, and in many places, and not all are for you or for anyone."

Maguire laughed lightly, and searched in his bag and took out coins, which caused the blind ancient to put out his hand, though his face was turned away. He felt the coins as though counting them, and put them away in some pocket within his robe. The two young men mounted, quiet now, and turned to go. The blind man was smiling as they started downhill.

⁓

Those waiting had felt living persons come near them, and go away again. They had touched the living ones in the darkness, but they could not be known to a Catholic *flaith* of this age who refused to see, nor by a knight who believed more in his sword and his horse and his friend than in anything else.

Those waiting had tried to speak, in the soft language of branches in the wind, of falling leaves striking the ground, but they had not been heard. They knew blood was to be shed and they spoke of it in the flowers of the creeping goosefoot, *blonagán dearg*, now red in the grasses. In their continuous and noiseless speech they spoke of heroes who had not failed, and of those whose feet stood yet on the earth; of the High King who was to come. In the next turn of the sun, which they would not see, the walls of Cruachain would again be covered with the goosefoot, red as the invaders' blood. They spoke, but could not be heard; and returned again to sleep.

The two living men returned at sunset to the place of the battle, to the dead horses and the broken weapons, and at dawn next day they went north, drawing their fighters after them.

A PAVILION ON THE BANN

*t*hat last year before the world turned upside-down was terribly beautiful. In every summer before, Hugh O'Neill had gone on progress through his country, sometimes sleeping in a bothy or pavilion woven of branches and flowers, hunting a little, fishing a little, but mostly receiving his allies and the men and boys and women of the septs, putting his hands on the heads of children. In this summer there was all of that and yet it seemed that nothing moved, everything was still: all over the Isles, from Scotland and Wales to Munster and the north of France, summer was deep, dry, and golden, even in the often-rainy North of Ireland. The folk lived outdoors in all the months from May to October, sleeping in the grass and beneath the trees, boys pursuing girls or the girls in pursuit; it was the world as it was in the time of the High Kings and the heroes and the lovers.

Hugh with Mabel and her Niamh went out along the sun-shot tributaries of the river Bann, to places he remembered from his young days, when Turlough Luineach shepherded the people on progress. Some had been mounted then, crowned in leaves and flowers; some led a lowing cow for milk. An ox pulled a wagon with foodstuffs and children, and two beeves followed, to provide the meats cooked over open fires.

Hugh had brought along a pair of old crossbows, thinking Mabel might be amused by them; the long prods, to which the bows were bound with whipcord, were of fine wood rather than steel. One had a windlass to draw back the bow-string into the lock. The other's bow-string, a thick length of cured hide, had to be pulled into the lock by hand: that's the one Hugh chose. While the kerne prepared the camp they shot bolts at targets, laughing at each other's misses; he watched her eyes, her joy in summer now, far from her old cold home at Newry. That there was a thing in her that was fragile, and made her often sad, he knew now: a sullen apathy that grieved and frustrated him. Not here, not amid the harpers and the leaping salmon.

They reached the old fort at Castleroe, and Hugh called a halt for the night—he thought Mabel would now want a real bed, though the castle hardly furnished one that was better than the grass. But next day they heard Mass in the chapel and trestles were set in the court-yard for a Sunday dinner. Mabel whispered in Hugh's ear: *Who is that sad fellow there who stares so at you?* Hugh glanced to where she looked.

"A cousin," he said, returning to his breakfast.

Later, Mabel saw Hugh and a man she knew as his *brehon* go with the sad cousin, who was talking eagerly and somehow desper-ately with them; they went into the castle and two of Hugh's men, men of the O'Hagan clan she knew as his guardians or foot-soldiers (she found it impossible to sort out whose duty was which, despite Hugh's instruction), stood by the door.

She went with Niamh among the women the rest of the morning, admiring the babies and the children, touching their sweet heads in a sort of laughing grief, kneeling to watch the women weaving on the small looms they had carried with them; Niamh told her what they'd said. One sang to an instrument she'd never seen before, like a little lyre: *I bathe my face in the nine rays of the Sun,* she sang, *as Mary bathed her Son in the rich milk.* Everywhere the people lowered their eyes before her, but only for a moment; their smiles were quick. One old woman squatting on the ground lifted Mabel's skirt and kissed the hem, raised a long hand to touch her belly, murmuring. *I will stay with them,* Niamh said to her in Irish, and Mabel touched her cheek and went away.

At noon she was at the castle door, about to go in to bring out her husband, when the men appeared: Hugh, the *brehon,* and the sad fellow, now appearing more desperate than sad. She heard him say in Irish, "Well, God be with you, my lord." Hugh looked blackly on him and said, "May God be at defiance with you till night." Those O'Hagans who had brought him to Hugh now stood close around the man, who was very afraid, that was clear. Hugh walked away from them, and seeing Mabel not far off stopped for a moment, unpleasantly surprised.

He took her arm. The black face she had seen at the door soft-ened. "We'll take a boat upriver," he said. "Perhaps we'll glimpse the woman of the water, coming up from her house."

"Who is she, where is her house?"

"Her house is under the water in the river. In every river. She isn't seen often. But she makes glad those who do see her." She knew he was teasing; she wasn't a child to be told tales. "She is the spirit of birth, of coming-to-be. In the land and in women. We might hope she could touch you." He laughed to see her draw away in horror, and embraced her. "Better she than the Morrigan, who's said to be her sister," he said into her ear. "The great crow, the mother of war and murder." And he laughed again.

It was a large wooden boat that she had seen tied up at the water-stairs. An aged man and his son—or so she guessed them to be—waved to them to get aboard. Since he had brought it along, Hugh took the crossbow with him in his lap while he and Mabel were rowed, smaller craft coming along behind them. She thought she'd fall asleep with the soft slap of the oars and the heat of the day. She watched Hugh choose a steel-tipped bolt from his kit, and with a stick of charcoal he found there he wrote Mabel's name on one vane of the bolt, and on the other an open hand—the sign of the O'Neill and of Ulster. "It should be red," he said, "but I have no color."

"Prick a finger," she said, "and paint in blood."

He regarded her for a time, and she seemed to see a feeling come and cross his face, but she couldn't read it; he said, still gazing at her, "There will be plenty of that in the times to come. Enough to paint the world." He drew down the rawhide string of the crossbow, hooked it at the lock, set the bolt, and lifted it, looking around for a target to aim at. On the bank a cluster of slim trees seemed to change places as in a dance while the boat passed by them. A bright bird and a dull one, male and female, flitted within the grove, but couldn't be seen well enough to name. Hugh put the crossbow to his eye like a musket, and pulled the lever that let the bow-string go. There was a noise compounded of the snap of the lock, the bow-string released, the whir of the flying bolt; Hugh and Mabel fol-lowed its flight, but it vanished soundlessly into the grove. The birds had hidden themselves.

"A prize to the man or boy or woman who returns that bolt to me!" Hugh cried.

They came to Portglenone, five miles from Castleroe; a pavilion had already been built for them, and from somewhere the smoke of fires and seared meat could be tasted on the dry air; they went up from the bank and the people withdrew, as if they knew what the pavilion and the privacy were for.

"Our friend Mr. Spenser tells tales of fairies," Mabel said. "More gentle than your Irish ones."

But Hugh was silent now, darkened again, this time not to be teased out of it. The sun was low when a man of Hugh's named Gallagher came to the pavilion with food for the couple. What was said between them then was later reported, by Gallagher most likely, though it's not known to whom he spoke, nor who passed it on further; it remains in the record, with so much else that would paint the world in the time to come.

Why have you been so long? the Earl is said to have asked.

I was seeing to the doing of an ill deed.

And what is that?

The killing of Phelim M'Turlough.

And is he killed?

Aye.

And is his son Donal Oge killed too?

Aye, both, killed and drowned.

Perhaps Hugh looked to Mabel then, to see what she had understood of this; and he turned again to Gallagher, and in a different tone he said: *What became of my shot that went over the river?*

Mabel cried out. She clapped her hands and pressed them to her face as though to shut her mouth: *Sorry, as should seem, of that which happened.*

There is no more of the record; Gallagher understood no more of what was said, for they spoke in English. Hugh O'Neill rose and came to Mabel, rubbing his fingers against his thumbs, and for a moment she thought he might kill her too. "You should not have been here," he said. "You should not." The slight Irish that Mabel knew she had learned from her nurses and the servants at home, when she was a little whelp racing from kitchen to garden to wash-house, exclaiming over puppies, absorbing language as any child will do, as Hugh had done in Sir Henry Sidney's house. It was enough. He could see she had understood what had been done, and that it was Hugh who had ordered it.

"He was a spy and a traitor to me," he said, motioning behind him with a hand to dismiss Gallagher, who nevertheless remained.

"Did they kill him, your O'Hagans? The frightened man? And his son? I know they did."

"You are not to ask such things, you have no right to be told them. You are now and henceforth to ask me nothing of my actions and my judgments. It is for your own peace and comfort that I say this."

"You are monstrous."

"You know nothing."

"How many have you ordered killed, by O'Hagans, by other men? Is it many? Is it hundreds?"

Till dark they stayed alone face-to-face, Hugh in fury, she fighting tears of rage. Whoever overheard them there would not have understood. She said that her brother and her father were right, that the Irish were murderers, she knew it now. And he: Did she not know how many Gaels her brother and her father had sent to die, on gibbets, broken on the wheel, bound like bullocks and their throats cut? Children too, as at Rathlin Island, where her dear father Sir Nicholas Bagenal had commanded the rear while the leaders had women and old men shot and sworded, babes torn from the arms of mothers and dashed upon the stones?

That wasn't true, she cried. That was only another tale, like the others he had told her, of battles and murders and rapes in the long-ago, when anything could be said to have happened but had not, not in truth. She had stood near him this day and listened to him order a man murdered, *a cousin*, he'd said, with no more soul-fear than he would have in ordering his horse, or his dinner. *That* was true. That was not a tale. She knew his faults, and had learned them quickly; she had not much minded his attentions to other women, in his own house or in others' houses—he was what he was, and what he was had possessed the force to draw her to him.

But he was this also. And this she could not abide. She went out of the pavilion and into the stillness of the evening. The singing and the calling of children, the lowing of the ox, were stilled. The great calm, the branches of the willows lifted on the evening breeze— how she had loved it all, how she had taken to it all, as though her lover had carried her to a kingdom she had not known to exist. *And is he killed? And is his son killed too?* She wished she could weep, but no tears came; day darkened to night as she stood shaking in anger and fear.

By the end of that summer she had returned to her first home, and rarely left it thereafter. She told her family only that the Earl had mortified and disgraced her by his behavior with some light women of his house, and that she could not ignore it; it was plain to her brother that there was more to it than that, but weak and distracted as she was he would not press her. When Hugh O'Neill came and begged to see her, Niamh sent for Sir Henry, who returned a refusal: there was a cold satisfaction in his account to Mabel, how he had seen off the Earl, that hurt her almost as much as anything Hugh had done. He had turned away at her door. It seemed to be the reason she could not rise at morning, could not sleep at night—at length could not see clearly the face of her sister or her servant: the sun burned her eyes. Daylong, in a whisper, she'd tell her beads, or count the heads of animals on a golden chain. She wished her husband would win his way to her, heal her, lift her up and take her away again, but he didn't and couldn't: the last red war he would ever fight, a war nine years long, had begun at the gates of the North, a war that would sweep down through the counties and destroy men and houses, as David did in the Bible from which her brother Henry daily read to her: *Saul has slain his thousands, but David his tens of thousands.*

OUT

two ways led into the Ulster interior: in the east, a thin road came and went through a narrow pass, steep and wooded: the Gap of the North, also called the Moyry Pass. It climbed from Dundalk over the Black Bank to Armagh, passing by the White Cairn of Watching where ages ago the sentinels of the Ulaid kings had looked southward, and—some said—still did. The other way was from the west, by Sligo and Ballyshannon and along the southwest shore of the Lakes of Erne. At Enniskillen, a long island near where the two Lakes joined, a Maguire of times past had built a castle, never captured or surrendered (so the Maguires asserted). The English war against the Maguires and the North was widening, had been widening since Bingham's disgrace at Tulsk, and now an English force was coming down from Sligo and could take Enniskillen.

O'Neill's messengers brought reports to Dungannon: on the western lake, the English had floated a great barge, covered in hides and hurdles to ward off Irish shot and javelins, and large enough to carry a hundred men and women, English colonists, to Enniskillen. As it went south the barge had to stop constantly to clear boggy islands of their dense green cover so that it could pass. The commanders and the guardian troops rode and walked down along the shore, wading through the tangle of branching streams and passing right under the high two-towered castle. Farther on, where the Irish had driven long stakes into the river-bottom to stop boats, they stopped. No activity could be perceived at the castle, and after some days of watching, sappers with picks were sent to breach the barbican.

Gaels, though fearless in the open air, in bog, mud, scree, or forest, hate entrapment, even in strong castles; if besieged they surrender, or flee if they can, rather than sit inside walls and be fired on or blown up. When the English soldiery broke into the Enniskillen barbican they found only some sixty defenders inside, and those were quickly slain. The high fortress of the Maguires was in English hands.

Before the end of July, the Maguire lord of Fermanagh had raised a large force of his family's fighters and their dependents to go with him, by ways known to Ulstermen, and recapture the castle. Red Hugh had ridden hard into Donegal to call up hundreds of Scots from among the MacDonnell redshanks that Gráinne O'Malley had years before ferried into Ulster—those ones she'd told old O'Donnell to put by till their time came, which in the eyes of O'Donnell's son Red Hugh, was now. The Earl of Tyrone wrote a rapid scrawl to Dublin so they would know that the doings of Red Hugh and the Maguire had nothing to do with him, he had not heard of it, did not concern himself in it. Dark Man did promise to set out with a force of his own to join his lordship the Queen's Deputy; but Pale Man couldn't do that, and never intended to. Meantime Dark Man sent a force of shot and infantry to Maguire's aid.

The ordered progress of an English army following its drums and trumpets—infantry here, horse there, supply-wagons protected on both sides, the sutlers and merchants who managed them, the camp-followers trailing behind—all of it was impossible on narrow Irish roads, no more than tracks worn deep by walkers and cattle. The Irish were at the English heels the whole of their hard journey northward, striking at laggard troops with swords, throwing javelins, then vanishing away. As they came near Enniskillen the commanders ordered the army into a narrow pass through bog and deadfall to where the Upper Erne fed into the Lower at a fording-place in the river.

In every true story there is a ford.

The cavalry was ordered to dismount and walk their horses, which made them useless till they could mount again. When they came near to the ford, a huge number—it seemed huge—of Irish caliver-men hidden amid the tangle of brush rose up as one and fired *en masse* on the English front. The calivers—nine-pound matchlock guns—threw one-ounce lead balls three hundred feet, and a good caliver-man could load and fire his weapon in less than a minute. As the English musketeers hurried to set up and fire their own heavier weapons blindly into the trees, a strange cry or scream began to be heard above the guns; it came from the rear, out of the air, a sound made by banshees or demons . . . no, it was Red Hugh's Scots redshanks, brought in time, and coming on at a heedless run. Some wearing the old-time chain-mail of their grandfathers, some bearing the claymores of their fathers, they charged still screaming into the rear of the English train, felling soldiers and civilians alike. Maguire, from where he sat his horse on higher ground, shouted in glee, lifted his sword to call the Irish horse into the fray.

The only escape for the English was to toss away weapons and armor, abandon the wagons and horses, wade through the ford to the far bank, and try to reach another crossing-place farther up; those who reached it headed away north as fast as they could. They might have been pursued, harried as by hawks—but the abandoned baggage-train at the ford was of far greater interest to the redshanks. In no time they were contesting with one another for plunder, but there was plenty for all: the English soldiers and their officers and the camp-followers had all stowed their belongings—purses of money, clothes, prized possessions—into the wagons for safekeeping, expecting them to be guarded by soldiers who were now on the run toward Sligo with the sutlers, laborers, wives, children, merchants, and wounded men. Maguire's captains tried to keep the provision wagons from plunder, but the men in their search for valuables turned out barrels containing the hard unleavened biscuit that was the staple of soldiers as of sailors; great amounts of it were thrown about and tipped into the ford, where it floated till it sank.

Maguire and O'Donnell, Dog and Fox, met at the ford and embraced, laughing.

"Now the world changes," Maguire cried. "Now it runs backward to where it begins again!"

They would call this battle at the beginning-again of the world to come *Béal Átha na mBriosgadh,* the Battle of the Ford of the Biscuits, and it would enter history under that comical name. Enniskillen Castle was again—for the time being—Maguire's. The Irish and their redshanks herded together all the disarmed English fighters they had taken prisoner and put them all to the sword, every one. Those waiting at Rathcrogan, at Caher on Black Head in Clare, in the spiral depths at Newgrange, at the Grianán Ailigh of Donegal: they all soon knew of this, and breathed in pleasure, and then were still again.

five

VICTORIOUS

CLONTIBRET

Gunpowder is easily made. Great quantities of gunpowder are not.

First, wood is cut and burned—willow or alder were thought best, and throughout the English island stands of those trees were disappearing as the demand for powder increased, but in Ireland the willow was plentiful; all that kept it from the Irish powder-mills was the willow-tree's tendency, in legend, to pull up its shallow roots and go walking in the night, following the lost traveller or the midnight reiver and wrapping him tight in its withies. When cut safely by day, the willow's and the alder's limbs and trunks were burned under a cover of ash or sand to keep them from the air; they had to sleep until, still bearing the likeness of the trees they had been, they had turned entirely to black carbon.

Next came sulfur, foul-smelling brimstone, plentiful in Hell but harder to acquire on earth: great jugs of water drawn from sulfurous springs was let to evaporate, leaving the crystal behind.

One element remained, rarest and most peculiar: saltpeter, niter. It accumulated, glittering palely, on the walls of caves; crystals of saltpeter flowered on the droppings of beasts, and in sewers too. Those who gathered it there (horrid trade) were employed by Crown contractors—saltpetermen, who came with warrants to scrape the walls of privies and stone barns and oversaw the boiling and refining of what they got.

The mills where gunpowder was made were built in a peculiar way: tall, thick stone walls and light, thin wooden roofs. If mishandled powder went off—which it did, commonly—the roof would be blown away but the building would stand. There were just such powder-mills now in the west of Ulster, in the Blue Stack mountains, where the English officials did not go, and in the Antrim hills. Those boys who'd learned to shoot with hunting guns given them by the Earl long ago had been taught how to make a low-grade powder from charcoal and sulfur and the saltpeter scraped from Ulster walls and styes—they were full masters of the art now, and trained up others. The soft smoke of the mountains that settled at evening in the glens did not all come from cottages and farms. The booms echoing in the valleys weren't the sound of dead heroes underground, playing at bowls.

But dank caves and smelly privies weren't enough: Hugh O'Neill needed the barrels of saltpeter that came by ship, in the long galleys of the pirate Gráinne O'Malley, negotiated for by Dom Pedro Blanco, purchased with O'Neill's silver, put aboard at Malta or Tripoli and hidden or disguised in the holds until the *Richard* or the *Moon* drew into a sheltered Donegal harbor or at Rathlin Island, where the goods were handed over to Pedro and his crew. Of gunpowder as of men, there was always a supply, always spent.

⁓

"This is Clontibret church, and the road from Newry. All this is Monaghan town. This is the strong fort, where the garrison is. The garrison has not been supplied in weeks. The English must relieve the fort or let their soldiers starve."

Three men—O'Neill, Maguire, Red Hugh—looked down on the map that O'Neill had spread before them, on which houses and hedges and a large church and the gates of the town were drawn and colored. Tiny soldiers in colored coats, horsemen with a forest of lances, an absurdly outsized cannon, laborers digging ditches. The Earl for a moment felt the vertigo that had come over him that day when he'd looked down like a flying bird on the earth shown in Doctor Dee's map in Mortlake.

Maguire, who like the Fox had become a fine cavalry leader without much interest in shot, had moved east from Enniskillen into Monaghan and taken Monaghan town. His war on the English and Bingham was his own: whatever he'd sworn before the Queen's officers and bishops he privately renounced, without saying so to the Earl of Tyrone or to Red Hugh O'Donnell, who hardly needed to be told.

O'Neill's *spiall* had made him aware that troops were being gathered at last to go out from Newry, under Sir Henry Bagenal, to relieve their desperate garrison. O'Neill could almost see them crossing the map in columns, the drums and the red jackets.

"Maguire riders out of Fermanagh can hold the garrison there easily," Maguire said, waving a hand at the map as though to brush away the fort. "Not more than three hours to reach it, once mounted."

"Why is it good to take the garrison?" Hugh O'Neill asked. "The English occupying the fort there are helpless, without provender, arms, powder, or shot."

"Because," said Red Hugh, "Dublin is on the march, the Marshal at its head. So *you* say, Uncle."

"And so it is. But not every quandary can be settled by men on horseback."

It was Maytime, the flowering trees were as though white with snow. Red goosefoot was appearing, "prostrate" as the gardeners say: low to the ground and spreading fast, as though leading the march toward Monaghan. When he had got near the town, Sir Henry Bagenal could see that forces of the Earl, his brother-in-law, were moving alongside his own troops, but at a distance. Just as the Irish shot and cavalry turned at a signal and came down upon him, Bagenal saw his sister's husband amid the Irish fighters, on a tall black horse, unmistakable in black graven armor.

In fact the Earl of Tyrone had not been at the fight for the Monaghan garrison. What the Marshal saw was another man, or no man at all but a vision, a shadow. The Earl that day was at home, spider at a web's center tugging at his spectral lines, some strong, others not so. Through the cold winter, alone at Dungannon, he had written his endless letters to the Council, to the Marshal, to the Queen's council in London; went early to the bed he'd shared with Mabel, hidden within the rich hangings, never warm enough; played chess against himself before the fire.

"Tell me that I am wrong to go out," he'd said to long-faced Pedro Blanco.

"I will not say your Lordship is wrong nor right," Dom Pedro said. "As to that, your heart and hand will tell you. I am here but to aid the both." His mournful countenance seemed to lay before the Earl all the promises he'd made over many years, to the Queen, to the Lord Marshal, to the council in Dublin. Could a man simply smash such things, as though they were clay pots badly thrown?

Out in the yard there was shouting, his own people hallooing. From the gate Hugh saw two young riders racing toward the castle, and when they came close they leapt off almost before the horses had ceased running. The people waiting there for the sun to rise pointed them to the gate, and took their lathered beasts to water and rest.

The English were assembling to depart with drums and trumpets next morning from the Monaghan garrison they had just retaken, the young men said. But look you, they are to go a different way back to Newry . . . Listening to them tumble over one another's speech it became clear to O'Neill that the English would take the old road that passed around the church at Clontibret. There was time, if O'Neill moved quickly, to line the Newry road on both sides with Irish shot and pikemen—a gantlet that the English would be forced to run. He sent Pedro Blanco to wake the O'Hagans sleeping in the yard; they must alert their fighters, assemble O'Neill adherents from every village and farm, see that they were armed and gathered at a place he named. The time was short, the prize real. He went to his armory, explaining to the two young messengers as he unlocked the doors that one of them must return to Monaghan, and tell Maguire and O'Donnell *this* and *this*, and here for them were banners showing the red hand of Ulster that no one would challenge. Now go!

The Ulster horse and shot were gathered and on the move before noon, and would be in Clontibret while the sun still stood high, even before the slow-moving English army reached that church. Hugh on his own best horse would set out soon. In the dim armory he had found the jack-of-plate that was sent him as a wedding gift by Sir Christopher Hatton, the Queen's "dancing chancellor"—not a man the Earl of Tyrone had expected a present from. It was a doublet of heavy canvas, within which were sewn overlapping steel plates, like the scales of a fish. As his hand reached for it on the wooden form that held it up, like a beheaded torso, he heard words spoken: *Will you don Sir Christopher's gift, and dance on my grave one day?* He paused, hand on this garment, as though warned, or mocked. His body servants, who had tracked their lord to the place, now took it from the frame themselves, and fitted it to him without a word. *We'll talk of graves,* Hugh replied in thought, *when this day's done.*

What amazed Sir Henry Bagenal as he rode by Clontibret church at the head of his soldiers wasn't the Irish forces hedging him in along the road, massed in good order as though by an English commander, but how many were wearing red coats. Red! The Queen's own color! For each troop, their horses lifting their heads and nodding in readiness, there was a banner: the red hand of Ulster. For a mad moment Sir Henry thought it possible that these red-jackets *were* a force of the Queen's, whether Irish or English, and ready to join him; then they stirred in masses, the shot raised their weapons, the pikemen came on following their pipers, the cavalry beat the earth, and the Marshal realized that he was hemmed in and had no retreat.

The fight went on as the sun sank. Hugh O'Neill, arriving late, took command, racing from one stand to another, urging, cursing, pressing fighters forward, calling them back. One brave English cornet, making out the Earl amid the smoke and the noise, spurred his horse into a run at him. Hugh turned to avoid the horse, and they both went down, grappling. The cornet, crying *Traitor, Traitor,* began stabbing and stabbing at Hugh's breast with a short sword, unable to draw blood. Two O'Cahan men ran to the Earl, crying out; they attacked the cornet and cut and wrenched off the arm he stabbed with, and Hugh O'Neill ran his knife into the man's groin.

As night came on the Earl withdrew his exhausted forces, and Bagenal was able to make camp. He hadn't seen the real Earl in the midst of the battle, nor the man in the black graven armor either. But he had seen an Irish force fighting in ordered ranks, at the command of officers, with seemingly limitless powder and shot. The Marshal was not a fool. He knew very well he had suffered a defeat there by Clontibret church, and he saw no reason why the same outcome might not occur again. In darkness his forces withdrew toward Newry, harried all along the way by flying squads of Irish fighters. When at last he returned home he found that while he was fighting at Clontibret his sister Mabel, Countess of Tyrone, had died. She had been dying since the day she arrived at this house in flight from her husband. Still and cold she lay now awaiting her brother, her hands wrapped in the glass beads of her rosary as in shackles, Niamh by her weeping without words. He dismissed the child, lay down by his sister in his filthy clothes and wept until at last he could sleep. For days and nights after, his lands around Newry town were burned by O'Neill raiders.

His Irish tenants dispersed, many of them running after O'Neill's captains and calling for weapons.

~

Beneath the jack-of-plate and shirt that his body-servants removed from him with care, stopping when he groaned aloud, Hugh O'Neill was badly bruised: the Englishman's sword-point had not broken the skin, but a mass of purple and black spread across his chest and stomach where it struck and hammered the steel plates against him. Almost too stiff to walk, he leaned upon his servants and was helped to his bed. He wouldn't allow them to put him in it, and sent them away. On the wall by the bed was one of the fine large mirrors that Mabel had bought, along with the other extravagances that he had rejoiced to see her enjoy. What he saw of himself in it now was so hideous that he laughed, and when he laughed he groaned in pain. He thought then of the lesser, or greater, mirror that he had never removed since Doctor Dee had first hung it around his neck. Had it got lost at Clontibret church? No, it was there, hiding in the hair of his battered breast.

And she was there in it. The black mirror was an infinite light-less hole, but he heard her speak. *You have crossed me in every way you could,* he heard her say, *and it has now lost you my good favor. You have cost me fortune upon fortune by your rebellious acts. I have dropped gold continuously on that island's earth like a stream of piss, and got me nothing but treason in return. You are stiff-necked, my lord Earl, and without good reason to be so. You must bend or you will break.*

How badly he wanted to speak to her, to tell her what her counselors and officials had done to him, to him and his family and his tenants and his allies, all the dead, the boys Red Hugh O'Donnell and Art O'Neill locked for years in Dublin prison for no crime, all of which she cared nothing for. Virgin and mother, she had never aided him except when it aided her; she had never heard him. He had sworn to Dublin, to the Council in London, to the Queen herself, that if he were made President of Ulster, he would serve her with all his heart and all his power, and keep her peace in the North. And she had spurned him coldly, gazing silent and motionless from the mirror like a great hooded serpent. She would not grant him a provincial presidency or any other position which would give him authority to govern Ulster. Whatever her Council offered was only a further demand: Hugh knew that before he asked, and before he asked again. In the tall silvered mirror on the wall, beyond the grotesque image of himself in pain, he saw a different face: the dim retreating face of Mabel, his Countess, in her satins and her coronet, and he knew that this day she was dead. With a sudden gesture he had thought he could never make, he took hold of the gold-chased stone and with one tug broke the chain. Crying aloud he flung the thing to the wall and heard its clatter, like a tiny cry in answer. He turned away, his heart racing.

The Earl of Tyrone had put away the Queen. There was nothing left to ask for, no one to obey. Pale Man and Dark Man must now become not two but one. All along the only true allies the single man had were the invisible ones he had known since childhood. He must put all his faith in them, and believe his faith was enough. It was all he had.

I am myself alone. Whatever came now, the O'Neill was out.

BLACKWATER

The Lieutenant-General of the Queen's army in that year was Thomas Butler, Earl of Ormond, the Queen's friend from childhood: Black Tom, whose hair and beard would by now be more silver than black, if he didn't dye it with care. No new Lord Deputy had been appointed. The army that Ormond had been given to bring to Ireland was a poor lot; he was almost ashamed to ride at its head, and sequestered most of it in Dundalk town when in July he went to meet Hugh O'Neill for a parley.

A parley! Everyone on both sides knew that parleys, dealings, letters sent and orders returned, month after month, were for Tyrone nothing but the twiddling of thumbs in wait for the Spanish to come again: awaited by the Irish who needed them desperately when war came, awaited by the English who feared and hated them. But the Council had insisted: one final chance for O'Neill to be brought to heel.

The meeting was at a brook, the water whispering and chuckling while the people on either side spoke. Ormond had brought Thomas Jones, the Anglican Bishop of Meath, the man who had married Hugh and Mabel. The Bishop had brought two secretaries, to write down what the parties said. Ormond and the Bishop first asked Hugh to give over his sons, Siobhan's boys, as hostages to the Crown: a safeguard, as the English saw it, against the wild impulses of the Irish.

"No," he said.

"But every gentleman in Ireland sends his sons out of this barbarous country," the Bishop averred mildly, "to be trained in civility, as you were—"

"You are wrong, Sir Bishop," Tyrone said. "You don't know the North at all. Civility! If my sons went out of the country to be trained up as Englishmen the people would despise them."

"I was not despised," Tom Butler said. His hearing was failing, and he could not follow all that was said. "When I came home I was received as what I was—"

"Mine would be treated as I was treated by Sir Henry Sidney,"

Hugh went on, ignoring Ormond. "When my father was killed, Turlough Luineach was made the O'Neill, and Sir Henry supported him against me. And Turlough was supported by every Lord Deputy thereafter *until the day he died.*"

No Englishman had ever heard Hugh O'Neill talk this way. Except to himself he had never spoken so to anyone. For a time no one spoke at all.

"I beg you, sir," Ormond said with a harsh gentleness, "that you remember Her Majesty's goodness to you. How she lifted you from the dust, gave you a pension, preserved you by her motherly care—"

Hugh felt a motion to put his hand to his breast, and pulled sharply at his reins instead. More fiercely than he had meant to—his nervous horse moving under him—he shouted at Ormond: "The Queen's motherly care! She never gave me anything but what belonged to me, which I got by my own scratching in the world, and not from her *goodness.*" He felt tears of rage fill his eyes, but he wouldn't stop, not for these men. "Haven't I spent my blood for her? Did I not keep my peace for thirty years? *Offer her my sons!* You shall get none of my sons."

Those sons stood by him, Siobhan's sons on their ponies, in slight armor: boys of twelve and thirteen, who had been fostered by the O'Hagans as O'Neill himself had been. The O'Hagans had brought the boys to Dungannon and to this meeting: *Let them learn.* On the hillocks not far behind Hugh, O'Hagan fighters stood patiently, lances erect. "And between me and God," the Earl said, "if these boys had been in your hands all this while as *pledges,* as *hostages,* I would have done just the same as I have done."

The Bishop leaned over to speak in Ormond's ear, then turned to O'Neill and took a few steps toward the brook that divided them. "Let us consider the matter more, and then meet again."

"No, no more *considering,*" O'Neill said, and turned his horse. "I have done with this day."

Toward Moon-rise Red Hugh arrived at Dungannon. He stood silent for a time, slapping one glove idly into the other gloved hand, watching the boys play chess: their father also watching, and sometimes instructing.

"The whole world talks of how you told truths to Tom Butler," Red Hugh said.

Without looking up, the Earl replied, "Your whole world is smaller than you suppose."

In a single motion Red Hugh drew a stool to the table and sat. Even such a small gesture showed the man's grace and certainty. Sir Fox. "Would you have me with you tomorrow, when you meet the Bishop and Tom Butler again?" Red Hugh asked. "I have a few thoughts I might express."

O'Neill laughed aloud at that, the first time he'd laughed in what seemed Moons. "Well then we will go, and *express our thoughts* to the mighty."

"You will be pre-eminent in this and in any meeting," Red Hugh said. "I will stand behind."

"I want no pre-eminence over you. But in the old way, walking or riding and travelling together, the elder should be on the right hand."

"Be on my right hand, Uncle," Red Hugh said smiling. "And together we will grant them nothing."

The second day's parley was no more successful than the first, and shorter; the presence of the young Lord of Tyrconnell, who'd smiled but said little, seemed threatening in some way Tom Butler couldn't assess. What he knew was that the parleying had failed to bring any useful agreements, and left him more certain than before that it was hopeless to treat with the Gael; they never said what they meant, and acted only on their own certainties. Next day he sat down at his Dublin desk with his pen and ink-pot to tell the Council in London what he knew, what the Earl had said, what he himself had argued for. Elizabeth's secretary of state, Lord Burghley, after scanning the Earl of Tyrone's new proposal for a presidency in Ulster, dismissed it all with a single word: *Ewtopia*. The Earl was in no position to re-make the world, bad as it surely was. Upon receipt of letters from the Bishop (*A traitor will always be a traitor*, he wrote) Burghley placed before the Queen the draft of a royal proclamation naming Hugh O'Neill a rebel and a supporter of treason, whose life any loyal subject of the Crown could take without fear of punishment, and in good expectation of reward. A fair copy was brought to her at evening, and she examined the stiff sheets for some minutes, as though for flaws; then she dipped a pen, signed with care, and pressed the royal seal into the warm red wax as into a face.

By then Tom Butler's ragged Dublin army was turning into a rabble: terrifying the citizens, selling their weapons for drink or food, which Tom Butler could not or would not supply. But he would have to march on O'Neill soon or he would have only fools in his train with nothing in their hands.

What had happened? How did men of England—poor men, granted, desperate it might be, ill-housed by necessity, but sons of English yeomen—run mad? What had caused it? It might, Butler thought, be the weather. But it was not the weather, bad as it was. Neither the Earl of Ormond nor his English officers knew anything of the presence of certain beings that cannot be perceived but who seem to be seen when they need to be.

Those waiting had brought them forth. Motionless themselves, dreaming in stillness their ancient dreams, they still must act, and could. They brought forth the *leipreachán*, to appear in the roads and in the taverns and even in soldiers' quarters, kindly ones not kindly at all: grinning trolls no larger than piglets or small children but ancient-appearing, wrinkled and brown, each one bearded like an old goat. Everyone knows how they incessantly cobble shoes, steal beer and drink it, hoard gold—but in truth they can do none of those things: cannot cobble, cannot drink, cannot steal or hoard. What they can do—what they do because they can't do the things they seem to do—is to lead the living astray. A man or woman might see just one *leipreachán* in a lifetime, yet that one can appear to be dozens when there is evil work to be done. The English soldiers and the Irish recruits went wandering after them, smelling gold, inveigled into bargaining for the pike or the caliver they had already sold for beer, losing their way, thinking that their trousers had been stolen, that they were drunk when they'd taken no drink, sickened on food they had not been given. Soon there was hardly a healthy Christian fighting-man in all of Dublin.

~~

Meantime O'Neill's crops were sown, his colts grown into war-horses; his powder-mills were busily washing and sieving, his pike-men practiced Spanish-style marching and wheeling under Pedro Blanco's tutorship. Someone, some being, had whispered into Ormond's ear that the way to take Tyrone was to establish a garrison on an island of Lough Foyle, the great lake at the far northwest point of Ulster; it opened to the North Channel and could be provisioned by sea. The miser-Queen considered and counted (*two thousand troops, with ships and provisions, to continue two years at the least*) and couldn't summon the will to consent.

Hugh O'Neill did not stay at home awaiting that decision, which he had been given notice of by friends at Dublin. He set out instead to besiege a new English fort built on the Blackwater River, well to the south—a dagger pointed at the heart of Ulster. When his fighters had surrounded it, sappers began to build out fortifications and embed sharpened sticks so that the garrison couldn't be resupplied. The Irish recruits within the fort—every English force had its component of kerne—prayed to the Virgin, begging that She deliver a message to Sir Henry Bagenal that would move him to march out and relieve them. And so She did—at least they thought She had when at twilight English redcoat scouts were seen racing to the fort. Yes, these scouts told them, yes, the Lord General Butler is coming, with a great force, with guns and mounted men, soon, perhaps in a week, perhaps by the feast of the Assumption of the Virgin in August. All would be well. And could they now have food and drink? And the starvelings of the fort could make no answer to them.

⁓

"There was a little tributary near that fort, that flowed into the Blackwater River," Hugh O'Neill said. "But I think you do not know that part of the North. There where your unseen See at Armagh is, and Saint Patrick's cathedral."

It was evening in the small walled garden of the Palazzo Salviati in Rome. Candles had been lit; a servant poured wine from a silver ewer into the two men's cups, and withdrew.

"What I know is in the accounts I was sent," said the Archbishop, who held a goose-quill lightly in his long fingers. "No doubt there is more for me to learn."

"Your pen is of no use now," O'Neill said gently. "Day is going."

"Tell me then," the Archbishop said.

The Earl drew a deep breath, as though quaffing memory. "The river Callan. To relieve the Blackwater fort—which was their aim and goal—they would have to cross it, and the crossing-place was called the Yellow Ford, for a discolored water that sometimes flowed there."

"Strange that such a queer *nomen* will live in fame," the Archbishop murmured.

"Beyond that river-bank there was a long line of hedgerows. The oncoming English couldn't see through or past the hedgerows, where I'd had pitfalls dug and covered over with wicker and grasses. Musketeers, as good as any the English could show, were hidden both before and beyond those pitfalls. Other traps were dug along the road and the line of march."

"What I know of the Irish in battle does not comport with all this forethought."

"Which is why so many battles were lost."

The Earl lifted his face to the sky above the garden. Blue satin, spangled with stars that seemed to him gracious. Was he proud of the battle at the ford, or was he a fool to be proud, seeing (as he did see now) what must come of it: the later battles that he could not win? But yes, he was proud. The sin of pride, so often harshly punished, was still in his own eyes a lesser one: he was proud of his pride. He had asked for forgiveness. The stars now proffered it. "It was the Feast of the Assumption of Our Lady into Heaven," he said softly. "That August day."

Marshal Sir Henry Bagenal was called by his captains "Henry of the Battle-axes" for reasons no one would care to remember later. They set out early from Dublin in six regiments, beating the Diana—the morning drum. Sir Henry rode in the van, where he'd have the best chance of seeing O'Neill and with luck taking him on single-handed. How he hated the man! On this morning Sir Henry was armed *cap-a-pie*, head to toe in shining steel, including a helm, breastplate and backplate, cuirass with faulds and tassets, gauntlets, vambraces, couters, and sabatons. His horse had armor as well: a shaffron for his face, and flanchards too for his sides. The Marshal had not, perhaps, considered how conspicuous he was, and not only to the armies of men.

"They brought up the sakers—the big cannon that oxen had dragged all the long way from Newry," Hugh told Peter in Rome. "But before they could be employed or even set and loaded with powder and ball, one after another the oxen were felled by our lances and our shot, or they fell into the mantraps and dragged the guns in after them. The Marshal seemingly couldn't bear to abandon those guns, and drovers and soldiers were put to pulling them out: bellowing oxen, shot soldiers screaming, the captains mad with fear and rage, and our skirmishers at them like wasps. I can hear it even now. Until then the Marshal, in the lead, didn't know that the rearward part of his army was being felled and dispersed in great numbers by Red Hugh's and Maguire's cavalries. They made an English retreat impossible when retreat was all that was left to them. The Irish soldiers among the English—there were many—threw down their weapons and just vanished into the earth, or so Red Hugh later told me, laughing. He was the only great fighter I ever knew who laughed in battle, winning or losing."

Late in that day an English captain broke through the hedgerows with his regiment. As he came into sight of the besieged fort he heard the faint shouts of men trapped on the ramparts, who could see what would happen: the musketeers that O'Neill had hidden in the trench rose up and began firing, as though they had materialized from the gunsmoke and the bodies. The pikemen, in the ordered ranks that Pedro Blanco had taught them, came in after the musketeers, pressing the English regiment all the way back down the road they had come up. As they struggled to get away from the pikes, some saw a wondrous thing: a length of fuse lay along the earth. The captain saw a man with a pot of fire rush up to the fuse and light it, then run away. He shouted a warning, and the press to escape became murderous; the fuse, sparking and crackling, reached the barrel of Ulster gunpowder hidden in the brush, which went off with a terrific noise, flinging bodies and parts of bodies for yards around.

Henry Bagenal had heard the explosion and now turned to see his terrified soldiery on the run from the device, in fear of another. What was it, what had happened? Bagenal lifted the gleaming visor of his helm to see better—to see anything, in the fog of powder smoke— and instantly a ball struck him in the forehead. He fell backward in a clatter of steel from his horse to the ground; the horse tried to run away through the mob, his flanchards flapping. The English retreat was so chaotic by then that the soldiers were unable even to drag the body of their general to shelter.

"It would never be learned who fired that shot," O'Neill said to Peter Lombard.

"If it *was* a shot. There are powers that can aim a certain sort of bolt more perfectly than any human gunner."

"So there are, Father. So there are."

Days after the battle, when all the remaining English soldiery were in O'Neill's hands, the Council in Dublin sent a letter saying that *since your great enemy Bagenal is dead*, might the remnant of their army be allowed to depart? Which O'Neill did allow.

"It was an odd thing, my friend, to be solicited in that way: as though I had made war on the Marshal, and not he on me. But I lost nothing by agreeing. The Lord of Tyrconnell and the other chiefs who had won the victory wanted to return home, gather the harvest now ripened in the fields; let the poor defeated English and their allies go, and a blessing go with them."

"Magnanimous in victory," Lombard said. "God and His angels knew your cause was right, and that your mind was unsullied by anger."

O'Neill acknowledged the remark with a lowering of his great head.

"But," the Archbishop said gently, "might you not in that moment of triumph have moved against Dublin, and in one fiery sword-swipe brought the—"

"Perhaps," the Earl said. "Many thought so. If I had been sure of all my allies, and sure of Spanish aid coming quick; if I hadn't believed that the mercy I extended then would be remembered when the time came that *I* must sue for mercy . . ."

Peter put his hand on Hugh's where it lay on the marble table.

They sat in silence then, in the flicker of the candles, both of them thinking of the days and years that followed after that singular, that unparalleled victory: years when despite the Masses said at Rome and Madrid and the prayers of multitudes, God had not seen fit to aid the O'Neill and the Irish lords. In the end came failure, and then further failure, as though going down Time's marble stair one broad step at a time, leading the Earl at last to the ship that departed from the coast of Ireland to bring him here to Rome and this darkening garden.

News of the great victory was given to King Philip II—the details whispered in his ear, his eyes almost closed, his body nearly motionless for days. Hugh O'Neill had fought and won, he was told, a singular event, never repeated, at a place called the Yellow Ford. Yet there is always a ford: men contesting which of them will cross, and which will not.

Soon after that singular battle, John Dee in Prague received notice, through the slow and painful processes of steganographia, that Philip of Spain was dead. The message, when drawn out of its thousand identical angelic letters in a dozen alphabets, was that a great victory of the Irish general at the Blackwater had given comfort to the dying man. The angel-courier who took away the King's last breath, which became words that she must carry, might have marveled at the task, if death meant much to such beings. John Dee thought it remarkable: that the running beast Tyrone was in the last thoughts of the Most Catholic King. Had he, John Dee, been wrong, in time past, to chain the Irish *dux* to the Queen by the arts he possessed?

SLUAGH SIDHE

UNDERTAKERS

*t*he laughter of those waiting in their hills and in their castles beneath deep lakes cannot be heard. But the O'Neill, listening to the stories told by the surrendered English captains gathered before him, wrists unbound after the battle at the Yellow Ford, he certainly heard. They told him how their soldiers and recruits had been played tricks by imaginary beings, or perhaps it was by devils, for devils are real enough—everyone knows. Who could fight when such foes had already sapped their faith and their courage?

Hugh O'Neill laughed to hear the tales. He knew what unseen persons the soldiers had perceived: those be-hatted and bearded ones, squat and sullen, holding out things of value that could not be grasped. He himself had had business with one, in the dawn of his life, at the Dungannon rath to which O'Mahon the bard had taken him: blind O'Mahon, who could yet tell young Hugh of the person that had come up from the earth.

What had been forced from the earthy man's hand on that evening was nothing, a chip of flint engraved as by a child who liked pretending. And here it was, it was in his own hand, voiceless yet seeming to speak, command, advise. He stroked its grained surface with his thumb. What it had done in the making of a victory at the Yellow Ford he couldn't know; he'd summoned no help by means of it, yet he believed that over the four parts of *Eirann*, North, South, East, and West, those who had chosen him had laid a net or a network, and it still held: from the North, courage in battle and in peace. From the West, learning and the repeating of histories, so that no great thing would be forgotten. From the East, hospitality and song, to praise both learning and courage, and to reward the kings who keep the world as it is. From the South, Munster, there came music, the coming-forth of good things from the earth, women of great power, deathless, beautiful.

Those four. Yet within Hugh O'Neill, and within everyone, there is another four, different and the same: Left, Right, Before, Behind.

And within each four there is still a fifth part, as great as the others: the name of that fifth part was the answer to the riddle that O'Mahon had set for him in that long ago time when he learned the names of the four great divisions of the land. Turn and turn about: the fifth part is not far nor is it near, not before, not behind, but *Here:* and that part keeps all the rest unchanged amid constant change: the one part that can't be departed from. Hugh O'Neill pressed to his heart the hand in which he held the stone of the *Sidhe,* command and promise, and whispered *Here.*

News of the amazing victory in the North flung out Old English lords and Irish clans of the South, sending them in raids through Connaught and Leinster, like a great sea-wave that washes boats, stones, dead fish, and driftwood up the strand by its power and then rakes it all back to the deep. After the Yellow Ford, whichever among the septs had been afraid of Thomas Butler, or Lord Marshal Bagenal, or the Queen on her throne, need be afraid no more. Fear was for the colonists: they were abandoning their houses, and their titles too, which were being reclaimed by families who'd owned them for three hundred years. By October, Tyrone's Ulster captains, with Red Hugh, Lord of Tyrconnell, and Hugh Maguire, Lord of Fermanagh, and a thousand mounted fighters, had crossed the line of low eskers where the land of Leith became the land of Mug.

"Uncle, will you not lead us?" says the Fox. He had asked once, twice, and got no answer but silence. As now, too.

"Let each lead those that follow each," says the Dog. "We'll need no chief of all."

O'Neill smiled upon the dark rider. His black hair, which when undone reached nearly to his waist, was twisted into a knot on the back of his long skull. His broad, wide-nostriled nose pointed south. "Would you, sir, follow me if I led?" he asked gently. "Be a dog nipping at my horse's hock? You are too proud a man for that."

Maguire looked from the Fox's smile to O'Neill's, uncertain whether he was teased or not.

"I am not too proud to be led," he said to O'Neill. "I will be a dog for you, my lord, at need. But I will not be your dog."

"Then you are off the leash, sir. Ride on." He gave his hand in friendship to Maguire and turned his horse to go, touching Red

Hugh's shoulder as he passed by him; then away, through the men and captains he'd brought this far.

They rode south with them, Fox and Dog.

⁓

And now the dead of Munster, those hanged or beheaded by the Lord Lieutenant Henry Sidney or by Sir John Perrot or another, the dead who had lain unburied winter and summer since the Desmonds had failed in their rebellions, rose from the bogs and the low places, the woods and the poisoned fields. They gathered themselves into an army, women and children among them, bearing on their spirits the wounds that English arms and English sheriffs had made. Some carried their heads, some their severed limbs, but unimpaired: a walking army unburdened by need, hunger, or thirst, turning upon the colonials and the local New English squires who had dispossessed them. Living fighters and their captains felt themselves pressed forward by the dead behind them; they couldn't be seen but they could be sensed, tireless numbers, always growing. The dead couldn't burn the houses, kill the landholders, but the armed men surely could and did; all the neat villages that old Warham St. Leger and Walter Raleigh had built up were put to the torch. The rumor of their coming on terrified all but the bravest, old Gael names spoken that the English undertakers of Irish lands knew well enough, names of the dead and of the living. They began to flee, leaving their stone houses, their family graves, their English bedsteads and leaded glass windows, their pots and pans. From county Kerry, from Waterford and Tipperary, they tried to make the ports where surely ships would arrive to take them off. The Anglican bishop of Cork fled his estates and barely made it alive to his fortified palace in Cork city. At Dublin the fare for a place on a ship to London had multiplied by ten.

Among the living Munster raiders, bearing actual steel weapons and guns, were the McSheehys of the Awbeg valley, where the poet Edmund Spenser had rebuilt a ruined castle and laid out gardens and farmlands. He had written a description of the abject and degraded Ireland he had come into, and a complementary vision of a new England that Munster could be: an allegory of peace, justice, love, and plenty. The clan McSheehy had long felt robbed by the English and above all by Mr. Spenser, taking what was theirs with his patents and royal grants; and when just before dawn they came out of the woods at the edge of the north pasture and attacked and fired the house, the poet had hardly time to flee with his wife and infant child. Clan McSheehy wanted no English house, only the land on which it sat, which was and always had been theirs and not Spenser's. And it was the McSheehy himself who drove him out, as the poet had foretold in his verses:

> *He, armed with blindness and with boldness stout,*
> *(For blind is bold) hath our fair light defaced;*
> *And gathering unto him a ragged rout*
> *Of Faunes and Satyrs hath our dwellings razed;*
> *And our chaste bowers, in which all virtue reigned*
> *With brutishness and beastly filth hath stained.*

Leaving their burning house, the Spensers made a night journey with a loyal servant, down the hard road and through a dark dream-wood; soon after he couldn't remember whether he had invented that wood, or if it had been invented by ghosts for him to suffer in. In London he took to a bed in a King Street inn, and as soon as his knights and ladies, fauns and satyrs, were safely in his publishers' hands he died of exhaustion, with their adventures nowhere near done.

Robert Devereux, the Earl of Essex, the richest nobleman in England, paid for Spenser's funeral and burial at Westminster Abbey, near to Geoffrey Chaucer. Something of a poet himself, and friend of Philip Sidney, Essex invited the poets and writers of the city to gather at the Abbey and toss into the open grave their messages in verse, their sonnets, their pens too, many weeping openly. Not only had the chief poet of the realm died in misery, but in misery caused by one single man, the Earl of Tyrone; nothing would wipe away the stain but his heart's blood on an English sword.

Tom Butler was recalled, having failed so completely as Lieutenant-General of the English army in Ireland. There was then only one person in England with the standing, and the Queen's approval, to end the Irish upheaval: the Earl of Essex. And the Earl wanted nothing more than to lay a great victory before her. *By God I will beat Tyrone in the field; for nothing worthy Her Majesty's honour hath yet been achieved*, he wrote to the Queen's Council. He recruited Charles Blount, Lord Mountjoy, with whom he'd once fought a duel for the Queen's favor. "It was fit that someone or other should take him down, and teach him better manners," the Queen had said of Mountjoy in the hearing of the Court. Like Spenser's noble knights, the two had since made up, and become fast friends.

The old men of the Court warned them: Beware the Irish promise; it lasts as long as it is needed and then is tossed away. Beware the tears of reivers and captains: they weep like dark clouds, without sense. Beware their praise; ignore their curse. My lords: Beware the weather. *Beware the weather?* What did they think of them, Essex and Mountjoy, English knights? That they would flee a rainstorm or a wind, like a maiden? He had stood out in all weathers, sword in hand, in the Netherlands; he'd led the cavalry at Zutphen where Philip Sidney died—and where he, Robert, *at the age of eighteen*, was knighted. Hardship held no terrors for him. He knew what he must do: as soon as his force was on Irish ground and Lord Mountjoy in charge of them, he would immediately make an expedition into Ulster and find and take on the Earl of Tyrone: English soldiery against a mob of kerne. Bring him in caged, to answer for his insults and his crimes. Or his head alone, if it came to that. There would be no factitious truce, no waste of time, of men, of talk. It was the only course: on paper, and in his mind, it had already been accomplished.

As this scheme was taking shape, a council of war was called at Dublin Castle that included Lord Mountjoy and a cluster of knights, some Irish strivers, and the graybeard Lords Justices, including Archbishop Jones. The Council could not agree to the Earl's plan, which Mountjoy had put before them in expectation of the Earl of Essex's arrival. It was too risky, the Council argued; the gains promised did not warrant it and the likely losses were clear. The general opinion was that Essex should go into the South, and there win over or defeat the clans that were O'Neill's supports.

Having arrived and heard from Mountjoy what the Council opined, Essex on the following morning came through the chamber door, sublime in black and silver, thanked the members, and announced that he would set aside their opinion. He withdrew Mountjoy from the Council, and forewent an invitation to discuss his plans further. It was Tyrone he wanted. Yet within a week he had agreed to go into the South with a large force, cannon, cavalry, victuals, and all. He would first kick out the props beneath the Earl of Tyrone, and, at a later time, meet Tyrone on the field, he and the rebel.

Why had he chosen to accede to the Council? It was hard for him to explain it to himself. The strangeness of Ireland perhaps, and the little he knew of it, which he did not admit. The softness of the weather, making everything unreal. The clinging mist, which could feel like ghost fingers touching his face. The darkness of the nights, total beyond the city bounds.

The English colonials who had hung on in Connaught and Munster came creeping out of their walled towns and half-burnt farmhouses to greet their savior and cheer him on as he passed on his tour. Old English magnates welcomed him, a force for peace and justice, protection for their holdings, or for their safe evacuation at the least. Gloved hand shook mailed hand: all would be well. What the Earl did *not* do there was to engage an enemy. None appeared; there was little Essex could send as news to London. By now the mists had become wearying winter rains, and even when glimpsed, or their tracks discovered, the enemy could not be found or fought. Once, in rain at evening, a troop surprised an Irish camp and overran it, slaying some twenty black sheep that had seemed to be fighters sleeping in their mantles. By Christmas Essex was feverish, sick. *The weather.* He returned his army to Dublin, and took to his bed. He would not reprove himself for it, but under the combined influences of casualties, desertions, disease, and the garrisoning of distant outposts, his army was melting away, and he had somehow accomplished nothing. The Queen discarded his missives.

Summer and the returning sun revived him. His first plan had all along been the only possible one: take O'Neill in a swift, brilliant assault. The Dublin Council may go hang; he would do as his Monarch had commanded. He wrote a fine letter—a last letter, it might be—to the Queen: *Since my services past deserve no more than banishment and proscription into the most cursed of all countries, with what expectation and what end shall I live longer?* Then, with a picked fighting force rich in young knights that he had made by his own sword, he went

out into a gold and green June, a noble knight like Spenser's, prick-
ing on the plain. Unseen, O'Hagan and O'Cahan scouts followed
him along the ways through the woods between Dundalk and Louth
Castle, sending runners to O'Neill, returning with his orders: on no
account may they attack or interfere with the Lord Deputy's force.
Essex called a halt at the castle grounds, where he was approached
by a man on foot, hatless, unarmed, signaling for a word with him,
as though they were acquainted. Essex kept to his horse, hand on his
sword.

"A parley," the fellow said to him. "The Earl of Tyrone invites you.
He lies not far from here, where there is a ford called Bellaclynthe."

There is always a ford.

Essex, unsettled by the fellow's boldness, thought to ride away
without a word, but halted and looked down on him. "Queen's officers do not *agree* to parleys," he said. "They *call for* them."

The fellow seemed unabashed. He nodded as though to show he
understood, and then he said, "Your Irish cohort here can surely
bring you to that ford in a matter of two hours. A branch of the river
Dee."

Essex was caught between doubt and possibility. "If this be not
what you say, but some entrapment," he said, "your head will pay
for it."

The fellow bowed, as though pleased to be addressed in this way,
and then he turned and was gone as though he hadn't been there at
all, and the woods gathered again around the Earl. He summoned
his Irish captain. "The Dee," he said. "A ford, Bellaclynthe."

~

"My lord of Essex," O'Neill called from the farther bank, taking
the hat from his head. "I have come alone and unarmed before you."

For a long breath Essex simply stared at him. This was he, the
running beast. It seemed possible—easy—to leap the stream that
ran between them, climb the far bank, and put the Irishman to the
sword. "What is it you want of me?"

"I wish, firstly," O'Neill said, "that you might intercede for me
with the Queen, for her mercy to me. My honor and my name have
been blackened, and my credit with the Queen whom I have served
and honored stolen away."

"I have no such power," Essex said.

As though he'd had an answer, O'Neill rode into the shallow river; at midstream he waved to Essex to join him there. Essex looked around at the nervous horses and men of his regiment; they sensed something, but Essex didn't believe it was treachery; he didn't know what it was. Lifting his hand to stop anyone following him, he guided his horse through the reeds and into the water. O'Neill turned upstream, already talking, and Essex could only follow.

"I know that Sir Philip Sidney was your friend," O'Neill said smiling. "He was my friend too."

"I was near him in the battle when he died fighting."

O'Neill nodded solemnly, as though he'd been there as well. "We were boys together at Penshurst. See there ahead? That little island. Let us go onto it and rest in the shade of those trees."

Essex paused, knowing he was entirely alone; but now he had no honorable choice but to follow; he was armed, he saw no reason to fear. They went up onto the islet, their horses shedding water, stepping through the rooty bank with care. A wide flat stone like a table, supported by other stones, filled almost all the open ground at the islet's center; and around it, as though conferring, was a group of children or small persons, silvery-pale, wavering, insubstantial. He heard laughter, and at that the children slid into the water all together, like startled frogs at a lily-pond.

"Will you dismount?" he heard the Earl of Tyrone say. He had almost forgotten that the man was here with him; he was at the table, sitting calmly on a stone seat. On the table was a jug and cups. So the children were most likely just servants, preparing a refreshment . . . He dismounted and took the seat opposite O'Neill. A cloud covered the sun, and passed.

~

How long they sat together was afterward unclear to the Earl of Essex, but he remembered day going; he remembered the insistent argufying that the Irishman wouldn't cease. He wanted Essex, Essex himself, to bring his appeal again to the Queen, make the Irish case to her. He rambled, seemed at times near tears. And all of it was surely falsity and ill-dealing.

But if that were true, he would later think, how could it have changed him so?

"Why," he said sharply, "do you suppose I would intercede for you with Her Majesty? You are her enemy, a rebel to her wishes and commands. You have her hate, not her love."

"There was a time when she spoke to me with kindness, with approbation. Motherly care." He paused, blinked away tears, displayed his honest open hands. "My lord, you and she are two stars: one in the ascendant, one in decline. Your fortune rises and hers cannot."

"You are a soothsayer as well as a fighter," Essex said. "All Irish are so, as I have learned."

"Then I will tell you what I see," O'Neill said, suddenly firm. "The Queen is no divinity. She is only an old woman, a woman who is as though encased in a younger woman, with her dresses and her whitened face and her wigs."

Essex half-rose from his seat, hand on his sword-hilt, hearing a titter from nowhere. "Beware, sir," Essex said. "You may not speak to me of our Queen in that way."

"You know it to be so. It's what any witch or sorceress does, puts on beauty to beguile a man before taking possession of him. And the way to avoid possession? It's only this: Take possession yourself."

Why, Essex wondered, does he turn and turn that stone shard in his fingers?

"She is inflamed by your youth and strength, your honor, your sword," O'Neill said. "Bring home to her a peace we together have made, lay it before her, and prove to her that *you*, my lord, are what she once was and can no longer be: peacemaker, subtle as the serpent, a wise old fox, unafraid and yet so very cautious."

"Too cautious. She wants peace and yet she wishes for victory."

"She wants what you want: that you should take up her burdens, and she be allowed to rest, with every honor and all praise. Don't you see?"

A sudden flash of heat went through the Earl of Essex's body. For a moment he couldn't see, and then could again. The white transparent children were once more around the islet; he saw them, thought he again heard laughter infinitely small. He didn't see one boy who held, sheltered in his two hands, a sort of golden fly— O'Neill glimpsed it, just as the pale hands released it. Then it was all as before: two men at a stone table on a river island, where green rushes grew.

"My lord," Hugh O'Neill said softly, as though to wake the Earl's attention. "My lord, I wish to propose a truce, to extend from this day six weeks, renewed upon both our agreement, as often as needed."

Essex hardly heard this. He looked around himself, to east and west, not knowing what he sought, not seeing it. "Very well," he said.

⁓

As though truly she was a witch, able to transform herself into fire, the Queen raged against her Lord Deputy to the court and in her private chamber. She wrote in fury, at first in her mind and then to a secretary sent for in haste. What could they be doing on that island of lies? She could not and would not bear being lied to. "If sickness of the army be the reason, why was not the action undertaken when the army was in better state?" she said, and the secretary wrote it in his scribble hand. "If winter's approach, why were the summer months of July and August lost? We must conclude that none of the four quarters of the year will be in season for you and that Council to agree to Tyrone's prosecution, for which all our charge is intended." The Queen paused then in her dictation, her secretary pausing too, pen in mid-air. She folded her long hands with deliberation and laid them in her lap. When she spoke again, eyes raised to the distance, she spoke without anger to one not present: "We require you to con- sider whether we have not great cause to think that your purpose is *not* to end the war." She held out her hand for the sheet and in her own hand she subscribed this: *Her right noble and beloved cousin is not to leave Ireland until Tyrone has been attacked and captured or killed.*

When Essex had left England—not in a rush of banners, drums, blown horns, but in pouring rain from Welsh ports—no one, not even himself, had expected glory. The Queen had agreed to send him, but not in any certainty he would do what others hadn't been able to do. She loved him, in her cold and yearning heart; she wanted him not to die. She wanted him by her, but she wanted much more that her Irish isle cease to roil and stir. She wished it to be at peace, and also prayed that it might be humbled. She wanted it to sink beneath the sea. She prayed for Essex too, every day, and didn't know that while she was at her prayers on a morning in 1599, her commandment still making its way to him, he had quit Ireland accompanied by his closest supporters and friends, and was on his way home with intentions he could not have explained to her or to anyone.

For weeks he had felt that something was eating his brain, and that only if he came home again would it cease; it was a thing close behind him that walked where he walked, stood where he stood, and he often flung his head to the right or left to catch the thing, but it was not to be seen. He never spoke to his council or his company of this Irish disease he had acquired, yet they knew he was in some way possessed. He could conceive only one cure: to kneel before the Queen and throw his wretched soul before her and beg her pardon, without hope or expectation. When he talked that way aboard the ship to England, Charles Blount, Lord Mountjoy, gripped his arm and stared into his eyes, mouth drawn, until Essex righted himself. The Queen is no longer a power, Charles Blount told him; she has lived on past her time, her counselors are flatterers and old men, there is no other course but to . . . *No!* Essex would not hear the words, no matter that he'd said them again and again in his own buzzing head.

The knights disembarked at London and dispersed into the city; Essex crossed the river and made for Nonesuch, the palace where he knew he would find the Queen. He was no longer thinking of a coup; he simply needed to see her, be in her presence, be cured by her royal touch of what had seized him. Feeling as much pursued as in pursuit, he mounted the stairs, flung open the doors, and walked in, fluttering the ladies-in-waiting like a hawk in a dovecote, and there she sat: on a stool. Her face unmade, her hair her own—white, wispy, a grandam's—but he saw nothing of that. It was she.

She did nothing foolish. He might have come to kill her—he looked as though he might—but she was unafraid. She only told him to go and change his filthy clothes, wash, and come back to her. When he returned she was herself again—the person she had made of herself. Though they chatted into the night in the old way, nothing in the old way would stand now. What would become of him would take months of letters, comings and goings, pleadings and submissions and rages, the passage of lords and counselors. Winter came and a new year, and still the Queen had made no decision.

Was it odd that stories were told in that day that the Earl of Tyrone had all along been in league with the Earl of Essex? Tyrone had known the Earl's father, Walter Devereux, and had even gone raiding with him in the North when he was young and witless. Folk talked in the North that Essex might become King of Ireland, and who else could have started such a rumor as that? If it had been reported in England it would have brought the man to his end all the more swiftly.

"Yet did you not," Peter Lombard asked Hugh in Rome, "write to the rector of the Irish College in Salamanca that Essex was soon to turn Catholic, abandon his Queen, and make *you* King of Ireland, with Spanish aid?"

"We understood each other, Essex and I," Tyrone said, smiling.

In the second month of the new year, four senior sharers in the Lord Chamberlain's company of players were gathered toward evening by the sea-coal fire at a Southwark inn: John Heminges, Augustin Phillips, Tom Pope, Will Kempe. The day was raw, February icy air; a fireside the place to be. They had been approached that day by an adherent of the Earl of Essex, Sir Gilly Merrick; he'd crossed the river to Southwark with an offer for the players: thirty shillings if they would play the play of King Richard the Second. It was obvious why the Essex faction wanted the play to be played, and Sir Gilly made it clear: the City and the people should see that at least once in history an anointed sovereign had been unseated.

Well, the players told him, the play was an old one, and they would lose money on it, and it hadn't been much liked when it was new. *Forty* shillings, Sir Gilly said, a huge sum; and—though they were only a plurality of the sharers—they agreed. Now though, when noises of horsemen and cries and shouting in the street reached them, they were unsure. What might become of themselves if they offered the play and thereupon the mad Earl went down? And they were implicated? No one spoke of it aloud, but each one thought it; the thought was a slight grip to the throat: that sort of thought.

"I'd suppose our John Factotum could with little notice make a play that would suit as well, and yet be new."

"No, no, not so: our Poet he is, and not a play-carpenter. Plenty of those, yes. Our Will's not that."

"The whole play played?"

"Sir Gilly said nothing about selecting parts to play. But the whole'd be clumbersome to do."

"Clumbersome!" said Will Kempe. "A dog of a word, sir."

"I do remember me," said Heminges, "that the old Earl of Essex walked with a clumber spaniel of evil temper. Perhaps a wicked spirit."

"To the point. What they'd like are the scenes where Henry Bolingbroke returns from Ireland with his army, and Richard gives up the throne."

"*Here, cousin*—seize *the crown*." Will Kempe, holding out an imaginary crown with a slack hand. Just the way Burbage had done it.

"But it isn't Henry in the play who returns from Ireland," Augustin said. "It's *Richard*. Which seems inapt."

"It's an ill day for playing," Tom Pope said, looking out into the fog. "Few seats filled, over in an hour, lights put out."

"And all for an old historical."

"I call that play a tragedy."

"Tragical historical then. Like the one this day may well bring. And we playing our parts."

~⁓~

All the next day from dawn onward the Earl's friends and armed supporters gathered at Essex House on the Strand to which the Earl had repaired, ready to support whatever he determined to do, so long as he would lead them. What did he want? They had to know. Did he mean to attack the Court, denounce the royal council, take possession of the Queen's body? Should they raise the city, the citizens who had cheered and tossed their hats in the air when he went out to conquer? He'd lead them to Whitehall and overawe the court, he said; but then instead he led them out to walk to the city along the Strand, having no way to get horses. They poured into the city by Lud Gate, but the city sheriffs, constables and churchwardens had already been ordered to keep the Cheapside citizens within doors, and the citizens obeyed. The Earl might be their hero, but the Queen was their queen. At Greyfriars, the theater where in winter the Lord Chamberlain's troupe played indoors to gentlemen, the old play of Richard II tumbled across the boards until the Provost Marshal's officers appeared and shut it down, and the players disappeared for the day.

The gate that Essex and his companions entered the city by was now chained shut by Court officials. He had to walk down to the river, to be rowed back to Essex House, followed by a faint chatter of sweet voices he could not interpret; at his water-stairs he heard tiny laughter from behind his left ear; he felt a needle's prick whose source he no longer sought for.

He would barricade his house, he decided, fight to the last, and called for his servants. But it was too late; the Lord Admiral had now arrived with a large force. From his windows he saw artillery brought up; he marveled at that, thinking for an instant that he was in Ireland, reducing a rebel castle; then he knew he wasn't. He drew himself up, and with a sign (he found it difficult to speak, with all the voices murmuring in his ears) he had the servants unbar the door. He stood in the doorway mocked, bewildered, trembling, and bathed in sweat—the Lord Admiral had expected defiance, or hauteur at the least. At the Admiral's gentle request he surrendered the sword he had drawn, and was taken to the Tower. The Queen once, and then again, postponed the thing she must do, and then at last let go. His execution was set for late in February.

The trial, the sentence, the appeals, and the execution were all past, and Essex's head and body had been laid in the Tower Yard church of St. Peter ad Vincula alongside the other noble dead at rest there. The Queen's mother, Ann Boleyn, who'd also been beheaded for treason, had whispered a welcome to the newcomer.

When Essex's gadfly at length ceased its hovering over his sealed tomb and returned to where it had been born or made; when Charles Blount, Lord Mountjoy, had gone into Ireland as Lord Deputy at Her Majesty's command, having finessed his own part in the coup; when the Spanish were on the sea again and the Irish and Ireland still unquiet, a royal archivist brought to Queen Elizabeth a summary of certain historical documents stored in the Tower of London. She read the summaries of the reign of good Henry III, the horrid death of Edward II. She stopped then at the reign of Richard II, and studied it. When the archivist asked why, she said, "I am Richard II, know ye not that?" And for a time she said no more.

MIDWINTER

I have dreamed a strange dream, my lord," Red Hugh said. "I will relate it to you."

"You may do so, but expect no interpretations."

Red Hugh sat down on his uncle's bed. "This was the dream," he said. "I was in a foreign court, rich, vast. Crowds of courtiers and officers in fine clothing; windows of colored glass, figures of saints and kings. What court I couldn't tell, but when I was spoken to it was in Irish; they all spoke in Irish to me, and priests blessed me in Latin, and a bishop placed his hand on my head."

"You dreamed of being in waiting for a crown."

"Not so. I had no idea why I was there except to win help for us."

"Then it was Spain."

"Perhaps. But then, Uncle, a steward or butler of some sort poured wine into a silver cup and gave it to me. Everyone stood very still as I drank. And then the round-dance of these figures began again. And I began to feel ill. Gripings in my gut that woke me."

"I can explain *that*. You were poisoned. Common in those parts."

"Well so I was, and I hardly got to the privy in time."

"I do not dream," Hugh O'Neill said. "Your sister Siobhan said I lay like the dead. I awake to the day without any memories, or memories of nothing."

"Then you can't tell me the meaning of my dream."

"I can tell no one the meaning of a dream, but I think that yours was given you by an imp or a night-mare bestriding you, and that you should discard the memory of it like a used bed-rag."

O'Neill's son Hugh, tall and thin and unlike his father, laughed in glee.

"Very well," Red Hugh said. "But if one day you come to have news of me abroad in some foreign court from which I can never return, remember my telling you of this."

"I have forgotten it already. Let's talk of daylight things—there is enough to do." He stood, and called—bells and bell-ropes had not been installed at Dungannon—for Pedro Blanco. Called again, and louder. There was a sound of activity in the hall, servants calling the man. Then he appeared, tall, thin, solemn of face.

"Dom Pedro," he said, bringing him forward with a hand. "Would you tell my lord of Tyrconnell the news you've gathered from Spain and the Portingales?"

"Ships have departed from Lisboa," Pedro said. "My information is, they each carry four thousands of soldiers. Some are men of the Azores, like myself, others from over the *Imperio Español*, from the Americas to the Diocese of Macao."

"Cavalry?" Red Hugh asked—he would command it.

"Sir," Pedro said, "the great ships are few, that would carry horses. But," he said raising a long finger, "I am informed they carry above a thousand saddles."

"They'll get horses in Munster," O'Neill said. "They'll be given them, gratefully." A small silence fell. Perhaps those around him (Pedro, Red Hugh, the Earl's own son) were not as sure as the Earl; the Earl was less sure than he seemed, looking from face to face. "However that may be," he said, "what's before us is a worse thing than that." He held out his hand for Pedro's papers, and the copies of his own missives.

He'd pled with the King of Spain's officers, he had written and written again: that if the promised troops numbered six thousand or more, they should be disembarked at a southern port, Cork or Waterford; they could be supplied by sea, the ships could hold the harbor against attack, and the disaffected Munster lords would surely join them. If, though, they were not more than four thousand, Limerick: the town could sustain no more. Only if the force was small—and he prayed it was not small—it should it go to a port in the West, Killybegs or Teelin on Donegal Bay for a preference. But what the Spanish captains had at length decided (Pedro translating the dispatches carried in on fast *petaches*) was to land at the little port town of Kinsale, down near the southernmost point in the island—the port that in O'Neill's opinion was the last of all the Irish ports, in the South, the West, the North, to settle on. It was as far from him and from the Fox and the Dog as the Ulster forces could be. But there would be no dissuading them, for the ships great and small were reaching the port even as the dispatches were being sent. Kinsale was three hundred miles from Dungannon. Winter was coming. The English forces would prey on him like following wolves as he went south to join the Spanish, they and the Irish allies of the English. Red Hugh, desperate to move, begged his uncle every day to send riders to all the allies, call them in, set out.

The Earl of Tyrone chose not. He knew what would happen next. English forces now at Dublin would soon move south, and lay siege to Kinsale town before the winter rains set in. The Spanish, with all their supplies and arms, could hold their own against even a long siege. The Earl could take the risk of leaving Don Juan Del Águila and his cannon and his bishops and his *tercios* bottled up there until spring. It was they, after all, who had picked the place.

All that year the new Lord Deputy, Charles Blount, Lord Mountjoy, who had been sent to Ireland as punishment (so he believed) for having been a friend and a supporter of the Earl of Essex, had bent his mind and his forces to confining the great Irish rebels, the Earl of Tyrone and the Lord of Tyrconnell. He built a circle of forts to keep Tyrone in the North, in a land of few resources, out of reach of allies. He had known—all the world had known—that the Spanish would in time come again to Ireland, and by establishing themselves on the island, have world and time enough to try England once more; and a southern port would be most useful to them. Mountjoy supposed that if the ships did not make landfall in the North to join the rebels, then it would be the great ports of Cork or Waterford. But little Kinsale was after all perfect: he felt he could grasp it in his right hand.

The first Spanish ships came into Kinsale harbor on the twenty-first of September, feast-day of St. Matthew the Evangelist. Don Juan Del Águila entered Kinsale town two days later, and the English garrison there fled away into the woods and fields beyond the town.

With Mountjoy and most of his army now in the South, the Earl of Tyrone, leaving his son to be Lord of Dungannon, took his kerne with their javelins and gallowglass with their swords and axes, and broke out of the ring of English fortresses that hemmed him in. Once out he went to war, taking great preys of cattle, burning the corn of the settlers and sending them into Dublin city for protection. Mountjoy wrote to the Queen that the affrighted settlers deserved no protection from the Crown: *They would not stir, nor raise the crie, but suffer themselves to be used, out of the malice of their own hearts, being the worst sort of people in all the kingdome.*

Pedro Blanco went into the Antrim highlands and sought out whoever remained there of those men who had been rescued from the Spanish ships broken on the Galway coast, sailors and soldiers who'd forgot all their martial arts, which he'd knock into them again. By October, when Hugh O'Neill turned his four thousand fighters and his wagons and his head of cattle to the South, Mountjoy had set his siege of Kinsale in place. As in a London play of kings and commoners, all that had gone before, scene upon scene, had placed the players in certain relations with certain actions to take, and they must take them, until all is accomplished and the last grave player steps forward and speaks the epilogue.

⌒

At the end of November the Spanish forces were still bottled up in Kinsale town; Spanish caliver-men and musketeers raked the English from the castle ramparts when they attempted to overwhelm the foreigners. When Mountjoy sent a Trumpet to demand surrender, the Spanish sent a messenger out to say that Don Juan Del Águila held the town for the King of Spain and for the Lord Jesus Christ, and would defend it *contra todos,* and all the while Spanish soldiers on the ramparts hurled taunts and obscenities at the English party. Mountjoy was sufficiently roused to bombard the eastern gate of the city nightlong. It came near to falling, and would have, but that Spanish engineers worked through the rainy night to repair and strengthen it.

Where was O'Neill? Red Hugh, and his riders? No word had come from the Earl. Don Juan Del Águila, desperate to get some clear measure of success, challenged Mountjoy to single combat. Mountjoy replied politely that, as he'd heard, the Council of Trent had forbidden such duels to Catholics. But Mountjoy's men were deserting in numbers; he had a week's rations in hand, no more; the wind was blowing in the wrong quarter and he couldn't be resupplied by sea, the roads were too dangerous, Tyrone possessed them. Where *was* the man? When would he strike?

In truth he wasn't far. After the great ride through the South to the sea, the hooves of his horses shaking the earth and the cots of the poor, he'd paused, hidden in Coolcarron Wood, just a few miles from Kinsale. Red Hugh and his riders were swarming through the wood, gathering to charge. O'Neill waited. His mere presence in the neighborhood with an army of thousands was enough to cause Mountjoy to draw in as soon as word of O'Neill came in. For the Lord Deputy was in bad case: spies had told O'Neill that famine and exposure were withering his army.

He waited. This would be the last battle of this age of the world, and he knew it; no one had told him or made it plain to him that from this day, from the morning after this night, up would be down, wrong right, high low. It was as though he held in his hands the leashes of great black dogs rearing to be released, and he could release them, and others would join the hunt, others who couldn't be named. Until that time—until that star had risen, until there was nothing else at all to do but cry havoc—he would wait. He could wait.

For years afterward he'd be condemned, his hesitation would be called the reason that all was lost, that his divided mind could not decide to come down on the English. Águila begged in a letter to O'Neill and Red Hugh that they come in, come in now. But Hugh O'Neill, then and in all those after-years, knew the reason he kept still, and it wasn't any reason that any friend or enemy ever named. The reason was that chip of flint that lay in his pocket, moved from garment to garment for forty years. Either he would have aid insurmountable by the English or he would not.

It was the night of the winter solstice, *mean Geimhreadh*, midwinter: yet a summer storm seemed to have rolled in from the north. A sharp wind rose. The last of day illuminated clouds black as furred beasts leaping in play. All around the Earl, Red Hugh's men readied themselves and their mounts to ride down on the English encampment two miles away. The Earl sought Red Hugh among the riders, laid a hand on his shoulder; Red Hugh turned, and saw in his uncle's face what he needed to know. "We'll lead," he cried against the crashing of thunder. "Follow as close as you can."

O'Neill watched them stream away like ghosts, whitened by sudden lightning. He called for the captains of the Munstermen and the Ulstermen who had joined his army with their fighters, joined it for all sorts of reasons. He watched, holding back his own fearful horse, raising a hand to keep them from moving. Scouts had returned:

a mass of soldiers and horse was seen moving toward them, banners unreadable in the dark: Mountjoy, at last out. The black clouds fought the white as though to see which would reach the battle first.

They were not clouds, though: not made of air. O'Neill knew it and his heart leapt. He took the flint from the glove on his left hand where he had hidden it. As though the pages of a book fluttered rapidly together through his fingers, he remembered the night on which he got the stone; he saw, however altered by time, the ghostly prince who had ordered it to be given to him; he saw the pale troop coalescing out of the rath the day the bard O'Mahon was put into Lough Neagh. He felt the awful cold in the stone the *leipreachán* had given him, a power that now ran through his hand and through the bones of his wrist and arm, and like a priest lifting the consecrated Host at Mass he lifted the stone in his bare right hand. Without spoken words he called to them. He demanded of them, in the name of their Isle, in the name of the sons of Mil, of the Tuatha De Danann, the *Sidhe,* whatever the name: if they did not gather now, here, then all would be lost and they too would fail.

And they came.

From Cruachain, city of the plains, Maeve's dwelling; from Emain Macha of the Ulaid kings, from Dun Ailline, Tullahogue, and Tara, from Newgrange where always the midwinter sun sought within to wake the sleepers; from sepulchers and holy hills large and small, from their feasting and their fighting, rising up into the middle of the air, the Underfolk were out, knowing that they had been called, and answering.

There was a transformation of the rain and the night above Kinsale: from the gray East a roiling cloud pressed through, rushing toward this battlefield, brighter than the thunderheads. The *Sidhe* were borne in it, riders on skeletal horses, figures male and female with hair streaming and weapons held aloft. The Irish kerne serving in the English army, their white faces upturned to the sky amid dark English heads doggedly pushing forward, cried out in fear and mad elation: they knew what they saw. Hugh O'Neill scanned the sky, watched the cloud-borne beings grow larger and more numerous, the Wild Hunt that the blind poet O'Mahon believed could be summoned by song. And now he could see their bronze axes and flashing shields, their horses' iron anklets bristling. Their mouths were open, screaming, a sound like wind trapped in mountain caves.

They turned in air, rising and falling, nearing the earth and turning away again.

Strike, Hugh cried in his heart, *strike! Come down on them, the false powers, the foreign ones, the stony hearts! Defend us who live under the sky, as it was promised long ago in the division of the lands, as you swore you would!*

The swirl of beings intensified, seeming to bear a light of its own; the figures transmuted, female to male to beast to god. The wind blew them and they mounted higher and again descended. But they could not come to earth.

They could not.

They could terrify the few among the enemy that could perceive them, and those few would always remember, and always fear their return. But they could harm no one. Hugh, staring upward into the ceaseless wind, understood: they had no true strength, no power. Their weapons were smoke, their battle-cries were silence. The Hunt had already begun to tatter with the gray dawn, horses and warriors losing their shapes, turning to nothing.

Nothing was what they were, all that they had ever been.

The Irish army was turning now, fleeing away from the oncoming English, their pikes forward, black heads down, musket fire sparking. They fled, discarding weapons as they went, trampling over the dead and the living who had fallen. The battle broke. It had all taken an hour and part of another; no more.

Nothing. Hugh had held the shard of flint so tightly in his hand that his palm bled. All that he could do now was to help his fighters get away, return home; he could learn nothing of what had become of Red Hugh, nothing of Don Juan Del Águila and the Spanish force. It was over. The rain was ceasing, and stripes of blood-color were in the east. He dropped the flint on the trampled mud and even before he turned away he could no longer see it.

seven

SPINDRIFT

A PURSE OF GOLD

When on that day on Streedagh's strand Ineen was at last able to rise from the stony sand where she had fallen, when Sorley had gone away out of sight with her child, she looked to see if anyone of the town had observed her with him, and she thought none had; the beach at that hour was nearly empty, the few women in black shawls, waiting for their men, looked only out to sea. After a time she took up the purse he had given to her, feeling the strange sleek leather and the coins moving inside as she carried it. She went up from the beach and to the village, and the people, the women, watched her pass; she knew that they did, and she neither looked toward them nor avoided them. Doors were shut as she passed. She took no notice of that.

The old church where her father had been buried, where her false wedding had occurred without solemnity or joy—she had come to think that her story was not uniquely sad, except that it was: for when she had first come here the story, the thing, the sin, had already progressed beyond escaping. She pulled open the door against the grasses that grew now so densely there, almost as though to keep out human souls, to forbid them entry to a holy place into which they had no right to go.

Foolish, foolish.

The altar, now without cloths or furnishings of any kind, was gray in the small light through the pointed windows. She went to the altar and knelt on the one low step before it, and crossed herself; then she rose and placed the purse on the altar. She stepped back into the aisle, and knelt where Cormac Burke had placed his mother's ring on her finger, where it still was now. She bent forward, put her hands on the cool stone, and then lay facedown; she spread her arms open so that she was a cross there before the altar.

Take it, she said without words. *Take it and consume it, or do as you will. It is not mine. I have nothing that is mine. I pray to die here now, but if my prayer is not to be granted, I ask for the power to live.*

Later she would have no memory of how long she lay there. She prayed to feel her sin and her pain, and never to cease; she grew deathly cold and thought yes, she would be allowed to die, and for a time was dead: and then felt a hand upon her.

Not Cormac. Not Sorley.

A young priest of the abbey not far away had been given the duty to care for this little church, which was consecrated no matter how ruinous now: to sweep, to repair, to lay flowers on the altar. He spoke to Ineen, softly, for he too supposed that she was dead and he did not dare to call her back, but she stirred then, lifted herself up, and turned to see him. The gold remained on the altar where she had laid it. The priest helped her to rise farther, as far as to her knees, and he began to pray: the words soft as rain, his hands folded before him and his eyes closed.

She wouldn't die. She had been ordered to live, and she would, she would have the power. *In nomine Patris, et Filii, et Spiritus Sancti,* the priest murmured, moving his hand over her in a cross.

~

She went to the women, the ones who had cared for her in her waiting and in her giving birth to the offspring of Sorley. She knew that they remembered all that had happened in her house in those days, but they didn't speak of it, and neither did she. *Just a slip of a boy,* they had said to her, and never afterward asked what had become of it. She went with them on rounds that never ended, one birth following another until the last day; she watched closely everything they did and wrote in her memory everything they said, which was written down nowhere else. Whether three went to a house or only one she went also. In time one of those whom she followed would allow her to come forward, and with her ears full of the mother's cries and curses and prayers she'd observe the crowning of the infant head glossy with slime, blind and inanimate; and then when a child came fully forth, she was taught how she must put her hands upon it. Every one that she saw appear in the year of her watching, and then in her own attending, was only a human child, a boy or girl that lived or died. But when she walked the beach alone she could in some weathers perceive creatures made as if of spindrift or smoke, who came and vanished and returned again all in a moment. She knew well that the sea could bring forth things that could not be understood or grasped, not by her, though perhaps sailors or sailors' wives could know them; but she was sure these came not from the sea but to the sea. They were of earth, or had been, and now of nothing, or nearly so. Where from here would they go? What land, if any land, lay in the West?

Often when the women were gathered in Ineen's house, putting up their remedies and their possets, crushing leaves or boiling them, each with a prayer to say with it, they told stories; and on a day in winter one told of the king who was born with ass's ears. He grew up still having them, she told, and he hid them under a great hat if he could, or he spoke to his knights and his *brehons* from behind a curtain, so his secret would not come out.

They all nodded, and shared a smile; they knew the story.

Well so, the teller said, the one man who knew the king's secret was his barber, who could not cut the hair of the king's head if his hat was on, and in that way he came to know. And the king made him swear that he would never tell no one what he knew. But he was a garrulous fellow, you know, and liked to talk, and he lived in fear that he would let the secret out of his mouth, as he longed to do.

Ineen put down the bunch of rosemary she was tying up with straw, and was still.

And what, said another, did he do then to relieve his heart?

Why he told the stones, and he told the reeds in the river, the storyteller said. And he told the secret to a *tree*. It was a spruce, and somehow it happened, look you, that a harp-maker took that tree, and from it made a harp. And when the king's harper first played on it in the hall, the harp sang out that the king had ass's ears; and the king hung his head and put off his hat, and there they were, believe it or not.

None of the women had ever told Ineen's secret: if they had done so she surely would have known of it. But had they told it to the stones, had they told the seals?

What I have heard, another woman said, is this: that the king left his hall and wandered in shame, until he came to the place where St. Brigid was. He knelt before her in his grief and laid his head in her lap and wept. And the saint stroked his head for a time, whether long or short I don't know, and when she ceased the ears were gone.

Gone like that, a woman said. The blessed saint.

Ineen was weeping softly now like the king with his ass's ears.

The women looked away, or to their work, so as not to break in upon her grief. Would he, her son, after years it might be, find a saint for himself, who would remove for good the webs between his fingers, the mossy fur on his back, his teeth small and sharp as a saw's?

"Look there," one woman said, who had turned to the window—the one from which Ineen had once seen the Spanish ships founder. She got up to see. Out on the harbor waters was a narrow ship with a prow like a dragon, its long oars plunging and rising and plunging again into the gray sea, coming toward shore.

BROKEN

*t*hey had dropped a ship's boat from the high deck to the water's surface; the navigator didn't want to bring his ship in farther. Streedagh's strand was not a place that their Queen visited often; there was no trade for her there. Men had come down to the shore to help bring the ship's boat onto the beach. Ineen no more than the others knew what it was that they had brought to shore, even when the men from the boat lifted a long wicker cradle of sorts, and something wrapped up within it which Ineen could not perceive. She started down along the path alone. The other women went to their houses and shut their doors, as they often did when something they didn't understand came from the sea.

Lastly a large woman with wild wings of dark hair streaked in gray was helped by the others out of the boat; she gave a signal—a wave of a long arm—and the sailors lifted the wicker basket and started up toward the village. Now Ineen began to feel that this had something to do with her, was bringing whatever it was to her, and she felt no fear; she had not in a long time felt fear. She wrapped her shawl around her tightly and went to meet the strangers, who now made toward her.

The woman was now summoning her with her hands. When Ineen had come within calling distance, she cried in a louder voice than Ineen would have expected, and what she cried was *Where is Ineen Fitzgerald?*

"I am Ineen Fitzgerald," she answered. The woman nodded, and called Ineen to draw closer and see: she bent to draw away the wrappings of the thing in the basket, and in wonder and certainty that it could be so, Ineen knew what she would see.

"Is he dead?" she asked in English.

The woman shook her head. "Not at this hour," she said in Irish. "Not so much longer, perhaps."

It was hard to see him as a living man, though he was nonetheless the man she had wedded and lived with. Hurt terribly. He was trying to speak, but a part of his jaw and face had been knocked away like the jaw of an old statue; he tried to rise but couldn't, though his hand moved as though seeking. Seeking her. She knelt on the sand by him, and took his hand in both of hers. Only because of what she had done in the dozen years past, what she had seen of broken and half-made life, could she look at him and hold his hand in pity and solace.

"Cormac," she whispered. His battered head turned toward her with great effort, but he couldn't speak. She looked up at Queen Gráinne where she stood with her sailors.

"He begged us to bring him here," she said, in an oddly gentle voice, almost a girl-child's voice. "He has no family, certainly none that love him, or might be willing to take him in."

"I am his wife," Ineen said. "I must take him in."

The sailors lifted the wicker cradle. Ineen went ahead and they followed her up to the house. Old women and children now came out and watched the procession pass, though they knew nothing of what had happened or who she led. When she opened the door to her house Gráinne said, "He must first be washed."

For a moment Ineen's soul refused the task, sorry she had spoken so quickly, saying that he was hers to care for. She had never loved him. She took a great black kettle and went to the small well she kept, and filled it. They had stirred the fire meanwhile, and she hung the kettle there. She bent to Cormac in the basket, and gently pulled away the sweated and filthy cloths that covered him. Queen Gráinne gave her no help until Ineen had water to warm the well-caulked wooden tub she'd brought and put before the fire: her great joy on cold nights. Then together, with the sailors looking on ready to put a hand in if needed, the two women with patient care took hold of the naked man and found where they might lift him, and they did, though he groaned piteously, and placed him in the tub. In something like shame he looked up at Ineen, and tried again to speak, failing again; and an awful pity, greater than for any malformed newborn, flooded her. She took cloths and washed him: his face, avoiding the shattered jaw. The twisted ropes of muscle. His breast seamed with wounds already becoming scars. The male parts she'd never seen nor touched.

Lifted from the tub, Cormac was wrapped in clean linen and placed on the bed, with what supports around him she could place. His eyes, unhurt, searched the room, her face, the sky out the window; but he couldn't speak. Gráinne regarded him with a curious gentleness. He was a gunner, Gráinne told her; yet he was not a very good gunner. It was not a trade that he was suited for, but he loved the guns and knew them and tended to them, and those who knew them better taught him what there was to know about that craft. And yet, here is a strange thing: he never had fired one but once. He was as though shy to, or felt undeserving, she couldn't tell.

There were only three on the deck of the *Richard*, she told Ineen, the ship you see out there now. And one was his favorite, as though they were his kids or his scholars, and he a tutor, and the favored one was a black iron one, the oldest, bound in iron straps to keep it whole. Now what was to happen then was my fault, if you must needs have me to blame . . .

The navigator and the cannoneers and Gráinne in the galley's boat had slipped between the Spanish ships at Kinsale harbor and to the besieged town, to do trading business, to acquire necessities, including powder, if any could be had. On the galley the rowers had lifted their oars and were sleeping or doing nothing at all; the *Richard* rocked gently at anchor in calm water, as close in as the navigators dared bring her. Cormac on the little gun-deck looked toward the rampart that guarded the port, trying to determine what ships those were at the docks, Spanish or English, but his eyesight wasn't good enough to make them out. He could, though, see the rocky outcrops that guarded the port on the left and right, and the number of harbor seals that lay there in the sun, and hear them too: what Ineen had called their song, though it sounded like no song to him. She had sought the seals, and also shunned them; seemed to hate them, and yet always watched them. When they put up their heads they seemed to be human, peering about and sounding, then collapsing again on their fellows. He loathed them, though he didn't know why.

He put his hand on the black *mortero*, warmed by the sun. He racked it leftward, so that it pointed at the rocks. For a time he only watched, feeling some enmity from the dark shapeless animals, and laughing that he felt it. He remembered following Ineen across the beach, well behind her, watching her watch, her shawl drawn over her growing belly.

Damn them anyway.

The iron balls that the *mortero* threw weighed some twenty pounds, just at the limit that Cormac could lift. He wrestled a ball from the stores into the carrier and brought it to the gun-deck, an effort that almost made him give up, but he managed to lift the ball and ram it deep into the cannon's mouth.

The powder chamber—the beer-mug shaped vessel—went in last, and the match-cord he'd light went into it. He felt a huge elation, as though he had set out to commit a mortal sin that could not be punished. He framed the view toward the seal-rocks in the square of his thumbs and forefingers, as the cannoneers did, sighting along the barrel. Yes, it was right. He got the flint and steel and struck them, shedding sparks into a char-cloth and when the cloth began to smoke he set it in the tinder. He got a small flame going and with it lit a splinter of wood.

Now. Now. His heart was hammering but his hands were steady. He put his bit of burning wood to the match.

At that moment a big wave on its way into the harbor, the third evil wave, rose beneath the *Richard*. The ship was lifted and turned away from the rocks and toward the town. Cormac lost his footing and fell, clambered up, reaching for the sparking match, but it was too late; the cannon belched, arching backward in its frame, heaving the iron ball high in the air; at its height it fell toward the ramparts of the port. He lost sight of its impact. The seals had left the rocks for the water. The world stood motionless. Then a cannon from the ramparts fired, in answer to the perceived attack. Cormac saw the puff, and a moment after heard the blast, and then saw the ball coming toward the *Richard* at impossible speed with perfect aim. He should have dropped to the deck, or thrown himself down the gangway, but he did neither; he only stared frozen at the oncoming ball. It had a face: a face he had seen in a book, a head of Medusa, fierce and wild, hair of tangled snakes. As it revolved toward the ship, ridden by its cannon angel, her mouth wide in rage or delight, it split into pieces. Stone balls do. And the rain of fragments large and small scattered across the decks, tearing at the mast, the decking, the ropes and barrels, and everywhere in the body of Cormac Burke.

～⚬～

He was near to death when they returned, Gráinne told Ineen. They had no doctor, only their own small skills. They had had to leave that harbor before the English blockade sent out battleships to sink the *Richard*. How it was he lived, Gráinne couldn't tell; but when he could speak—he'd not be able to for long, as the wounds to his face and jaw began to close—he asked to be brought here. And now here he was. Gráinne told Ineen how she had loved him, for his mildness and for his griefs, and Ineen would see (she said) that he was still a man, for all that he had suffered and all that he had lost.

She stood then, with great effort, an old woman with aches in all her parts. She blessed Ineen in a few words; and with her men she turned down the lane and to the ship's boat where her crew waited, and to the now repaired *Richard*, to make for Clew Bay and home.

She supposed he'd die soon. She fed him with a spoon, like a babe: milk and gruel, mashed greens and apples, pushed in past the broken teeth; water from a cup she held for him that ran down over his wispy beard and chin. He needed her help to stand, to reach the privy. When she left him to go about her rounds in the village, she might come home to find he'd wet the shirt he'd been dressed in. Like all such labor it seemed both useless and endless. But in time he began to heal a little. He would sit and try to close his hands and open them, over and over, until he could grasp and lift a spoon, a cup—at last a pen. The women who came to Ineen's house credited this to his being a priest, which they assumed he was because he could read and write; if Ineen said he was not a priest, they nodded, and went on treating him as one. In time they began to come to ask him to write for them: a letter to a landlord or to an official from whom they hoped to receive justice or avoid ill treatment; to a son or husband in prison, who might have the letter read to him. In exchange they brought bread or fish, or a small coin, which he'd refuse. He still couldn't be understood when he spoke, though Ineen had come to know what he meant. He sat in a chair now like any man, though he struggled to rise from it. And she knew that though he had not died quickly as she supposed he would, still he was failing; the deep hurts would not pass.

She asked him at last: Why had he fired on the town that day? What had he thought? Were they the pirates' enemies? He twisted in his seat, the ropes of his throat tautened, and he made his mouth say *Seals*. She studied him in wonder; his eyes searched hers as though for understanding. Word by word she drew the story out of him, appalled and sorry.

And so the seals were spared, she said then, and she could almost see that he laughed, or would if he could.

Dark was rising. She put her hands together, still regarding him, and then she took his crumpled ones in hers, and told him what she never had, what he had no right to hear: of Sorley and her unresistance, her yielding, her desire and her choice; of the son she bore, more his than hers; of her grieving for that monstrous child. How she still grieved: now, this day.

The firelight colored his face, and she saw that though he had sat as stiff and constricted as ever the tears fell from his eyes and down his ruined face, and he made a sound that was pity and anguish, and would not draw his hands away from hers.

***

When he was dying from the cannon-ball fragments buried in him, when the stone had stopped his guts from working his food, his lungs from taking and releasing breath; when he ceased to speak and couldn't rise from the bed she had laid him in, which had been her own bed, the one she and Sorley had been in together on the night of the ships when everything began, then she went for the priest: the same priest that had raised her from the stone floor of the tumbledown church. She rang the little abbey bell until she was answered, and the young priest was found; and when he had assembled his sacred things, without words she took his hand—the others were shocked to see that—and pulled him with her toward the hill paths and the stone house. And when Cormac had whispered his confession to the priest and been blessed—his lips and his ears and his eyes anointed, his poor hands too—and the circle of bread given him, he ceased to move and then to breathe at all, and the taut strings that had held him rigid slackened and let him rest.

He was buried beside her father, where there was a place that would have been for her, but she no longer cared where she would be laid. She put into the place his book of Latin lessons and his book of psalms, and he was closed up with them.

After that nothing more happened.

Only this: when she was old and alone and had ceased her service to the women who bore children, when the whole of the island that lay beyond Streedagh's strand was as though skinned and burned of living things by the armies, and the dead lay unburied as they had before, as Time knew they would: on a night as she lay in her bed, hers again, under a thick mantle in the cold, the fire low, she woke to the door-latch lifted and dropped: someone in the house. The Moon was down; she could see nothing of the being come perhaps to murder her, but she felt no fear. A slight, sleek figure it seemed, neither tall nor short, but dark as though dressed in dark, close things, jacketeen and hose. She had heard from many people, many women, how a dark figure might come to you at the last, to bear you away, either to a place of rest or to another place, and she had only partly believed them, but now she did for a moment, and then again did not. It was not Death in her house. She dared to lift herself in the bed, to meet the one who stood now at the bed's end, but she didn't dare to speak or question him.

It is I. Spoken in a soft voice that would not frighten her. She wasn't frightened. *Sorley,* she said or thought.

Not he.

Then she knew who he must be, though it wasn't possible that it could be he; and she knew that Sorley was dead. She told him without speech that he must not kill her, because of who she was, and who he was: it would be a greater sin than any that she and his father had done. He came closer to her, and the face that she could now see, she knew: Sorley's constant faint smile. As though this one could know her thoughts just as Sorley had, smiling and setting them aside. *My father was a great lord in our country,* he said. *And so therefore am I.*

The ash fell in the fireplace, making a small burst of sparks, and she saw him clearly. He put out his long dark hand, a hand without the web between the fingers, as Sorley had told her: a man upon the land. *Come, Mother. Take my hand. We'll go to where your mother is, for I know the place.*

And she took his hand, and rose and went with him where he would go.

RUNNING BEASTE

It was on a hill eight miles from Kinsale town that Hugh O'Neill and Red Hugh O'Donnell met at last after the dawn of their defeat. Clouds hastened across the sky and augured further rain. Below were the exhausted soldiers, the horses of Red Hugh's cavalry, their heads down-drooping.

"Lost," Red Hugh said. "The night and the rain. The scouts were baffled."

"You never met with the English forces."

Red Hugh said nothing. When O'Neill was sure his cousin would say no more about that, he looked off to the north. "Did you," he asked, "see a thing in the sky, toward dawn on that night?"

Red Hugh studied the Earl, trying to discern what he meant, and what answer he would want. "I saw," he said, "lightning in constant play, as I've never seen before. The black rain-clouds. Wind-tossed crows." He waited to see if what he'd said was enough. O'Neill looked far off, but not as though to perceive something. At length he said: "I have news that Don Juan Del Águila will surrender."

"He will be well treated."

They said no more while the cries of wounded men begging for water came to them. Then Hugh O'Neill said: "It's over. There is no more to this. The Spanish will want peace."

"We must make them want war. They have made promises, to protect our religion, our people. God wants this war. It will end in victory."

O'Neill made no answer to this; his answer was clear in his deep-scored cheeks. He had got old, Red Hugh perceived; he had seemed ageless till now.

"I'll lead as many of the men as can walk or be carried," O'Neill said. "We'll go north."

Red Hugh's horse shook his head and took steps, as though making objection. Red Hugh looked over the weeping, stirring, huddling mass. "They have no weapons," he said.

"Men in retreat throw away their weapons. They are only a burden to them."

"I'll go on," Red Hugh said. "Maguire was lost to me in the night—I can't tell what he did or could not do. My brother Rory will lead my people back to home. I'll go speak to Don Pedro Zubiaur, who is holding supplies there. His Spanish soldiers won't retreat. He'll bring more." His uncle Hugh was regarding him as though deaf. "I'll go to Spain," Red Hugh said. "I will."

Hugh O'Neill leaned from his horse, bridle in his left hand, right hand extended to the man he believed was the finest leader of horse, the finest swordsman of his time. For a moment the Fox only regarded the gloved hand held out to him. Then he took the hand firmly. He turned his horse, and started down to where the horses and the riders waited.

After the battle in the hills beyond Kinsale, English captains brought to Mountjoy—along with all of O'Neill's abandoned baggage and supplies, his wagons, his cattle, and his arms—more than a hundred Irish prisoners of war, many ill or crazed, others near naked. To Mountjoy they were nothing but rebels against their rightful sovereign, the Queen of England. They had risen against her treasonously in full knowledge of what they did. He ordered them all hanged immediately, but his own soldiers were too weary to carry out the order. Prisoners wept, begged for a priest, or sat silent and unmoving. Beginning at dawn on New Year's Day, every one of them was hanged. It took a long time.

Red Hugh at Castlehaven sat with his brother Rory and his secretary and beloved friend Matthew O'Maolthuile, and together they compiled documents that gave all the O'Donnell rights and lands to Rory, who would in time take the title of the O'Donnell that Red Hugh now and forever resigned. There was every chance that he himself would not live long, Red Hugh told him, and their house must be secured.

"Suppose you do live," Rory wanted to know.

"Then good Matthew will scrape the ink from these papers, and write another thing. Come, kiss me, ride for home."

Days later Rory O'Donnell knelt before his mother Ineen Duvh at Donegal Castle, with no enemies' heads to lay before her, no ensigns captured, and told her all that had happened in the South. That Red Hugh was gone to Spain, and here were papers she must read, or he would read them to her, because he could. He passed over nothing, told no lies—he had never told a lie to her that she had not seen through. She listened in silence.

Meantime the Earl of Tyrone, going north too with his dependents, tried to gather his Southern allies as he passed through their lands, at least to take their hands and promise all that he could, which was solely the promise itself. The Lord Deputy saw little threat from this combination; it was not enough to mount any serious challenge. He wanted O'Neill. A huge reward was put on the Earl's head, surely enough to tempt any reduced Irish lord or defeated captain. Not a one of them came in, only a number of liars who could be seen through and tossed out with a warning or a whipping. Mountjoy wrote to London that it was *most sure that never traitor knew better how to keep his own head than this, nor any subjects have a more dreadful awe to lay violent hands on their sacred prince, than these people have to touch the person of their O'Neills.*

O'Neill made no last stand: there was no stand he could make. *A running beaste, and nowhere he might run to,* Blount had written to London. He stayed away from Tyrconnell country lest he draw Mountjoy's army that way; when word came of English forces on the move he went down into Maguire country, or north into the country of the O'Cahans, his last powerful allies. Only then did he learn why Maguire, his Dog, had never reached Kinsale. With a few riders he'd left Red Hugh and gone to reconnoiter in Munster, perhaps raise more cavalry; and as he rode a band of English fighters appeared, racing toward him. Maguire—his companions later described it all—turned his horse, sword drawn, and rushed into the oncoming English; but before he or his companions following could beat them off, one man had struck Maguire with a sword. Maguire struck back. The other pulled a pistol from his jack, and shot Maguire full in the face. The shooter, severely wounded, fell from his horse some yards on and died.

Who had he been, the Earl wanted to know, this attacker?

A fellow named St. Leger, he was told.

Warham St. Leger?

Yes, but not that man. A nephew of the same name.

The circle of Hugh O'Neill's life seemed to close to hear this, as though the years marched not in a straight line into forever but in a circle: like caterpillars marching around a post, each following the one ahead, the first following the last.

Dog, he thought: Oh Dog. Good Dog.

While O'Neill went to ground, Lord Deputy Mountjoy began building again: a string of stronger forts along the Blackwater that would keep the Earl hemmed in until he could be drawn or dragged out. As though under a compulsion to repeat the same action over and over, the Lord Deputy built forts and more forts, from Lough Neagh to Toome, from Toome to Dungiven Abbey. O'Neill could ride out and watch them being built; in his heart a hopeless anger such as he hadn't known before was growing, and would come forth when it would. When word reached him at Dungannon that the O'Cahan had at last capitulated to Dublin, he shed tears of rage. His elder son, now twenty years old and holding the title Baron Dungannon—the son who had kept the house safe in that worst of years—feared for his father's mind: but he could not comfort him.

Then the Earl took the last and only step he could. He would go where he could not be sought. And when Mountjoy had completely surrounded him on the east with his forts and reached for Dungannon itself, he would find his enemy gone, and no Dungannon there for him to have. *Dóiteáin Rí*, King Fire, would do that duty, and the Earl of Tyrone would be his servant and no one else's. Like the chained bear he had once seen tormented by dogs in London, he raged, he struck out at anyone who came to his aid; his closest men—Pedro Blanco, the young captains he'd brought to Kinsale, Hugh his heir—they avoided him, afraid even to try to stop him. From morning to noon he gathered flammables and stacked them in the chambers, the towers, the kitchens. Only then did he call the castle people together, the cooks and the horse-boys and the pigkeepers, and told them what they must do. He would not be exempt: stripped to the waist he cut branches of pine and spruce with them, had them dragged into the halls, thrown down. *Yes, that will do, that will do*—they heard him speaking, as though to someone near beside him, though there was no one.

At last he ordered all who were in the house to take branches to the kitchens and set them afire, and return to him. They stood stock-still and only stared at him; he waved and shouted at them, as at a testy horse. He took thick spruce branches in his own hands and went and thrust the branches into the kitchen fire. When they caught, he raised them high and bore them into the hall, the household coming after him, some now with burning brands, others pleading that he cease. Whatever he saw that would burn he ordered torched; he himself fired the great pile of pine and spruce in the hall, and when the smoke drove them all out he ordered them up into the bedchambers, and there they set fire to the beds, to Mabel's splendid hangings that he tore from the walls—they would not burn easily. He set the pictures on the walls afire, the closets with their clothes, the chairs and tables, anything that he could. Mountjoy would find nothing here to seize, nothing of his or hers he could mishandle.

The choking pall of smoke drove the servants away at last, but Hugh still roved the rooms, seared and panting, until the women took hold of him, threw damp cloths around him and pulled him away. Hoarse with the smoke, he ordered them to build fires against the walls, more fires. Bring powder-kegs, set them round.

He sat then, wrapped in the cloths they had brought, and with all the voice he could summon gave his orders to the chief men. All the cattle that could be herded in quickly, as much of the stored food as was in the outbuildings, all the weapons and armor, all which had to be put aboard wagons, the oxen hitched to them; and the people must go with the wagons up into the hills as fast as their feet could carry them. When a week had passed they had prepared for the journey as best they could and gone out. His fighters, mounted and on foot, followed Hugh as he went out; some of the O'Hagans turned to look back, but the Earl did not; when the powder-kegs were lighted and blew up with a great noise, and parts of the outer wall fell with a noise even greater, still he didn't turn his head, only rode on.

Left behind in the ruination of his house, there in a dusty corner of the chamber where Mabel had first asked to see it and looked into it, was a small mirror of obsidian, cased in figured gold. The heat of the fire melted the gold and erased the Monas sign that had given it its power—if it had power—but the stone itself was unharmed.

Years before, when Phillip II lay dying, he had heard with great satisfaction of the victory of the Irish over the royal forces at the Yellow Ford. Now the Queen of England, Phillip's great antagonist, was herself dying: not in a bed or couch but standing upright, in her richest gown, waiting for the on-creeping of Time. And among the last things she thought of and spoke of was the running beast, the great rebel Tyrone, who could no longer see her, whom she could not reach. When the gossip and townsman Nicholas Harington returned from Ireland he was summoned to her chamber; and the first question she put to him was *Have you seen Tyrone?* And with an answer given her—no, he had not—the black glass in Ulster went dark forever.

Hugh O'Neill and his great extended family, horsemen, pikemen, pregnant women, naked children, old men, cooks, armorers, Spanish sailors, husbands, sons and daughters, went into the deep glens of Glankankyne, into which no English force dared penetrate. As O'Neill had foreseen, Mountjoy soon occupied the ruin of Dungannon and began the work of turning it too into an English fort, and then gave that up. In a different place, though, the Lord Deputy destroyed instead of building: he took men the few miles to Tullahogue, where on a low hill the crowning-stone of the O'Neills stood, the *Leac na Rí,* Stone of the Kings. He ordered men with hammers to break the ancient throne into pieces: like a deserted husband smashing the pictures and ornaments of his wife in futile jealousy. All that day the breaking and scattering went on. Some people from the farms around came to see, but not too close; and the women covered their faces, and went away. Never again would the O'Hagans, stewards of the place for time out of mind, put the white staff into the hand of an O'Neill; no more would those attending listen for the faint ring of St. Patrick's bell in acknowledgment and blessing.

His Lordship held the laborers to it, himself kicking away the dusty fragments, till there was nothing, nothing at all. He put a piece of the stone in his pocket, mounted, lifted a gloved hand, and took his troop of soldiers and the workmen and their sledge-hammers and rode away, in a cold spring rain and the wind close. Not one of them had heard the voices of the Underfolk in their stone beds down within the wide, rath-encircled hill: voices of the kings crowned here even before there were O'Neills, awakened now by the shattering of the stone; whisperers who in their sorrow would not rest or sleep again for a century of days, of winters and summers, of memories and forgettings, until at last they fell silent everywhere but in dreams.

DEATH OF A FOX

In the days when the league between the Irish lords and the Spanish Crown was being sealed, when the Duke of Lerma and Phillip III were writing in high hopes to Hugh O'Neill and to Red Hugh O'Donnell, when plans were being made for an invasion that would rescue the Catholics of Ireland from the English *heretics* and restore Spanish honor, O'Neill offered a pledge to the King that would make clear his accord with Spain in all matters then and in time to come. The pledge that Hugh offered was his son Henry, then fourteen years old, the boy he'd once refused to give over to Black Tom Butler and his archbishop, for fear of what would become of him. Henry was taken to Madrid on a Spanish ship with a Spanish captain; he never spoke later about what he felt in being carried away, though he had clung to his father up until the moment he was to board; thereafter he never looked back. The voyage was spent in teaching Henry the Spanish language, starting with the names of things aboard the ship, then the terms of art in regard to the management of sailing ships, then the ranks of Spanish nobles, generals, mayors, and court officials. Henry learned quickly.

The King was somewhat embarrassed by the pledge, which he had not demanded, and always thereafter treated the boy with grave courtesy and kindness. Henry became enamored with Spain, the Escorial, the great churches; he sat entranced before polyphonic masses and celebrations, a hundred choristers, their voices rising in praise to heaven.

His father had never schooled him in religious matters, and the hedge-priests of the dangerous days could rarely answer Henry's questions, about grace, about devotion, about sin and forgiveness. Here there were reverend fathers deeply learned in Greek and Latin texts, ready to answer him and to teach him what he did not know to ask. As soon as his guardians saw that he was ready, Henry was admitted to the University of Salamanca. After four years, and in the year of Kinsale, he entered the Franciscan novitiate and began to

prepare for ordination. That choice, made for him by God as he perceived it, was an earthly trouble for his Spanish protectors. Henry,
slight, pale, sweet, was beloved by all, and no one wanted to thwart
his pious desire, but the fear was that the Earl of Tyrone would feel
that his son had been misused. A Franciscan archbishop was sent
from Madrid to the scholars at Salamanca to learn whether the young
man might be dissuaded, and in time they issued an opinion stating
that Henry would be in mortal sin if he continued at the novitiate.

"He was always a good boy," the Earl of Tyrone said, perusing the
letter that had reached him from Spain. He gave the paper to Pedro
Blanco, whose face revealed nothing. "A Franciscan," O'Neill said.
"They are the poor men, aren't they, and loved by all." Without a
summons from home Henry remained in the Salamanca novitiate,
believing he would know when God had changed His mind; yet he
had not given up his holy intentions as ordered. The Brothers protected him when, now and then, the King's ministers remembered
that he was there.

Also waiting for a decision from the King—though Henry didn't
know of it—was his cousin Red Hugh, Lord of Tyrconnell, who had
come to Spain on a French vessel, desperate to reach Madrid and the
admirals, to beg for a new invasion. He was received at the port of
Corunna with royal honors by the Governor of Galicia, who accompanied him and the small retinue he'd brought across the province to
the coastal town of Betanzos: for it was from here, the Governor told
Red Hugh—spreading his arms to take in the broad fields—here,
in the gulf of past time, that the sons of Mil set sail for Eire. The
Galician spring was like Ireland's, Matthew O'Maolthuile thought,
misty and wet; from the fields he passed came the sound of pipes:
shepherds, his guide said, who love to play for their flocks.

At Salamanca, eight leagues from Valladolid, Red Hugh began
to feel unwell, feverish and weak, unable to keep down food. But he
would not turn back. He was taken to a Franciscan hostel, nursed by
nuns, and there for a time he seemed to regain health. Soon he'd be
well. That was what he told the novice in black cassock who sought
for him there, a tall, thin young man, shaven but not tonsured.

"Henry," Red Hugh said.

"Cousin." Henry took Hugh's hot hand in his. Red Hugh lifted
himself painfully, and a nun in voluminous white put a pillow under
his head.

"Tell me of my father," Henry asked. "Is he not angry with me?"

"Angry?"

"Because of my choice."

Was the Earl angry? Red Hugh couldn't remember if O'Neill was or wasn't. He seemed to be coming apart, in pieces that had forgotten one another and their former connections. He hadn't released Henry's hand. "No," he said. "He loves you. But he wants you to be with him."

Henry's eyes filled—Red Hugh could see it. "I have two fathers," Henry whispered. "The Earl, and God. I hear God's commandments in my heart and I must obey them."

Red Hugh released the hand he held. It was of no interest now to him whether Henry came home or did not. He struggled to rise; he must get to Valladolid, put his case to them, the Irish case; he sought for his clothes, demanded them. Good Matthew O'Maolthuile called the nuns, ordered them in poor Spanish to bring his lordship his coat, his shirt, his trews. He himself carried Red Hugh's sword and scabbard. "I will go with you," Henry said to his cousin. "As far as Simancas at least, the Franciscan house there." Red Hugh waved him off—somehow he could not see what was before him, or what was ahead.

Simancas was within the province of Valladolid, from whose cathedral heavy bells tolled unbearably. Red Hugh was greeted by the King's aides and taken in a carriage to a palace in the city, where eager and anxious Spaniards, priests, knights, and doctors surrounded him, took his hand. A servant all in black brought him wine. His hand shook as he took the cup, drank thirstily: and at that he realized with a strange loathing that *he had been here before*, in this company; as then, he could not hear what was said to him, or everyone had fallen silent. He bent forward, vomiting, the cup falling and spilling its blood on the tiles.

The worm, the doctor who attended him said, palpating Hugh's stomach, lifting his eyelids. The worm is fierce in this province; many have died. *In nomine Patris, et Filii, et Spiritus Sancti,* murmured the priest who touched him last.

⌐

It became Henry's duty to write to his father, to tell him that the Lord of Tyrconnell was dead, and would be buried in Valladolid with honors. Composing the letter took him a great deal of time; every word he wrote seemed to have a double meaning, to defend the course he had adopted, and also to comfort his father. He described how the King of Spain himself and his court had come to Simancas, all in blackest mourning, to accompany Red Hugh's body to Valladolid and see him buried in the Plaza Mayor. How Henry himself had walked with the Franciscans behind the cortege, singing the funeral service. And as he wrote, Henry wept—not for Red Hugh, but for himself, though he knew self-pity to be a sin: for during that procession to Valladolid the Archbishop had summoned him, and told him that he must now at last obey his sovereign, and leave his order.

He ended his letter to his father saying that he was to be sent to Flanders, to serve in the forces of the Catholic Archduke Albert, whose co-regent was that King of Spain's daughter once promised to Ireland. He hoped his father would be glad of this at last, that he was to be a soldier; and he begged him to tell his elder brother Hugh that he prayed daily for his well-being, and their father's.

That letter took a long journey to reach Hugh O'Neill in the Glankankyne woods. Henry's elder brother Hugh, Baron Dungannon, stood in a state of acute embarrassment, listening to his brother's words read aloud, watching his father mourn. His brother a priest, or desirous of being one: so strange. At last the Earl wiped the tears from his face—he had shed them for too long this day, for his Fox, for himself, for his island—and put down the paper. "Don't leave me," he said to his son. "Stay with me. No matter where I go."

There was then no place for them to go. Ulster was a province in ruin. What had happened in Munster when O'Neill was a young man was now inflicted on the North: some said it was worse in Ulster than Munster had been in the Desmond wars. There was plague across the island, and famine too, with the same stories of children starved and then killed and eaten, repeated into truths in the histories. The dead found with green-stained mouths from eating nettles and dock, the unburied bodies stripped of their wretched clothes. The rebel lords blamed the English for the suffering, the English blamed the recalcitrant Irish magnates who cared nothing for the people they supposedly loved and ruled. Now spring had come, and the Earl of Tyrone's dependents would starve too if they couldn't return to their fields. All the provender they'd carried into Glankankyne was gone. Thin faces and hollow eyes that turned to him told him so. When it appeared that no grain would be sown, no ground harrowed, Hugh O'Neill sent word to Mountjoy that he would surrender to Dublin without qualification or exception.

Mountjoy refused his offer.

It was richly satisfying to Lord Mountjoy, refusing the surrender of the Lord of the North. In not too many days, however, he'd begun to see advantage to himself in permitting the Earl of Tyrone to surrender, rather than have him lurking always in the corner of the eye, uncatchable. He sent Sir Garrett Moore, the Englishman whom Hugh O'Neill loved and honored above all the others of his nation, up into the hills to find O'Neill; and word of it reached the Earl soon enough. He and Sir Garrett met near the shattered seat of the kings at Tullahogue, and embraced. Sir Garrett took the hand of young Hugh and clasped his shoulder. "Never fear, your father will be well," he said. "I promise you that. No harm will come to him while I am by." They mounted then, and rode toward Sir Garrett's ancient abbey house, Mellifont, at the gates of Glenmalure valley where the frozen O'Donnell boys were long ago laid down. The two recounted to one another how Red Hugh had lost his great toes; and Hugh O'Neill told him that Red Hugh was dead.

"Sickness?" Sir Garrett asked.

"Or poison," Hugh answered. "It can't be known, until we meet again."

March mist blew across them as they rode, like curtains of clinging gauze. At Mellifont a large number of armed men lined the way up to the door, where—all in black as always—Lord Mountjoy stood. For a moment Hugh O'Neill thought to turn again and ride away: why should he place himself in Mountjoy's hands? But Sir Garrett, reading this thought in O'Neill's manner, reached to take his arm, and smiled and nodded *yes, this is what we have come to do and you will do it, on my life*. And the Earl could not shame his friend. He dismounted and entered the house; Mountjoy stepped back, step upon step, and Hugh O'Neill, Earl of Tyrone, came forward, head low. He bent his knees with effort, and knelt with Sir Garrett's help; and he began to speak, naming himself, his title, and his clan.

He submitted, in language given him by Mountjoy's secretary:

He surrendered all he possessed, his rents and his authority. He renounced his connection with the Spanish, and his title of the O'Neill. Still on his knees, his thighs quivering, his hand in Garrett's, he repeated after the secretary that he would abandon all *barbarous customs* if allowed to return to the North of his fathers, and there he promised to build English houses and good roads and make the people into English people if he could at all. He would honor the Queen in all he did and assist the Queen's officers in whatever they requested of him. In all that time Hugh wept, as Garrett Moore had known he would weep. Lord Mountjoy however was astonished: How could such a proud man bend so low, how could he shed shameful tears? He came to the Earl, and with a clumsy gentleness helped him to his feet; a great groan came from Hugh of pain or grief, and little Mountjoy held him upright. *My lord*, he whispered. *We have done a good thing this day*.

The Earl was taken within the house, to the fire, and given a seat. Lord Mountjoy sat opposite him, his spectral secretary behind him. "Be assured," he told Hugh, "your title of Earl will be restored; I have no power to take that from you. And all the lands you owned before. And no attainder will be upon your house or on your sons. You have my word for this."

Sir Garrett had told O'Neill as they rode to Mellifont that something like this would be offered him in exchange for his subjection, and Hugh hadn't believed it. Now, unable to speak, he stared at Mountjoy. A man who loved the work of killing, and who did it well, and thought well of himself for it. A long silence obtained. Then Mountjoy grinned, an uneasy grin, slapped his knees, and invited the two men to supper.

~⁓~

One thing remained. In the morning, Hugh and Sir Garrett, surrounded by Mountjoy's clattering guard, rode to Dublin to seal Hugh's promises and surrenders in proper form before the Council. Only then, at the gates of that prison he had so long escaped being buried in, did he learn what Mountjoy had known for days and not said or whispered: what every man there knew, and what every man who knew talked of.

The Queen was dead.

She had been dead a week when Hugh O'Neill mounted his horse and parted from his son; when he entered Sir Garrett's house; when he gave up his life to Mountjoy, the life he had lived beneath that Queen, the Queen who had scolded and wept and laughed with him, looking upon him out of John Dee's black mirror, before he tore it from his throat and cast it aside. For years she had hunted him as a stag is hunted, with her hounds the Lord Protectors and Lord Deputies and her serpentine tongue. She had never loved him: no more than she had loved any man. The officers of the Council looked away, or at him coldly, as he wept. *They* had all known. They had known that Mountjoy's appointment as Lord Deputy had ended with the Queen's death: he had had no legal power to take O'Neill's admissions at Mellifont, nor to deprive him of his name; and O'Neill had not known that he did not.

Dead. Hugh began to think, as he had at Kinsale in the midwinter night, that somehow Time was running backward, or running both forward and backward at once in a giddy spiral, the Queen still alive when he came to Dublin and the queen's Death running back to Mellifont to take her away even as Hugh came in to kneel and give up everything he had to her.

He began to laugh. At first it seemed sobs, but the gray rain was ceasing, it was April, and he laughed, and laughed louder at the shocked and puzzled faces of the Council and their secretaries and their guards; he laughed the laughter of the faded and powerless gods, laughter that could long ago destroy a world or make one new, and now no longer could.

May, and the trees of Flanders were in leaf; on the wide fields, so broad, so suited to the marching and countermarching of armies, the poppies bloomed, nodding their heads as if in assent to the shedding of human blood, as red as they; sweetening with their odor the memories of husbands and sons, fathers and brothers, asleep in those fields. Seven years had passed since Kinsale and the death of Red Hugh at Simancas. Henry O'Neill had become a soldier in a regiment of Irish expatriates in the army of Albert of Austria, Cardinal Archduke and ruler of the Low Countries. A captain now, Henry had summoned the courage to ask his colonel for permission to travel to Brussels and present himself before the Archduke and the Regent, tall Isabella Carla, the King of Spain's daughter. The colonel let him go, though he doubted that Henry could win such an audience. But Henry knew that Albert was aware of him, and of his father, and the long struggle against the English *heretics*. He also knew that, like himself, Archduke Albert had taken minor holy orders when young; in fact, he had been named a Cardinal (for reasons of policy) at the age Henry was when he entered the Franciscan novitiate. The Archducal couple welcomed the young man, who had a clear simplicity, a love of God, such soft eyes, and a rare common touch with soldiers. What did he want? He need only ask.

Nothing for himself, Henry told them. He needed, well, he needed the loan or the lease of a ship: A ship large enough for some dozens of people. A merchant ship would be the best, French rather than Spanish or Dutch, as arousing less interest. The Archduke lifted his clasped hands to his lips for a moment: England, that island of spies, held its secrets close, but the Archduke's own network had told him that soon the leaders of the failed Irish rebellion would be swept up and sent to prison for the rest of their days, no matter what clemency had earlier been offered. He summoned an aide, whom he instructed to take his young captain to the right men to meet his needs, which are just and Godly. And he held out his long pale hand to Henry, to kiss the ring of the Cardinal he had briefly been, and which he had always refused to surrender.

～～～

There was a man of Fermanagh in Henry's regiment of banished or escaped Irishmen, a Maguire, in fact a son of Hugh Maguire, Hugh O'Neill's black Dog. Henry O'Neill could not think of himself as strong or stolid, a stone wall, unafraid, but this son of Maguire's was all those things. By candlelight in Henry's tent they went over every detail of what must be done. A purse of money, bills of lading for the carriage of goods, Archducal permits: all of which, and a French flag, would allow John Maguire to pass into an Irish harbor unmolested. Would Henry not come too? No, Henry told him. His own voyage was not that way.

In August then, French mariners brought a French ship into Lough Swilly in the west of Donegal, carrying a load of wines and fishing nets, as French ships did, and tied her up at the village of Rathmullan. John had been told to alert first Red Hugh's brother Rory; then Rory's younger brother Cathbarr, and with Cathbarr his wife and infant son. Then Hugh O'Neill, the Baron Dungannon, and *his* young son Conn. John then must send out riders to reach the others who'd take passage on this black ship, whose name none of them would remember afterward; the French mariners who would sail her were actually Irishmen in the dress and gear of Frenchmen. This John Maguire was a patient waiter, but when some time had passed and it was clear that his masquerade couldn't last much longer, he hurried to reach the men and wives who couldn't be left behind, and went on drawing them in until the string broke.

Last of all those to be brought on was the man whose need to fly the land was greatest. With only a day before the ship must sail, a shipman—John Maguire—arrived at Sir Garrett Moore's house at Mellifont. Sir Garrett sent for O'Neill, who had been keeping safe, and when he came to the postern and saw the man, what he saw was dead Hugh Maguire saluting him.

Next morning the Earl went among the people of the house, the doctor and the cooks and the horse-boys, and blessed each one. He embraced Sir Garrett—who knew nothing of what was to come on this day, good kind man—and walked out into the mist, where gray figures on horseback awaited him, spears raised like the men of the rath who had come before him in the beginning of his life: O'Hagans, there to bear him away, the last task they would ever do for him. It was the fourteenth of September in 1607. The Earl, and all the others arriving that day at the Rathmullan dock, left their horses untied at the port: they'd not be returning to claim them.

TRANSFIGURED

In the year of the defeat at Kinsale, Peter Lombard in Rome completed his work on the long history and present state of Ireland, the *De regno Hiberniæ sanctorum insula commentarius*. His many correspondents were clear in what they told him now: the English had won; the *heretics* could now suppress the True Church without deep opposition; they would raise up the new possessors to their seats again, they would take the resisters to law and to heel. They would make the crooked straight and the rough places plain, and there would be no end to it until there was an end to all.

He went to his desk, where the huge manuscript lay. It would be printed in time, but it was incomplete. He thought of Kinsale, of the men of Ireland who died there and likely still lay unburied. He thought of the navy of Spain taking leave of that port, those proud admirals and captains who had failed their King and their God. He picked up the pen that lay there, nearly splayed, and dipped it; and at the bottom of the last page he wrote in Latin *Postquam nihil postea gestum:* After this, nothing more happened.

And yet: there was then a child growing up in wounded Munster, a child who almost from birth babbled in rhyme and meter, went a way that others did not; grew in summer and in winter, as the songs and the words grew stranger and stronger: *If you tell my story to the captives of Ireland it will be the same as if their locks and their bonds were opened.* Those who heard came close to hear more, or shrank away: *Unseelie* that a child should sing so, and reach the heart. How the child had come to know such praises and curses, put forth day-long, no one knew, nor could account for it, but they'd remember the child's careless walking-away from what parents or siblings the child might have had, and on to other villages and to other people with other tales and songs to be learned and altered. Fair-haired, lithe, strangely tall, dressed in trews and a shirt of linen and taken for a boy, low of voice when speaking, but light and sweet in song: Only those cottagers who offered a bed and fed the singer knew the bard was not a boy, nor yet a man: but her right nature seemed a *contúirteach focal*, a dangerous word to speak.

She asked from anyone whatever she needed, but she was not good at giving; she lampooned those who turned her away, the one and only of her kind, and it might be that such ones sickened, forgot how to question what they saw and heard, and other evils too. She passed through the courts of warlords and wasn't beholden to them; from those who did not do her honor, she walked away, knowing in what direction she must go but no longer where she had come from, nor where she would arrive, she went on: a bard making the world as she sang.

The Queen was six years dead, and John Dee was dying. His books and alchemical ware and even the gifts that the Queen had given him had been sold for bread: his long toil for her meant nothing to the new Scots king, who feared magic above all things. It was all gone but this small globe of moleskin-colored quartz, that had come to have a spiritual creature caught in it: an angel, he had long believed, but now he doubted. The war of all the nations that the angel had shown him had now paused, as in a storm's eye, and a calm had fallen over the half-part of the world: it would not last; it was passing even now.

When the coming of a second Armada had grown certain, it was clear to John Dee that the Spanish would have one great ally that the Protestant Queen did not and could not have: all the Dominions, Virtues, and Powers of heaven. For of course the angels would come in on the side of Catholic Spain: though they have no preferences in human enterprises, angels—many great families of them—love the Mass, love the ceremonies of the Church, in which they themselves are named in love and honor, the incense rising to their nostrils (all that they can ever sense of odor), the music of the choristers and the *scholae cantorum*. These angels had strengths never wholly catalogued, and if catalogued not mentioned by the Aeropagite or Aquinas in their writings. It would be his, John Dee's, duty to sequester, baffle, impede them if he could. Those that he had seen and known had committed themselves to the truthful answering of his questions; well, he would pose questions that they had never heard, nor the greater choirs above them: questions that would take years to answer. It was the last duty he owed to his Queen.

But when news of the defeat of that small second Armada out of Spain at Kinsale had been conveyed to him along the steganographic pathways, he was perplexed; angel voices, angel intercourse, had made no mention to him of the battle, nor of their part in it, if they had had a part. They seemed, as he sensed them, to be weary, veterans who had got a victory but only by sacrifices that left them diminished.

Now back in his own home again in Mortlake-on-Thames with only his eldest daughter to keep his house, he was regarded by those who remembered him at all as a ghost of some past way of the world, a slippered pantaloon in a play. Had he actually altered the outcome at Kinsale by a distraction of the heavenly forces, keeping them from the battle? Likely he had not. Whatever angel armies did or were compelled to do, they cared nothing for outcomes: those were fixed at the *Fiat lux* and were no concern of theirs. Yet he wondered if they had been seen above the battlefield on that Christmas night, giving hope without promise to armies whose fates they couldn't know. He could not suppose he had succeeded so completely.

What he saw now in the glass, when it cleared of cloud, wasn't what he had seen in former times. He saw not the armies of emperors and kings, nor the towers of heaven and their hosts, only a long stony strand, and he knew it was the western coast of Ireland; and there where the Spanish ships had once been shivered on the rocks, other ships were being built, like no ships men sail, ships made out of the time of another age, silvered like driftwood, with sails as of cobweb; and the ones building and now boarding and setting them out to sea were as silvery, and as fine. Defeated; in flight. They sailed to the West, to the Fortunate Isles, to coasts and faraway hills, to little woods and big that they had never known, that would perhaps come to exist only when they were reached. The voice at John Dee's inward ear said *This is soon to come. We know not when. Well, let it be.* And as he bent over the glowing stone, the empowered soul within him spoke in vatic mode, and told him that now when the end had come, and after it had long passed, the real powers that had fought these wars would be forgotten, and so would he, and only the merely human kings and queens and pikemen and clerics and townsmen remembered.

~

Hugh O'Neill too was dying, coming farther toward death a little faster every day, parts and powers of himself falling away or withering—it was just as he had seen it happen to old men, and now to him, though to witness it was not to experience it. Not the loss, not the weakness, which could be seen, but the shame; shame and guilt and fear. Embarrassment before the hale and cheerful, who knew nothing of this yet. Still he went out at morning from the Palazzo's gate, turned to the right, and, kept steady by the twisted olive-wood stick he carried, arrived by late morning at the foot of the high place called the Janiculum. This was the penance that the Archbishop had set for him: that on any day he could—no longer every day, but on those days when he knew he must—he would climb the steep way to the top, which grew steeper the oftener he climbed it, up to the church of San Pietro in Montorio on the heights.

He set out upward this day thinking that he would be unable to reach the church, the same thought that he thought now on every day when he began to climb; but as on all days before, he did arrive at the wide terrace. He stopped there, so that his heart and lungs could remember how to breathe.

San Pietro was founded by a Spanish queen, and was warm and plain, unlike the great Roman churches built in later centuries, orgulous and abashing. San Pietro was—it had the aspect of being—kind; or kind to Hugh O'Neill at least, seeming always to welcome him back, in sorrow, as was right, and yet offering him from the terrace the soothing stillness of the long view: the red-tiled roofs of the Trastevere, the solemn Roman ruins, the dark pointed poplars like no tree he had known in his homelands; the blue hills beyond, which had no name that he knew. His eyesight darkened as he looked on all this, then brightened again. He turned away, took the wide stairs up to the church doors, never locked.

The morning Mass had ended. Choristers and altar boys withdrew, their housekeeping done, each bending a quick knee at the altar, where the consecrated Host resided in a sunburst-shaped ciborium. Above the altar was what O'Neill had been told was Raffaello's

Transfiguration: Jesus, arisen from the tomb, wrapped in white—as long ago the blind poet O'Mahon had been wrapped—rising into the air, his feet bare, his eyes turned upward to what he saw above. Bearded figures that Hugh had never identified rose with him.

He went up the nave and took the seat he always took. Under him, beneath cloud-like slabs of Travertine stone, were bodies, laid there over the years. His own son, last bearer of the title and estate of Baron Dungannon, lay just there; Rory O'Donnell, Earl of Tyrconnell, there; and there, Cathbarr, Rory's brother. All three dead of Roman fever not long after O'Neill had brought them here, in flight from the English wolves. Would it have been a better death to have stood their ground, turned and faced them? Time would say nothing in answer to that.

In the sepulcher below was a place where he would himself soon lie alone—this honor had been decided on by kind persons, the Archbishop, the Papal officers, and he had not wanted to offend by refusing. He would have preferred to lie beside the others, in the hope of coming forth with them on the last day, in the meanwhile to sleep in their company. *D. O. M. Hugonis principis ONelli ossa,* the tablet on the wall would say: Here in the care of God lie the bones of the prince O'Neill. How was it he could see these letters, which were yet to come, deep-cut on the wall? A great foreboding shook him, and his eyesight again blackened. After a moment it again returned to him, but changed. It seemed now that the stones of San Pietro's floor, the creamy swirl of the marble, was a clouded sky that he looked down upon from above, as the gulls and the sea-hawks must see it. Yes, it was a thin and breaking cloud cover; beneath was a far, dark earth that rolled to the west, and it was winter there; years had passed. He walked it, the cold flakes flying by him as he went, the steps he took carrying him far and fast. He saw armies on the march, Spanish *tercios,* German *Landsknechte,* rabbles in arms; blood on the snow, houses afire, men and women hanging from the black torture wheels raised on timbers, but all of it motionless, like paintings on Roman walls. A war was now beginning, he knew, that would be more dreadful than any he himself had seen or fought in, more cruel, more useless, and it would last for years; not even the angels that he sensed bending near the earth could reverse it, nor would if they could. He knew he would forget all that he saw of it, and had already.

Black sea was before him, and he strode westward over that too, untouched by the rebellious waves just beneath his feet. And his heart felt full to bursting, for he saw ahead the shores of his island, where the armed English vessels were crowded into harbors, and the towns with their houses and new castles rose up. Beyond the shore and the headlands the land was green, no snow fell here or had fallen; the lakes and hills were all as they had been when he was a boy, they had been healed or had never been harmed, the cattle and the sheep, the running horses, the boys and the girls. He was altogether transfigured now; the hills of his own lost *Tir-Oen* came up into sight as though they rolled over in sleep. He saw ahead of him, crossing the land with quick steps longer than his own, the slight figure of the walking man, the courier who could never be explained, who looked back at Hugh as if to say *follow*. The long hill from where the poet O'Mahon summoned the pale warriors was before him now. He heard without any sound the clashing of weapons in celebration, and a woman, singing in his language without a pause for breath, the song rising and falling continuously like the far voices of seals on the sea-banks. He was known to all these, and he knew they awaited him; and when he came near, the doors of the hills were opened for him to enter in.

ACKNOWLEDGMENTS

During the years in which I began to write fiction, my imagination seemed to be a rover, seeking odd and unlikely subjects, most of which I'd discard as unworkable. Three or four though I found to be usable—a war like the Wars of the Roses of the fifteenth century in England, fought on a distant planet; a far-future America, depopulated, quiet, green; a science experiment that blends DNA to create a being half-lion, half-human. In all that time I was auditioning—so to speak—other options. One that couldn't be dismissed but which I wasn't ready to take up was the story of the Tudor plantation of Ireland and the resistance of Irish chieftains to English dominion. I found a book by the Irish writer Sean O'Faolain, a biography of Hugh O'Neill, and read and reread it. I began outlining events, seeking for a beginning, and not finding one. I put it aside, the book and the notes.

Some years later, I wrote a story based on the song "Silkie" that Joan Baez made popular; I was also deep into the life of Dr. John Dee, astrologer, angelologist, alchemist; and I began to see that the Irish story, which had never gone away, was akin to these. The late Gardner Dozois published the piece—now grown into a novella—and it reached enough readers whom I trusted, who'd urged the novella could be part of a novel, and that's what it is—a *mash-up* in old genre lingo, enriched with a few years of further study and thought, and now complete. In its writing it doesn't much resemble anything else I've written, but then almost none of my books resemble any of the others, which I'm very happy about.

So I acknowledge here my debt to Gardner Dozois, to Henry Farrell, to Patrick Nielsen Hayden, to Howard Morhaim, who convinced an editor and a firm to take it on; to the many scholars of Irish history I read and drew from, forgot, returned to, remembered; to L, my wife, critic and encourager, to friends who listened to what I could tell them at a moment in time; and to you, reader, one perhaps of not a great number who have come this far with me.

John Crowley, Conway, Massachusetts, September 30, 2021